midnight in austenland

shannon hale

BLOOMSBURY
LONDON • NEW DELHI • NEW YORK • SYDNEY

First published in Great Britain 2013

Bloomsbury Publishing Plc
50 Bedford Square
London WC1B 3DP

www.bloomsbury.com

Bloomsbury Publishing, London, New Delhi, New York and Sydney
A CIP catalogue record for this book is available from the British Library

ISBN 978 1 4088 4015 3

10 9 8 7 6 5 4 3 2 1

Printed and bound in Great Britain by CPI Group (UK) Ltd, Croydon CR0 4YY

For Jerusha and Steph, the muses of this book,
who, unlike a certain British actor,
will at the very least acknowledge this dedication
and probably even swear to me their eternal love.

prologue

NO ONE WHO KNEW Charlotte Constance Kinder since her youth would suppose her born to be a heroine. She was a practical girl from infancy, only fussing as much as was necessary and exhibiting no alarming opinions. Common wisdom asserts that heroines are born from calamity, and yet our Charlotte's early life was pretty standard. Not only did her parents avoid fatal accidents, but they also never locked her up in a hidden attic room.

At the very least, she might have been a tragic beauty. Though she eventually grew into her largest inheritance (her nose), she was never the sort of girl who provoked men to do dangerous things. She was . . . nice. Even her closest friends, many of whom liked her a great deal, couldn't come up with a more spectacular adjective. Charlotte was nice.

Eventually Charlotte met a nice man named James, whom she was convinced she loved passionately. They had a very nice wedding and two children who seemed perfect to their mother and adequate to everyone else. After raising them to the point that they no longer needed her constant vigilance to stay alive, Charlotte wondered, what now? That's when Charlotte Constance Kinder, who was nice, discovered that she was also clever.

She started a Web-based business, grew it to seven employees, then sold it for an embarrassing profit. With Lu and Beckett in elementary school, she had time, so why not start another? Her retirement fund was flush. She gave to charities. She bought James a fancy car and took the kids on cruises. Charlotte was content—toes-in-the-sand, cheek-kiss, hot-cocoa-breath content. Her childhood wishes had come true, and she wonderfully, blissfully, ignorantly reflected that life just couldn't get any better.

Until it didn't.

We may never know what turned once-nice James away. Was it the fact that his wife was making more money than he was? (A lot more.) Or that his wife had turned out to be clever? (That can be inconvenient.) Had Charlotte changed? Had James? Was marriage just too hard to maintain in this crazy, shifting world?

Charlotte hadn't thought so. But then, Charlotte had been wrong before.

She was wrong when she assumed her husband's late nights were work-related. She was wrong when she blamed his increasingly sullen behavior on an iron deficiency. She was wrong when she believed the coldness in their bed could be fixed with flannel sheets.

Poor Charlotte. So nice, so clever, so wrong.

Charlotte came to believe that no single action kills a marriage. From the moment it begins to stumble, there are a thousand shots at changing course, and she had invested her whole soul in each of those second chances, which failed anyway. It was like being caught in her own personal *Groundhog Day*, only without the delightful Bill Murray to make her laugh. She would wake up, marvel anew at the bone-crushing weight in her chest, dress in her best clothes, as if for war, and set out with a blazing hope that today would be different. Today James would remember he loved her and come home to the family. Today she would win back her marriage, and her life.

Eventually the time came when Charlotte sat in the messy ruins of her marriage and felt as weak as a cooked noodle. She would never be nice or clever enough. Hope had been beaten to death. She dried her eyes, shut down her heart, and plunged herself into an emotion coma. So much easier not to feel.

Once numbness shuts down a damaged heart, a miracle is required to restart it. Things would prove rough for our heroine. Her only hope was Jane Austen.

LET'S SKIP AHEAD. NO NEED to dawdle over lawyers and assets and custody, the sound of ten-year-old Beckett crying in bed, the glazed expression that thirteen-year-old Lu was perfecting. No need to belabor the Valentine's Day Charlotte alphabetized her magazines.

But before we leap too far, pause for one moment. Charlotte has just stepped out of the shower. The mirror is breathy, the air stifling. It's been months since her heart has felt Stonehenge-heavy each time she thinks of James; frankly, it's been some time since she's felt anything at all. She wipes the fog off the mirror and freezes, struck by the eyes of a woman she doesn't know. Does she always look this way? That line in her forehead—is she scowling?

Charlotte concentrates on the muscles in her brow, telling them to relax. Still they bunch up. She rubs the spot. Is she having a muscle spasm? Should she see a doctor? Then—oh. She understands. She can rub all she wants, but that line isn't going away.

"Wrinkle," she whispers. She didn't look the same as she had the last time she was single.

That's what she was thinking when her college friend Sabrina took her out to lunch.

"Kent is a couple of years younger than you, but really great," Sabrina was saying while salting her cheesesteak. "He's a paralegal, rides a bike to work, and, you know, only has as much baggage as your average unmarried thirtysomething."

Charlotte rubbed at the wrinkle between her eyes, pluckily trying to erase it again. It was this same can-do spirit that secured her the Ohio Woman Entrepreneur of the Year (or OWEY) award.

"I'm not getting remarried," Charlotte said.

"Marriage schmarriage. When are you going to let a little romance into your life?"

Romance. That word seemed silly to Charlotte now—so cheap, mass-market, high-discount. It was temporary insanity caused by the brain. It was a biological trick to ensure the survival of the species.

"One date," said Sabrina.

"Yeah, sure, okay," she said, then added, "Thanks," so Sabrina would feel she was doing Charlotte a favor instead of manipulating her into volunteering for torture.

Friday night arrived after Thursday, just as the calendar warned it would. Charlotte changed her comfy work-at-home clothes to irritating look-at-me clothes and found a mirror to take stock of herself. Her hair looked awful. It just hung, floppy, off her head, like . . . like . . . It was so pathetic that when she tried to think what it was like, her mind got overwhelmingly bored and slipped off to think about something more interesting. Such as the tax code.

Being single was ridiculous, with all its demands of blind dating and stock taking and hair doing. Could that be why James had left? Because she hadn't taken her coiffure seriously enough?

Charlotte flat-ironed her hair, rubbed at her brow wrinkle, and met Kent at a sushi bar.

She called Sabrina as soon as she got home. "I'm damaged. I'm sorry."

"Oh, Charlotte, what happened?"

Not much. Surely other women would have found Kent's informal lecture on the merits of homemade dog food fascinating, but Charlotte left the sushi bar with mild food poisoning and a heart that threatened to feel again. And what it almost felt was not good. She shut that right down. Be numb, cruel heart.

"I'm dumpy," Charlotte said without emotion.

"You're not dumpy," said Sabrina. "You're five eleven. How can you be dumpy?"

"I feel dumpy."

"Wait . . . did Kent call you dumpy? I warned him to keep his mouth shut."

"No, he was fine. I'm done complaining. And done dating. For now. Sorry. Thanks."

But it wasn't over. Word had gotten out among Charlotte's female network: she'd been on a date! That meant open season. Those weekends each month when Lu and Beckett were with James found Charlotte dressed up and trundled off on blind dates. To clarify, no men actually asked Charlotte out, but every married woman of Charlotte's acquaintance had a reserve of unmarried men just waiting to take her out once and never call again. Well, some called, but those were the "artists"—hopeful novelists, painters, glassblowers—who found dating women like Charlotte more convenient than applying for grants.

Charlotte was standing in the supermarket checkout, contemplating a strategy of dating avoidance that mostly involved never answering her phone again, when she saw a women's magazine advertising the article "10 Tips to Saying NO!" She bought it. The ten tips were mildly helpful ("Be gentle but firm, like a good flan! After all, no one wants a slouchy custard."), but it was a different article that tipped her world upside down.

> Common wisdom used to assert that a son needs his father more than a daughter does. Someone to play catch with, right? Well, don't neglect the daughters. New research warns that daughters of divorced parents can suffer from a dangerous drop in self-esteem.
>
> "Whether they like it or not, teenage girls do identify with their mothers," offered Dr. Deb Shapiro, researcher for the Minneapolis Center for Family Studies. "When her father leaves her mother, a girl often feels she is being rejected too. We're finding more and more that these girls can be desperate for male attention and approval, and are much more likely to become teenage pregnancy statistics."

The accompanying photo gave Charlotte chills: a pretty, somewhat sad teenage girl dressed in a short skirt and halter top, sauntering past a group of ogling boys. "This could be your daughter!" the photo seemed to scream. "She is out there fishing for affection in a swarm of sharks and it's YOUR FAULT because you weren't interesting enough to keep her father home!"

Charlotte put down the magazine and cracked the door of her home office. There was Lu on the couch with her new boyfriend, Pete, her legs dangling over his. Charlotte had instituted a no-boyfriend-behind-closed-doors policy, but what was this boy doing when Charlotte couldn't keep an eye on him? The thought haunted her like an overdose of MSG. She was not a woman who could statically fret—she had to *do* something.

Coming home from an errand the next afternoon, she just happened to pass by Pete's house. Oh so casually she parked across the street and watched for a few minutes. Or an hour. When a Jeep pulled up and Pete hopped in, Charlotte followed it to another house. She sneaked out of her car and peered in the basement window. Three boys, including Pete, were sitting on a couch playing a video game.

This is crazy, Charlotte, she told herself. You're crazy. You've lost it.

You really have, said her Inner Thoughts. You weren't this paranoid before James left.

I know, Charlotte thought back, hoping her Inner Thoughts would shush up and leave her be. If she stuck to Pete, she'd discover a secret, a greasy side, something she could tell Lu that would convince her to stay away from boys until she was older. Say, twenty-five.

It was getting dark. Charlotte crouched down to wait. A bush hid her from the neighbors, and with the lights on inside, surely the boys couldn't see out. Wait, where had the boys gone? The couch was empty.

She turned.

Pete was standing in the backyard holding a can of cola, squinting at her.

"Mrs. Kinder?"

Charlotte stood up, brushed the grass from her skirt, and said with forced nonchalance, "Hm? What was that? Oh, hello, Pete. Do you live here?"

His squint became even tighter. "It's my cousin's house. Are you looking for Lu or something?"

"No, no, I was just examining the various landscaping styles of various properties in various neighborhoods and so on and so forth. You know. For my work."

Without looking away, he took a long, slow drink from his soda.

"Okay then, nice to see you again, Pete. And such a great placement of a juniper bush! Excellent roots and foliage. Very healthy."

She hobbled down the slope of the front lawn, her heeled shoes aerating the grass. Not very practical footwear for examining various landscapes in various neighborhoods. Maybe he hadn't noticed.

No more stalking, Charlotte! her Inner Thoughts demanded.

Sure, okay, but by the way, did you know there's an entire section in the yellow pages devoted to private investigators?

Two weeks later she received an envelope of information and photos: Pete with his friends in the mall, Pete getting on a school bus, Pete at soccer practice. What had she been expecting? Pete sneaking into seedy motel rooms or sliding paper bags under bathroom stalls?

She put the PI's file into the shredder then went to find her daughter, who was in the basement, watching commercials on TV. It was time to try the direct approach.

"Hey, Lu. How are you doing?"

Lu sighed and pushed Mute. "Mom, if you want to talk to me, don't try to be all sneaky about it."

Charlotte sat beside her on the couch. "I have some concerns about Pete."

"Of course you do. He's a boy and you're my mom and Dad left. It all makes sense."

Charlotte shut her eyes and recalled an image of a three-year-old Lu in pigtails, twirling unselfconsciously in the living room of their old apartment.

"You're fourteen, honey," Charlotte said, returning unwillingly to reality. "That's just so young to be serious with a boy."

"Mom, please. Can't you remember being fourteen? You were my age once, and you came out okay. So lighten up."

Did I really come out okay? Charlotte wondered. For Lu's sake (and for fear of legal repercussions if she were caught hiring men to take photos of a teenage boy), she tried to remember what it was like to be young. That Easter weekend, when they visited her mother in North Carolina, she dug out some old boxes and uncovered a diary from her middle school years. The first page arrested her:

<u>Things to do before I'm 30</u>

- Get married [check]
- Have a baby [check, check]
- Walk in high heels without wobbling [check]
- Climb Kilimanjaro [um . . .]
- Understand physics [check-ish]
- Help save whales or other animals in danger [check! Thank goodness for those Greenpeace donations!]
- Read Jane Austen [???]

It was strange discovering forgotten goals in her own handwriting, as if she'd woken up at a dance club wearing fishnet tights with a group of strangers who called her "Sahara." Some of the goals made sense—who doesn't like whales?—but, Kilimanjaro? Wasn't that a bit much to ask? Jane Austen was doable. The only author Charlotte had read as an adult was Agatha Christie.

She'd inherited a fifty-book set from her grandmother and slowly worked her way through them whenever circumstances demanded a book. She couldn't remember why Austen had intrigued her younger self but was curious enough to take a trip to the bookstore. Jane Austen wasn't hard to find.

The next weekend the kids went to their father's, and Charlotte played the sick card to get out of blind dates. She was alone in the house for forty-eight hours and spent most of them with a book in her hand. She read like a woman drinks water after nearly dying of dehydration. The stories pulled out of her sensation after sensation: a fluttering in her belly, a laugh on her lips, a pounding in her heart. Austen's books made her *feel*, and that was new, and intoxicating too. And so hopeful. Hope had been that thing with burnt feathers buried in her soul, but now it was waking up, stretching, beating fresh wings in the ashes.

Maybe . . . maybe it would be all right to allow herself to feel . . . just a little? Not immediately, nothing rash. But fluttery hope suggested that when she was ready to open back up, perhaps all emotions wouldn't be stones-pressing-chest horrible. She had no specific expectations. She just contemplated that bird's heartbeat inside her and considered it was time to take a chance.

THE CHANCE CAME THAT SUMMER.

"Take a trip, Charlotte," her sister-in-law Shelby said over the phone. "When the kids are with James, go somewhere exotic. Meet someone."

There was no one Charlotte wanted to meet. Except the characters in Austen's books. Which was a ridiculous idea. Right? Wasn't it?

"Maybe I'll go to England," Charlotte said.

She called Sunny, the travel agent she used for business trips.

"I have three weeks this summer and I'd like to go to the U.K. Maybe . . . I don't know, do they have Jane Austen tours?"

"Oh sure," Sunny said, sounding up to her name. "There's some super great tours that take you through towns where she lived or places from her books. Bath is popular. It's so effin' quaint."

"That sounds nice." Maybe if she stood in the places where Austen wrote, where her characters lived, she could feel again as she had when reading her books—not like a girl who'd been wadded up and tossed aside, but like a woman with possibilities.

"Divorced nearly a year and never a vacation," Charlotte said to fill the silence while Sunny clicked away on her computer. "I should stop feeling like I don't deserve it and just do it. And it's not frivolous; it's literary, right? I mean, Sunny, have you read Austen?"

"Sure—well, not since high school." *Clickety-click.*

"There's something about those stories. That's where I want to be right now. Even if just for a minute, to be there would be so nice."

Sunny's keyboard stopped clicking.

"Charlotte, hang on a sec, okay?"

Hold music. Disco. Charlotte's toes tapped along. Charlotte's toes loved disco.

The phone clicked and a new voice spoke—deeper, velvety.

"Ms. Kinder, this is Noel Hess, owner of Endless Summers. Sunny told me of your desire for an Austen vacation. I have a suggestion for you—one we reserve for our exclusive clientele."

Charlotte listened. Charlotte swallowed. Charlotte rubbed the goose bumps on her arms. This Austen vacation would cost four times what she'd thought she'd spend. But Charlotte was breathless. She felt as if she were Ponce de León being guided to the fountain of youth and invited to dip in his toes. Surely Ponce de León would have preferred full immersion, but, hey, immortal toes are better than nothing. Even if they love disco.

The travel agent overnighted a glossy pamphlet emblazoned with a grand estate, a man and woman in Austen-era clothing walking arm in arm. It wasn't a drawing. It was a *photo* of an actual, brick-and-mortar, flesh-and-blood venue.

Charlotte opened the pamphlet and read the scripty font:

Pembrook Park, Kent, England. Enter our doors as a houseguest come to stay two weeks, enjoying the country manners and hospitality—a tea visit, a dance or two, a turn in the park, an unexpected meeting with a certain gentleman, all culminating with a ball and perhaps something more . . .

Charlotte closed her eyes and clutched the pamphlet. Lately the nonfictional world had been thin and drab. But in Austenland, life could be lived in full color. It was real! Well, real-ish. If she went, would the dead and frozen part of herself revive? Austen's words had started the thawing process. Imagine what could happen if Charlotte could actually step inside the story.

Everything was about to change.

austenland, day 1

AN ASTON MARTIN, COMPLETE WITH hatted and jacketed driver, picked her up at her London hotel. She'd been in the city for a week, ostensibly to start her vacation early, though she spent most of her time working on her laptop. Why relax and think when there was wonderful, numbing work at hand?

She'd been to England once before, while touring Europe after college with a backpack, a rail pass, and a "best friend" who'd ditched her in Vienna for a guy from Albania. She'd had no romantic notions of England then, her experience mostly revolving around the question "Will it rain before I can book it to the next hostel?"

Now she looked over the landscape with expectation. With hope.

Come on, she willed through the car window. Come on, change me. I dare you.

They entered a drowsy countryside of low green hills and hedged pastures. Trees engulfed any sight of the nearby town, and a building styled as an inn came into view. A woman of sixty waited in the threshold. She wore an Empire-waist dress, a lacy cap over her hair, and a smile that seemed to pinch a bit. Charlotte wanted to pat her on the back and say, Don't worry, you don't have to smile on my account.

"Welcome to 1816," the woman said as Charlotte stepped out of the car. "I am Mrs. Wattlesbrook, proprietress of Pembrook Park and your hostess for the next two weeks. Please come in."

The inn was cozy and quaint, with a fire in the fireplace, a table set for tea.

"Have a seat and refresh yourself while we get acquainted," said Mrs. Wattlesbrook.

"Would it be all right if I changed first?" It was weird standing there in jeans beside Mrs. Wattlesbrook in her old-timey attire, like being the only person at a dance who'd worn a costume. (Tenth grade: Charlotte went as a disco queen.)

Mrs. Wattlesbrook sniffed but escorted her to an upper room, where an ancient maid awaited. A full forty-five minutes later, Charlotte was dressed: socks, garters, boots, bloomers, chemise, corset, dress. The maid scooped Charlotte's shoulder-length hair into a well-pinned twist, and Charlotte inspected herself in the mirror. She squinted. She gaped. She flared her nostrils menacingly. Nope. No significant change yet. Her insides still felt chilled. She might as well have been dressed as a disco queen.

So it's not the corset that does the trick, she thought. It's not the dress. But it's a start.

Lately she'd become the Divorced Woman. She'd let herself be defined by what James had done to her. Now it was her chance to redefine things.

I choose this, she told the reflection.

The reflection didn't change. She hoped it wouldn't take its time. She only had two weeks.

Charlotte returned to the tea table. The corset was as stiff as a life vest. She couldn't lean back comfortably or bend easily to scratch her ankle. Which was the point, she supposed. Austen ladies didn't have itchy ankles or desires to lounge. Austen ladies were grandly pretty—like marble statues.

She kind of hoped she was pretty. She'd forgotten to check for that in the mirror.

Mrs. Wattlesbrook opened her folder and reviewed etiquette rules and the schedules for each day and, with the help of two silent maids, taught her to play the card game whist.

"You have read all of Austen's works?" Mrs. Wattlesbrook asked, playing a card.

"Mm-hm," said Charlotte.

"And in your papers, you selected *Pride and Prejudice* as your favorite."

Mrs. Wattlesbrook had sent her a thirty-page questionnaire to fill out beforehand, requiring more information than if she'd been applying for Special Forces.

"It strikes me as a completely perfect novel," Charlotte said.

"So it is," Mrs. Wattlesbrook said, making Charlotte glad she had chosen it.

Initially *Pride and Prejudice* had been her favorite, but two other books had impacted Charlotte even more upon rereading. *Northanger Abbey* made her laugh out loud. And *Mansfield Park* resonated because it was the only Austen novel that had an actual affair—married Maria Bertram with single Henry Crawford. The affair was exposed; Maria was ostracized and divorced. The starkness of it put into relief the rest of Austen's era, when marriage usually lasted all life long. No one in Austenland would pat Charlotte's hand and say soothingly, "Don't feel bad. Half of all marriages end in divorce, you know." In Austenland, leaving your wife for another woman would be shocking! She wanted to live in such a place, even for just two weeks.

"By the way, my dear, have you given thought to what you

would like your name to be?" Mrs. Wattlesbrook played the winning card, a slight gloat in her voice. "If there is no particular name that takes your fancy, I can design one for you."

Charlotte was relieved she wouldn't have to carry around the burden of *his* last name, not here anyway. She'd kept it after the divorce because it also belonged to her children. But it pinched, like Mrs. Wattlesbrook's smile. It reminded her each time she reported her name to the bank teller or insurance agent that she'd been someone else once, a missus to someone's mister. She'd been a wife, a lover, a companion—so much so that she'd abandoned her parents' name and taken his. Become for him.

An unwanted name was a heavy thing to bear.

"I could be Charlotte Cordial."

"Lovely," said the proprietress.

It was the first name to pop into Charlotte's head, her maternal grandmother's surname. Charlotte had been named after her grandma—a lovely woman with a wicked laugh and a keen eye, whom everyone had called "Candy." Now it sounded like a stripper's moniker, but in the early twentieth century, "Candy Cordial" was a darling name.

"But you wish to retain your Christian name?" Mrs. Wattlesbrook asked, peering over the top of her reading glasses.

"Sure."

"Hm . . ." said Mrs. Wattlesbrook, as if to say, *So, you're one of those.* "'Miss Cordial' it is."

"Actually, better make that 'missus.'"

"'Miss,'" Mrs. Wattlesbrook said firmly.

"'Missus,'" Mrs. Cordial said more firmly. She didn't care about disowning James, but in 1816, a "miss" could not have children and be accepted in society. She could change her name, her hair, her dress, her way of being, but one thing she could not change was her status as mother. She felt it etched into her very face, as indelible as her brow wrinkle.

"Mrs. Cordial," said Mrs. Wattlesbrook with a sniff, her approval rapidly dwindling. "A widow?"

Charlotte nodded. "Yes, my husband died tragically. It was a gruesome and exceedingly painful demise."

For the first time, Mrs. Wattlesbrook really smiled, and in such a way that Charlotte half expected the woman to extend her fist to knock knuckles.

"It is a shame when they die young," said Mrs. Wattlesbrook.

Charlotte nodded with mock solemnity, but she couldn't help smiling a little as well. She had a feeling Mrs. Wattlesbrook *understood* about unfaithful husbands. Maybe Mrs. Wattlesbrook was a fellow jilted wife.

The smile lasted a lightning flash, then the woman cleared her throat and cleared her face of expression.

"So, Mrs. Cordial, I would have you know that I take extreme pains to ensure all my Guests have a Satisfying Experience," Mrs. Wattlesbrook said, certain words clearly capitalized. "From your detailed profile, I have matched you to a gentleman character suited to your temperament and personality. My clients enjoy discovering their intended Romantic Interest and pursuing an innocent love affair under the rules of Regency Etiquette. We have had troublesome clients in the past. I trust you will not be one?" She raised her eyebrows.

"I don't think so. Generally I'm not . . . troublesome."

"Good."

"Can I ask you a quick question? What does 'Regency' mean?"

Mrs. Wattlesbrook pressed her lips then inhaled deeply through her nostrils. "In 1811, King George III was declared unfit, and his son ruled by proxy for nine years. He was the Prince Regent, and thus this era is known as 'the Regency.'"

"Aha! I am so clueless. Why was King George unfit?"

"Because he succumbed to madness."

"Oh," said Charlotte, feeling as shocked as a nineteenth-century woman who'd just heard the news. There was nothing like madness to make her feel unsettled. Madness and plane crashes. And ghost sightings. Also toxic mold and flu epidemics. And carbon monoxide leaks.

"If that is all, allow me to acquaint you with some of the characters in your session." Mrs. Wattlesbrook scanned some papers, speaking as she flipped through. "Mr. Thomas Mallery dotes on his dear aunt"—she indicated herself—"and has come to visit me at Pembrook Park. Mr. Mallery has invited his old schoolmate Edmund Grey along, as well as Mr. Grey's sister, the young widow Charlotte Cordial."

"I have a brother?" Charlotte asked. Clearly this Mr. Grey would not be her Romantic Interest. She was relieved there would be at least one safe gentleman in the house. She supposed romance was an integral part of the Austen Experience, but she was pretty well done with setups.

"You have a brother," Mrs. Wattlesbrook confirmed. "And note that while Etiquette demands a woman address a man properly, by his surname and with the designation of *mister*, Edmund, as your brother, may be addressed in the more familial sense."

Charlotte blinked. "What?"

"Mr. Grey's sister would naturally call him 'Edmund.'"

"Oh."

She doubted that would be natural, even if she *were* his sister. She had a prejudice against formal-sounding names, especially ones with an abundance of hard consonants. "Edmund" did not roll off her tongue. Neither did "Slobodan." Or "Abednego."

"There will be two other guests at Pembrook Park during your stay. Miss Elizabeth Charming has been with us for . . . some time. Miss Lydia Gardenside is new to Pembrook Park, like yourself. She is suffering from consumption and is here to convalesce in our peaceful country estate." Mrs. Wattlesbrook made herself busy, rearranging papers, looking down while she spoke. "I believe Miss Gardenside is a girl of some renown in the cities and in the papers, but at the Park she needs relaxation and anonymity. No hustle and fuss to disturb her recovery. We understand each other?"

Mrs. Wattlesbrook peered at Charlotte over her reading glasses.

Charlotte blinked. Was Miss Gardenside a famous convict recently released from an English jail? Or perhaps royalty?

"Of course," said Charlotte. She just hoped that this duchess or countess or whatever wouldn't feel slighted when Charlotte had no idea who she was.

Charlotte didn't have long to wonder. A manservant entered, dressed in a tailed jacket and white wig, and informed Mrs. Wattlesbrook that the carriage was ready.

"Very good, Bernard. Fetch Miss Gardenside from her room."

The servant bowed and went into a back room.

Charlotte finished her tea, brushed the crumpet crumbs from her chest, and looked up to see on Bernard's arm the very person whose poster hung on her daughter's bedroom wall, whose face graced Lu's school notebook, whose rainbow-colored name was imprinted on Lu's sheets. It was *her*, the twenty-year-old actress from the celebrity magazines, the Grammy winner, the television star. The British girl who'd gotten millions of American teens to use "fancy" as a verb and "brilliant" instead of "cool." So famous she only had one name: Alisha.

"Oh, it's you!" said Charlotte's mouth, completely without her permission. Because, of course, if Charlotte had been in control of her mouth, she would have smiled nonchalantly and said, "How do you do?" or something politely formal and indifferent. Oh, traitorous mouth! Now it was too late to appear unaffected by this incognito celebrity.

"It is I?" Miss Gardenside asked innocently. Her accent was more formal, like the queen's, than the rougher tone Charlotte had heard her use in interviews. Nevertheless, there was no mistaking a face that famous, though her long black hair was twisted up and set with silver pins. Her dark skin glowed against the yellow of her gown, and her black eyes looked simpler without her trademark long fake lashes. The girl was extremely thin but still very pretty. Charlotte considered putting an Alisha poster on her own wall.

"I am sorry, have we met?" asked Alisha—or rather, Miss Gardenside.

Had they met? No . . . but then again, she wasn't really Mrs. Cordial, and Mondays didn't usually find her in a corset and bloomers. Those fake-lashes-less eyes seemed to plead, I'm not Alisha, please pretend I'm not Alisha . . .

"I think so," said Charlotte, trying to play along. "In Bath last year? We were introduced at the assembly by . . . by Miss Jones?"

Miss Gardenside only blinked before saying, "Yes, I remember now. Of course. That was a lovely evening. If I am not mistaken, you were wearing a fetching little cap fit with cherries and a tiny cupid."

"Exactly," Charlotte said sportingly.

"I recall you danced *three* dances with that tall mustachioed officer, you scandalous thing!"

"Just so," Charlotte said, not without reservations.

"And you were so bold at the dance, humming out a tune for the quadrangle until the musicians finally arrived."

"Uh-huh," Charlotte said, losing heart.

Miss Gardenside clapped her hands. "I was simply enchanted

with you at the time, and swore in my heart that if we met again, I would keep you forever at my bosom. So now it is official. You will always be Charlotte to me, and I Lydia to you, and I claim you most fiercely as my dearest friend and confidant."

There was barely a trace of the hair-swinging, shimmying superstar. It would break the game to compliment her outright, but Charlotte wanted her to know that she was doing a good job, so she gave her a sincere smile.

Miss Gardenside took her arm. "Bosom friends," she said resolutely.

The carriage ride was short, too short for Charlotte's liking. It felt so perfectly surreal to be wearing a bonnet and jolting along a country lane—frankly more like a Terry Gilliam movie than a *Masterpiece Theatre* episode, but all the same, still very *interesting*. She and Miss Gardenside gasped in unison when the manor house emerged from the greenery.

Charlotte had been to parties in some impressive mansions back home, but they were weak sauce compared with this big, old stone house. A few dozen windows faced front, the glare from the sun making them opaque. Perhaps it was all those blind windows and the mystery of what might wait on the other side, or perhaps it was her mental library of Agatha Christie novels, but Charlotte thought at that moment, This is the sort of house where murders happen.

A line of manservants and maids stood out front. The very thin butler opened the door as the carriage stopped and helped out the passengers.

"Welcome home, Mrs. Wattlesbrook," he said.

"Thank you, Neville."

"Yay!" A brightly blonde woman of fifty ran out of the house and down the stairs. "More girls!"

She spread her arms wide, her enormous bosom shaking

violently with the exercise. The woman seemed to be coming in for a hug at full speed, and Charlotte took a step back, sure she would be crushed against the side of the carriage. But with a look from Mrs. Wattlesbrook, the woman stopped short.

"May I present Miss Elizabeth Charming, our beloved houseguest," said Mrs. Wattlesbrook, in turn announcing Charlotte and Miss Gardenside.

"How do you do?" said Charlotte with a curtsy and head bow, as she'd practiced at the inn.

"I do properly well, *rawther*," Miss Charming said in a stressed and twangy accent of no identifiable origin. "Jolly good to have you here."

Miss Charming's well-lipsticked lips quivered as she spoke, and for a moment Charlotte worried that she was suffering a mild stroke.

"Are you okay?" she asked.

"Miss Charming is of our native England," Mrs. Wattlesbrook explained.

"Oh . . ." Charlotte smiled politely. "I can tell from your . . . accent." Charlotte hadn't dared try to sound British herself. The only accent she could do was Brooklyn, and then only when saying words like "quarter" and "daughter." James had hated it when she did her Brooklyn accent.

Miss Charming beamed. She looked over Miss Gardenside, seemingly without recognizing Alisha beneath the bonnet, and took their arms, leading them up the steps.

"This place is so great!" she whispered, her tone settling into American Southern. "And the guys are *delish*, but I get lonely for girls between sessions. I can't wait until—"

She had to stop, because Miss Gardenside had begun to cough. Not a light there's-a-wee-something-in-my-throat cough, but a harsh, grating, suffocating hack. She bent over, wheezing and battling her lungs, while Charlotte stupidly patted her on the back and offered to fetch water, the universal language for you're-coughing-and-there's-nothing-useful-I-can-do.

Mrs. Wattlesbrook rushed inside and returned with a tall, blonde woman in a navy blue dress.

"I'll take her up to bed," said the woman.

Miss Gardenside appeared to be shaking her head no, but she couldn't stop coughing long enough to voice any protest, and her feet shuffled along as the woman walked her inside. Mrs. Wattlesbrook followed.

"Did you guys have popcorn in the carriage?" Miss Charming asked.

"Popcorn? Um, no. Why?"

"I once got a piece of popcorn stuck in my upper respiratory," Miss Charming whispered. "Had to go to the emergency . . . apothecary place."

"I see," said Charlotte. "No, Miss Gardenside has consumption."

"Ooh. That sounds contagious."

As far as Charlotte knew, "consumption" was the archaic term for tuberculosis, which was, in fact, quite contagious.

"But I can't imagine she would come here, and Mrs. Wattlesbrook would let her, if she really has a deadly, communicable disease. Right?"

Miss Charming shrugged. "I won't be sharing my toothbrush with her."

They entered through the front doors and into a grand foyer, where a huge staircase spilled scarlet carpet down to the marble tiles. Dark wood banisters and trim contrasted with bright white walls, giving Charlotte the impression of gashes against pale skin.

Gashes against pale skin? You're really morbid, her Inner Thoughts said.

Charlotte shrugged internally. She didn't think she was morbid by habit, but old houses did seem to bring that out in her. Given their many years of history, odds were that bad things had happened inside. Really bad things. Her imagination couldn't rest for wondering.

Mrs. Wattlesbrook returned and escorted Charlotte upstairs to her chamber. Its walls were painted a sunny yellow, her bed dressed in summery blue. A white-upholstered chair and pale wood table and wardrobe added to the perky atmosphere. Charlotte smiled. Maybe staying in a big old ponderous house wouldn't be so bad after all. Maybe it wouldn't tickle her nerves at night and make her shiver and long for home.

"Take a rest if you like," Mrs. Wattlesbrook said. "We convene in the drawing room before dinner."

"Thank you."

Charlotte smiled. Mrs. Wattlesbrook smiled. The maid left. Mrs. Wattlesbrook did not leave.

"Hm?" said Charlotte, expecting something more.

The proprietress stepped forward. "Do you have anything with you from home?"

Charlotte indicated the open trunk. The maid had unpacked her Regency attire into the wardrobe and drawers. All that was left was Charlotte's toiletries bag.

"If you have any medications," said Mrs. Wattlesbrook, "my staff will keep them in the kitchen at cooler temperatures and serve them to you with your meals."

"Nope . . . no, I don't have any medications."

"All right then." Mrs. Wattlesbrook still didn't leave.

"Was there something else?" asked Charlotte.

Mrs. Wattlesbrook cleared her throat. She looked uncomfortable—the way a boulder looks when it doesn't like where it's sitting.

"There are certain . . . modern accoutrements we don't allow at Pembrook Park."

"Yes, I read the papers you sent: no laptops, no cell phones. So I left all that at the inn. But when I registered, I explained that I need to call my children every few days to check in—"

"Yes, I have your request on file and we will see to it." Mrs. Wattlesbrook stared pointedly at the toiletries bag.

"Um . . . the papers said we could bring our own makeup and—"

"May I inspect your case?" Mrs. Wattlesbrook interrupted.

Charlotte stood back and watched the woman rifle through her powders and lipsticks and toothpaste. The tampons made her blush. The under-eye concealer made her blanch. The acne cream made her want to die.

Buck up, Charlotte, she told herself. You're not the only grown woman in the world who still needs acne cream. From time to time. No big deal or anything.

Mrs. Wattlesbrook cleared her throat, nodded, and left without making eye contact.

Charlotte shut the door and noticed that it didn't lock. She lay on her bed, clutching her toiletries bag to her chest like a teddy bear.

"You're an idiot," she whispered to herself.

Then she fell asleep.

home, before

AT FIRST JAMES SAID HE was confused. He needed a break. He was unhappy at work. No, he was unhappy at home. He needed to re-center. He needed new hair products.

This dragged on for months until the truth came out.

Another woman? At least existential angst had its roots in the fine tradition of melancholy poets and misunderstood teenagers. But . . . a mistress? It was just so cliché. Charlotte, lost and hurt, wondered if she wasn't also a little ashamed that the man she loved would succumb to such a hackneyed story.

If he was going to leave her, let the reason be explosive and alluring. Let him be overcome with a passion for trapeze artistry, or take an oath of silence and settle down in the foothills of Everest.

"He's been fighting the impulse for years," she could explain to her friends over tea and scones. "But he's an artist at heart. And he's never felt so fulfilled as he is now, living in Guatemala and painting gourds that he sells to support blind orphans. We'll miss him, of course, but . . ." And she'd make a cute, bewildered shrug.

But no. It was "love."

"I'm in love," he said. "For the first time in my life, *really* in love."

How blessed for him, and how opportune. Just when life was getting a little bit crunchy, a little stretched and strained, he conveniently falls in love with another woman. No more battling with kids, no more grumpy daughter or needy young son to worry about, no more slightly saggy wife who knows all his secrets and the scent of his back sweat. Falling in love in the middle of an old relationship was such a treat!

She handled the framed photo of their family taken the past Christmas. She dropped it in the garbage can. She fished it back out, wrapped it in tissue paper, and put it away with the holiday decorations.

austenland, day 1, cont.

CHARLOTTE WOKE TO A KNOCK. The curtains were drawn, the room dark and chilly. She sat upright, hugging something plasticky that was making her neck hot.

Toiletries.

Still clutching the bag, she ran to the door, rubbing the side of her face in case the pillow had left indentations. Why should she feel guilty? Mrs. Wattlesbrook said she could rest. She smoothed out her skirt before opening the door.

"Dinner is nearly served," the maid said quickly. "May I help you dress?"

The maid was slim and petite, and Charlotte considered that she probably weighed as much as Charlotte's right leg. The maid's hair was pale, her skin and eyes were pale. She seemed to be fading away. Or Charlotte's eyes were just dry. She blinked them hard.

"Thanks, I am dressed."

The maid looked pained to have to speak again. "It is the custom . . . to wear an evening dress to dinner."

Oh! Right! This was sounding familiar from her Austen read-a-thon and Mrs. Wattlesbrook's "Notes on the Regency Era."

"Sure, thanks."

The maid curtsied and entered, lighting several candles before going to the wardrobe.

Wow, Charlotte thought. I am in a place where people curtsy. And this is where I'm going to refind myself? In her sticky postnap haze, the prospect seemed doubtful. She went into the bathroom and closed the door. The mirror revealed the truth of her pillow face, and she employed the previously prodded toiletries before coming back out.

"What's your name?" Charlotte asked as the maid helped her out of her dress.

"Mary."

A common Austen name. There were Marys in several of her novels. Charlotte wondered if the maid's name was real or applied. Were the maids actors too, or were they just . . . maids?

Charlotte was practically naked now—in her corset, chemise, and bloomers. Standing before a stranger in her underwear was never a good time, but especially not in *weird* underwear.

"How long have you been at Pembrook Park?" she blurted. It was the sort of small talk she engaged in while undergoing a pap smear. If she was talking, she wasn't thinking about how humiliated she felt.

She made it a point to never go to the same gynecologist twice. There was always a reason to disapprove: chilly exam rooms, sweltering exam rooms, a doctor who hummed while she worked. Her most recent visit had gone smoothly, leaving her no easy excuse, until her lab results were mailed to her on the clinic's official letterhead: "Rock Canyon OB-GYN: We're GYNO-MITE!"

"Just two months, ma'am," said Mary. "Before, I was at Windy Nook."

"What a pretty name," Charlotte said, pulling the new dress over her head so quickly she tangled her hair in a clasp. "Is Windy Nook another estate like Pembrook Park?"

"It was." Mary said it like she didn't want to talk anymore. Or wasn't supposed to.

Which intrigued Charlotte.

"What happened to Windy Nook?"

"It's gone." Mary's voice was nearly a whisper.

Charlotte didn't press her further, but her mind was buzzing now, working over the idea of another Pembrook Park, something gone, some tragedy. What a delightful diversion. Was it true, or was this a little clue that would become part of the ongoing story of Pembrook Park? How curious. That was when Charlotte began to suspect that she'd fallen down the rabbit hole.

Mary did Charlotte's hair in silence and curtsied when she left. Charlotte curtsied back. Then thought maybe she wasn't supposed to curtsy to a servant. It was all very confusing.

She blew out the candles, and her formerly cheerful room was quieted of color. A shiver chased her into the hallway. She'd slept through the remains of the day, and an overcast evening skulked outside the windows. All the doors were closed. She tiptoed down the hall, strangely afraid of disrupting the stillness with her passage.

I don't trust old houses, she told herself, as if acknowledging the fact would make her more brave.

She was intimidated by the creaky, sleepy lurkiness, the nooks and crannies and doorways and passages, the unexpected noises, the many places a stranger could skulk. Who could rest easy in a house with wings and battlements—and, no doubt, dungeons?

A glimmer beckoned from downstairs, and she followed it into the drawing room.

At last, plenty of light—kerosene lamps (both real and electric, it seemed), candles, a fire, furniture upholstered in gaudy fabrics, and an enormous mirror with an ornate gilded frame holding court on the wall. The brightness and colors were briefly overwhelming.

"Mrs. Cordial!" Miss Charming bounced up from her sofa and took Charlotte's arm. She leaned in close and whispered in her ear, "Now you get to meet the men! It's the best part."

"Good evening, Mrs. Cordial," said Mrs. Wattlesbrook. "You look lovely this evening. I see I did well assigning Mary to you. She has a way with shorter hair. I am sorry she is such a skittish thing, but I hope you find her abilities outweigh the vexation of her personality. Yes, very good with short hair . . ."

Mrs. Wattlesbrook looked her over as if she were a cow going to market. Not that Charlotte had any personal experience with selling cows, or with *market* per se, but there just wasn't a good metaphor in her realm of experience.

"Well," the hostess said approvingly.

Charlotte's smile was genuine. Perhaps Mrs. Wattlesbrook had forgiven her the transgression of wanting to be a missus.

"Mrs. Charlotte Cordial, may I present our gentlemen guests."

At her words, two gentlemen, who had been sitting on sofas just out of sight, arose and came forward. Charlotte gasped.

In movies, we are accustomed to seeing handsome actors. It's so commonplace on the screen, large or small, that we barely note it as extraordinary. But in life, rarely do we encounter an onslaught of beauty, enter a hive of handsomeness, find ourselves awash in an ocean of attractiveness, drowning in a miasma of hotness. Charlotte was unprepared. She momentarily forgot her animosity toward dark old houses.

"This is Colonel Andrews," said the hostess. "The second son of the earl of Denton and a dear family friend."

Colonel Andrews bowed in a very pleasing way. He was darling—fair hair, a naughty smile. He must have been at least ten years her junior.

Oh, Charlotte, what are you getting yourself into?

"And of course you know your brother, Mr. Edmund Grey."

Apparently Mrs. Wattlesbrook only hired eye candy. While the colonel had a roguish appeal, Edmund was handsome in a cheery way. His slightest smile produced Death Star–size dimples in both cheeks, and his blue eyes sparkled in the candlelight. Not just metaphorically. Truly sparkled.

"Sister dear! How delightful that you should come. I was telling Andrews that you are jolly good company and game for anything, is that not so?"

To be honest, Charlotte didn't feel game for much. She felt as poorly disguised as Alisha, though instead of being a famous and talented starlet, she was a frazzled mommy playing dress-up. But Edmund Grey's blue eyes kept on shining, and she trusted their hopeful promise that he would get her through this somehow.

"That's right. The Greys ever were game." She thought she should say something more, something charming, tell a witty story about Edmund when he was younger and repay him for his dazzling blues, but she felt shy in a push-up corset and low-cut dress. Should she slouch to keep her bust from sticking out so much? Would her proper posture make them think she was trying to flaunt her cleavage? At least no one was obviously looking her over. Except for Miss Charming. Charlotte caught her eye, and Miss Charming nodded in an approving way.

"And where is Mallery?" Colonel Andrews asked.

Just then the front door banged open and they could hear loud footsteps coming down the hall. A figure passed the drawing room and headed toward the stairs.

"Mr. Mallery!" Mrs. Wattlesbrook called.

He paused, then came back, his stance impatient. He was the tallest of the three gentlemen, striking in a black cloak and riding boots, his long hair held in a masculine ponytail. Charlotte added the word "masculine" to her internal description, because normally she considered long hair on men weird and maybe a little bit sweet. But everything about this man pronounced Masculinity in no-nonsense terms. While the other two gentlemen would look comfortable on a *GQ* cover, Mr. Mallery didn't seem likely to feel comfortable anywhere—except maybe a castle on a moor. He had dark hair and dark eyes, and standing on the threshold as he was, he seemed too untamed and, well, *dangerous* to enter the prim world of the drawing room.

His look was restless, but he bowed to Mrs. Wattlesbrook.

"My apologies, madam. My horse stumbled in the field."

"That is a shame. Is she all right?"

"Of course she is, or I would not have returned from the stables."

Mr. Mallery's glance took in Charlotte, then his eyes returned to Mrs. Wattlesbrook. He left without another word.

Colonel Andrews laughed. "There goes the wealthiest man in the county, but twenty-five thousand a year cannot manners buy."

"Indeed." Mrs. Wattlesbrook sniffed, but Charlotte observed that her sternness seemed more affected than usual. In fact, the woman was downright pleased.

The butler entered, but Mrs. Wattlesbrook waved him off.

"We shall wait for Mr. Mallery, Neville."

"He shan't be long, I daresay," Colonel Andrews said. "The old boy dresses like he rides—fast and careless."

"Not careless," Mrs. Wattlesbrook corrected. "Mr. Mallery is never careless."

Colonel Andrews nodded assent.

Charlotte noticed Miss Gardenside, sitting on a lounge, her feet up, a blanket over her legs. Her face was shiny, her eyes wet, and she dabbed at them with a handkerchief.

Feeling a little unready for the gentlemen, Charlotte wandered over to the lounge and took a chair beside her.

"Can I get you anything?" Charlotte asked.

Miss Gardenside smiled. "Oh no, my dear Charlotte. I have never felt so well in all my life. I swear I could dance till dawn, were we haunting dear old Bath again. Stay and talk. I do not mean to be alone."

She shivered, closed her eyes briefly, then smiled again as if nothing were wrong in all the world.

"Your brother is the dimpled one there?" she asked, nodding toward where Mr. Grey was speaking with Miss Charming.

"Yes. Edmun—" It was such a trial for Charlotte's tongue to perform both *d*s. "Edmund," she said again, forcing the hard consonants. The name was too formal, too heavy. "Eddie," she tried out.

His attention turned toward the lounge.

"We call him 'Eddie' at home. Don't we, brother?"

He didn't miss a beat. "Indeed we do, Charlotte. It is good to see you. I would ask you all the news of home had I not received one of mother's tomes just yesterday. So I meet you well informed on the number of chickens in the henhouse, the dastardly conduct of elderly Mr. Bushwhack at the reins of his new phaeton, and the mud that just will not dry on the path to church. More news than that I cannot possibly imagine."

"Join us, Eddie," said Charlotte, indicating the edge of the lounge. "Miss Gardenside is under the weather and could use some company."

"Consumption, isn't it?" he asked, sitting. "The devil take it. But yours is seasonal, I shouldn't warrant, and so will clear up soon." He lifted his hand as if he would place it on her blanket-covered leg but then pulled back. His look was warm and sincere as he added, "I think you brave beyond words, Miss Gardenside. I had a bout of consumption myself years past and felt as if I had one leg in the grave and would not mind tossing in the other as well. I marvel at your strength to be here amongst us and put on a cheery demeanor."

"I prefer it . . . takes my mind off—" She started to cough, and her face took on a yellowish-greenish sheen.

The blonde woman who had taken Miss Gardenside to her room earlier approached, still in her plain-cut navy dress. She was holding a glass of water for Miss Gardenside, so Charlotte got out of the way.

She joined Miss Charming, who sat alone at the piano, picking out single notes in no discernible tune.

"Who is that other lady?" Charlotte asked.

"Miss Gardenside's nurse, Mrs. Hatchet," said Miss Charming.

"What a name."

"I know. It's weird. What's a 'gardenside' anyway?"

"I meant . . . um . . . So, how long have you been at Pembrook Park?"

"Oh, I don't keep track anymore."

"You must really like it here."

Miss Charming sighed. "It's home now. Though the food hasn't grown on me much, and I think I was a little happier before Mrs. Wattlesbrook had a special corset made to fit me." She heaved her chest, letting her bosom rise and fall.

Charlotte didn't mean to stare, but now that she'd made eye contact, she couldn't look away from the woman's squeaky-tight cleavage and the awesome expanse of her chest propped up and popping out. It was unnatural, surely. No human could support such weight, no woman (let alone man) could manage so much breast.

"Sometimes . . ." Miss Charming's voice dropped lower, and she looked Charlotte in the eye. "Sometimes my boobs *kill*."

Charlotte's eyes widened, her mouth agape. It wasn't until Miss Charming followed her shocking statement by rubbing her chest in discomfort that Charlotte realized "my boobs kill" meant "my boobs ache" rather than "my boobs fatally maim people." It was a natural mistake to make. After all, they really were large enough to suffocate a grown man.

"Here we are," Mrs. Wattlesbrook said, saving Charlotte from her thoughts.

Mr. Mallery had just entered, his hair combed, but not very well. His dinner jacket and breeches were somewhat finer than his riding clothes, though he lacked silk and velvet and lace and still wore boots—unlike Colonel Andrews, in his man slippers with buckles. Apparently, there was nothing that could be done to dress up his expression. When Charlotte fell into his line of sight, she felt, frankly, alarmed. Mr. Mallery, in a word, was formidable.

"That is better, Thomas," said Mrs. Wattlesbrook. "I cannot think what our guests' opinion must be of you, stomping in dirty and rough at dinnertime."

"Madam, I dress only for you."

His gaze returned to Charlotte, and he considered her unabashedly. She turned half away.

He's an actor, she told herself. This is a character, a part he's playing.

The knowledge didn't settle her nerves. It was as disconcerting as if she were watching a play and an actor scowled at her from the stage, and not for forgetting to turn off her cell phone or for fiddling with cellophane-wrapped candies, but for no discernible reason except that she *displeased* him.

"Well then, ladies and gentlemen," said Mrs. Wattlesbrook, "let us dine."

Eddie offered his arm to his sister and escorted her into the dining room, where Charlotte resolved to be witty and wonderful all dinner long.

She wasn't.

home, three years before

"WHO WERE YOU TALKING TO?" James asked as Charlotte hung up her phone.

"Jagadish, in India. He's my new programmer."

James nodded, but his expression was stern, as if he were working over a difficult problem in his mind.

"Why do you ask?"

"No reason." He shrugged. "The way you were talking, your tone, it was different than I'm used to hearing from you."

Oh no, she hoped she hadn't sounded like an obnoxious American, speaking too loudly and overpronouncing everything. Jagadish was fully fluent in English. How embarrassing!

"How did I sound?" she asked fearfully.

James started fiddling with his phone. "Confident."

austenland, day 3

CHARLOTTE COULDN'T KEEP BLAMING HER less-than-scintillating conversation on jet lag.

"Mrs. Cordial," said Mr. Mallery, taking a seat opposite her at the breakfast table. He looked her over, unhurried, unself-conscious. "You look well rested."

"I am, thanks," she said.

Nicely played, Charlotte.

"Sister!" Eddie eyed her plate as he filled his from the side-board with all things protein. "You cannot survive on fruit alone. I told the men in the smoking room last night that you were pleasantly chubby as a child and I swore to make you so again."

Oh, oh, that's a good lead-in, she thought. He's setting me up, feeding me a great idea that I can play with, make a joke. I've got to say something funny . . .

"Um, okay," she said. "I like meat too."

Yow, what a zinger!

She should be coming up with witty things. That's what made Austen women intriguing, wasn't it? Well, some weren't exactly the life of the party, but they were sweet, and their men loved them anyway. As nice as nice was, Charlotte wanted to be Elizabeth Bennet from *Pride and Prejudice*, she who didn't like to speak unless she could say something to amaze the whole room, she who could make a man like Mr. Darcy fall crazy-mad in love. If Charlotte couldn't become an Austen heroine, how could she ever immerse herself inside the story? How could she reclaim those sensations?

Colonel Andrews said, "Mrs. Cordial, do have some cherry preserves on your bread. We all enjoy the sweetness of a cherry cordial." He winked.

And Charlotte said, "Okay."

Score for the witty woman! And the crowd goes wild!

She wasn't always this numb-brained, was she? She had smart friends who didn't seem bored by her. But these men, these obscenely gorgeous men, how they muddled one. Charlotte's thoughts cast to the first time she'd visited an art museum. She'd seen prints of Van Gogh before and thought his *Starry Night* was lovely. But to view it in person—the texture, the brushstrokes, the rich gobs of paint swirled together—it took her breath away.

These real men took her breath away.

But how real are they? Charlotte wondered.

She glanced at Mr. Mallery. He was still observing her. Did she have jam smeared on her face or something? She wiped her mouth, smiled halfheartedly, and quickly looked away. He didn't.

After breakfast, the ladies adjourned to the morning room, where, in the absence of gentlemen and the proprietress, Miss Charming kindly instructed them on the finer points of needlework.

"It's called 'needlework,' you see, because you do *work* with a *needle*," said Miss Charming.

Miss Gardenside stared at Miss Charming a moment, and then laughed. "You are so funny! I love you. I love both of you hugely. Now you must call me 'Lydia.'"

Miss Charming, startled at first by Miss Gardenside's laugh, recovered and raised her fists in the air. "Yay, friends! We're going to have so much fun," she sang.

"*So* much fun," said Miss Gardenside.

"*So*, so much fun," said Miss Charming.

They sewed some more. Miss Charming sniffed. Charlotte looked out the window. She vaguely wondered when the fun would start.

"You know, you look kind of familiar," Miss Charming said.

Miss Gardenside blinked and just stopped herself from frowning.

"Lydia and I met at a ball in Bath last year," Charlotte offered. "Perhaps you saw her there as well?"

"Ooh, backstory!" Miss Charming repositioned her breasts as if preparing for a physical feat. "I'm descended from royalty *and* the Swiss, and my daddy is a peer. Or something."

"Why not?" Miss Gardenside smiled.

"Exactly," said Miss Charming.

They sewed some more. Now it was Miss Gardenside's turn to look out the window and sigh.

Colonel Andrews popped his head through the doorway. "Did I hear a sigh?"

Miss Charming screamed and dropped her needlework, and Charlotte jumped in her chair, knocking her knee against a marble coffee table.

"Ha-ha! Just the entrance I desired. For today, I am your guide in all things startling." He entered the room, rubbing his hands. "Such a treat have I for you. Nearby lies the ruins of an abbey, its Gothic arches withstanding the onslaught of rain and time. A most fearsome place."

Miss Charming squealed and clapped her hands. "I love excursions! It's like we're on a cruise ship. I mean . . ." She blushed. "I mean, an old-timey steam-powered cruise ship that's totally appropriate for . . . whatever year it is."

"Can you make it?" Charlotte asked Miss Gardenside quietly.

"Oh yes. I am simply expiring to explore a crumbling old abbey and can only hope, with a most fervent, wild hope, that some horrid murder took place amongst its ancient stones, and just by entering the sacrileged grounds we take upon us a mortal curse and are haunted nigh until death!"

Silence followed Miss Gardenside's monologue. Then Miss Charming clapped her hands again and said, "Yay!"

"Miss Gardenside," Colonel Andrews said, bowing, "I believe you shall be most happily satisfied. And Miss Charming, I am pleased to offer you a diversion you have not yet experienced at Pembrook Park."

The ladies applied their bonnets. The other two gentlemen awaited them out front, Eddie holding the door of the closed carriage, and Mr. Mallery at the reins of a light, two-wheeled open contraption that Ms. Austen might have called a "phaeton," but which Charlotte was tempted to call a "chariot," because it reminded her of the chariot races in the movie *Ben-Hur.* Except there was a seat. And no lethal blades swirling in the wheel hubs. At least, not noticeably.

Colonel Andrews and Mr. Grey helped Miss Gardenside into the carriage, followed by Miss Charming. Charlotte approached to step up.

"Now be kind, Mrs. Cordial," said Colonel Andrews. "You would not want to deprive us gentlemen the company of these fine ladies."

Mr. Grey nodded his head toward the phaeton. "Someone needs to go with Mallery. Be a sport, Charlotte?"

The set of Mr. Mallery's shoulders spoke of impatience. Charlotte became aware of the wrinkle between her brows. Surely this didn't mean that Mr. Mallery was her Romantic Interest? Eddie was her brother, so that was out, and Colonel Andrews did seem to pay more attention to Miss Charming than anyone else. But . . . Mr. Mallery? What in her personal profile urged Mrs. Wattlesbrook to pair her with this man? It was surprising, but flattering in a way.

"Eddie." Charlotte took his elbow and pulled him aside.

"Does this mean I'm supposed to go with him? I just assumed . . . he's always looking at me in a disapproving way."

"Disapproving? Of my sister? Impossible. If that were true, I should give him a most stern and scolding sort of look that would cause quakings and shakings of fear."

Eddie previewed his stern and scolding look, and she nodded emphatically to show she was impressed.

"Now here is the truth of Mallery: if he disapproved of you, he would ignore you altogether. He does not bother with anyone beneath his notice. No, I should say his attentions prove quite the opposite."

Really? Wow, that made her stomach drop a tad. "But Eddie, is he . . . safe?"

"Docile as a kitten." Eddie smiled and gave her a good-natured nudge. "Come now, you are not actually afraid of the old boy."

"Yeah, kind of. I don't know. Is that silly?"

"Yes. Completely. But so are you."

"Eddie, you say these things, and I know I'm supposed to come up with some witty retort, but I panic and my mind goes blank, and I think I'm embarrassing you."

He tilted his head. "How so?"

"Because I'm your sister. And you deserve a wittier sister."

"That is wonderful." He leaned his head back to look at the sky. "Allow me to absorb the wonderfulness of that for a moment. Yes, that will do. Now, you stop worrying about me or anyone. We are on holiday with not a care in the world."

She glanced over at her waiting escort's back. "I don't know what to say to him," she whispered.

"You do not have to entertain him," he whispered back. "It is his job to entertain *you*. Go on, Charlotte. You might enjoy yourself. I have the sense that you are long overdue some enjoyment."

"Okay. Thanks."

Charlotte approached the phaeton and stood beside it, taking in Mr. Mallery's profile, his eyes shaded beneath his tall hat.

"Are you joining me, Mrs. Cordial?" he asked, still staring straight ahead.

"I . . . I don't have to." She looked back at Eddie, who was watching her from beside the carriage. He nodded encouragingly. "But yes, I believe I will."

"And what is preventing you?"

She laughed a little because she knew she was hesitating idiotically, but she honestly didn't know how to get into that chariot-thingy with such a long skirt. Would it be inappropriate to hoist up her hem? Was Mrs. Wattlesbrook watching from a window somewhere, grading her on phaeton-side etiquette?

"My dress, I guess. It's so . . ."

Mr. Mallery put a hand on the edge of the phaeton and swung out onto the ground. He put his arms under her back and legs, picked her up, placed her on the bench, and then leapt in beside her. Charlotte tingled with an adrenaline rush, as if she'd just been pushed unwillingly off a high diving board.

"Well, that was . . . efficient," she said, placing a hand to her chest, trying to quiet down her heart.

Mr. Mallery gave the horse a tap. The phaeton took off so quickly that Charlotte held her bonnet against the rush of motion.

Her escort was quiet at first, and she found the silence comforting. He was not the sort to make idle chitchat, and she wasn't in the mood for it anyway. She was wearing a bonnet and riding in a phaeton. She needed a moment to absorb it all.

They rattled down the drive, past the inn, then took a country lane. Off to her left was the motorway, the occasional car zooming by, the sound as annoying as the pestering of a fly.

"You do not strike me as a flighty woman, Mrs. Cordial," Mr. Mallery said.

If you can't say something witty, she told herself, don't say anything at all.

"And yet your hands flutter about," he added.

"You make me nervous," she said, forcing her hands still in her lap.

"I am driving too fast?"

"No, not the driving. You."

He pressed his lips together.

"Does that offend you?" she asked.

He shook his head. "Of course not. It is curious, however, because I was just thinking the same of you."

"I make *you* nervous?"

That didn't seem likely. And yet, she couldn't be sure. Was he different when she wasn't around? She would try to be observant of Mr. Mallery. That would give her something to do for the rest of her stay. And there was the question of the estate-that-was Windy Nook and Miss Gardenside's consumption. She felt calmer already, thinking of these problems to answer, riddles to unravel.

Soon the trees parted and Charlotte spied the ruins. She wondered at them as Mr. Mallery helped her down from the phaeton (by holding her hand this time) and the carriage pulled up beside them.

The structure (what was left of it) was beautiful, and yet creepy too, as if the peaked shape of a Gothic window alone was enough to give one chills. She wouldn't have tiptoed through those ruins after dark for a month's income or an unlimited pass to a chocolate fondue bar. But by the hazy light of an overcast afternoon, the chills induced were pleasant. Charlotte was tempted by the feeling, so she indulged, outpacing the others to begin the exploration on her own. She felt *daring*, and found the novel sensation nicer than numbness.

Hard dirt paths wove between fallen walls and scattered

rocks, the hivelike remains of the nuns' cells still lingering in the shadow of one massive wall. Looking straight up, Charlotte got the dizzy feeling it would tumble down. She passed beneath a doorway and faced a countryside unblighted by human habitation. The air felt chilled there, as if she were a ghost or something, a being caught in a liminal space. She was neither here nor there. *Between*. She sat on a low stone wall and breathed in the summer sun. She was real—but not too real. Nothing felt thorny in her chest; no anxious errands prodded at her brain. For the moment, she didn't belong anywhere.

"Ooh, look at the old-fashioned woman!"

Charlotte started at the voice. Two college-age backpackers were coming straight for her, camera at the ready.

"Are you part of a pageant or something?" the woman asked in an American accent.

"Um . . ." Charlotte's hands fluttered to her bonnet strings then back to her lap.

Wearing the costume in front of civilians made her feel removed from reality, like standing at the top of a skyscraper and watching the cars move way down below. Her mind reeled with time-period vertigo.

Mr. Mallery appeared, climbing atop one of the fallen stones. He took in Charlotte's expression then glared at the intruders.

"You are upsetting the lady," he said. "This is a private engagement. You should leave."

The woman's eyes widened. "Oh man, you look *amazing*." She shoved her camera in her companion's hands and jumped up beside Mr. Mallery, posing with jazz hands spread out razzle-dazzle. The man hadn't yet gotten the camera to his eye when Mr. Mallery hopped off the stone and took it from his hands. He held it awkwardly, as if he hated the feel of the modern thing, but found the power switch and turned it off.

"It would be best if you left," he said again, only lower now, slower, and leaning in a little, his gaze locked on the man's eyes. The backpacker leaned back but seemed unable to look away.

His companion jumped down beside him.

"Hey—" she started.

Mr. Mallery looked her over, and the woman's confidence seemed to plummet. He took one of her hands and placed the camera in it, then put his hands on her shoulders and turned her away from the abbey.

"Now would be a good time for the aforementioned leave-taking."

Charlotte wasn't surprised when the backpackers started off, with nervous backward glances.

Mr. Mallery held out his arm to Charlotte. She took it.

"You scared them," she said.

"They were bothering you," he said simply.

He walked her back toward the others. Charlotte subtly moved her hand up from his elbow to his biceps, curious how strong he was. He glanced down at her hand, as if he guessed what she was about, and she felt herself flush but didn't move her hand. He did have mighty fine biceps.

"There you are!" said Colonel Andrews. "I was just about to regale our young ladies with the dark and sordid history of Grey Cloaks Abbey."

Miss Charming was sitting on the edge of a stone, her hands dangling between her knees, her mouth open.

"It sounds *sooo* spooky," she said. Then, as if realizing she'd forgotten to apply her British accent, she added, "What-what."

The colonel's voice dropped to a stage whisper. "Exactly three hundred years ago, this abbey was home to twenty-one nuns, the abbess, and one novice. Over here"—he walked to the edge of the ruins—"they worked a kitchen garden, with herbs of healing to administer to the town's needs. They kept goats and chickens on the other side of a yew hedge. The walk from the garden to the abbey was lined with fruit trees and pines, under which shade they contemplated the marvels of the world. It was a peaceful existence, quiet and without incident . . . until one evening in January.

"The sisters made their dinner as usual and sat down to eat. The abbess was getting older and not feeling well of late, so this night, after she prepared the tea and blessed the meal, she went to her chamber to lie down. She rose again an hour later to join the sisters in compline prayers, but when she entered the chapel, to her horror, she discovered all the nuns were dead."

"Ooh," Miss Charming said, nose wrinkled.

Miss Gardenside's face was shiny with perspiration. She shut her eyes against the colonel's story, or perhaps the pain of her illness. Charlotte sat beside her and put a hand on her arm.

"The good abbess went through the chapel, examining each body," the colonel continued, "praying to find someone alive. No wounds were upon their bodies, but their pulses had stopped, their breaths stilled. When hope was near extinguished, the abbess found Mary Francis, the young novice, trembling under a bench, quite alive. The abbess fainted from grief and fright.

"In the morning, the abbess woke to find that Mary Francis had laid out all the nuns' bodies side by side in the chapel and covered them with their blankets. She had cleaned up the dinner from the night before as well, washing each dish and tidying the kitchen. She had been up all night at this task.

"'What happened, Mary?' the abbess asked. 'How did the sisters die?' Mary Francis shook her head and would not speak."

"Sounds suspicious, rawther," said Miss Charming, her chin resting on her hands.

"Exactly so," said Colonel Andrews. "If the novice did not know, she might have said so. But why refuse to answer?"

He left the question hanging in the air. In the distance, a crow screeched. Charlotte shivered.

"Don't you just love a good horror story?" Miss Gardenside whispered.

"As long as it's light out," said Charlotte.

Miss Gardenside laughed as if it was a joke. Charlotte didn't correct her. A woman in her thirties should not be afraid of the dark. She also shouldn't be playing dress-up.

"No one ever hanged for the deaths in Grey Cloak Abbey," said Colonel Andrews. "The bodies were buried in the churchyard, and the abbey was abandoned. The poor abbess moved in with a niece and rapidly succumbed to dementia. She would sit in the garden and sing hymns, sometimes suddenly shouting, 'Either she saw who did it or she did it herself!'"

"Meaning, Mary Francis," said Charlotte.

"No. A nun wouldn't kill anyone," said Miss Charming. "Nuns are nice."

"My mother bears scars on her knuckles from 'nice' nuns armed with rulers," Miss Gardenside said.

"No one lives who knows the truth," said the colonel. "But there may yet be clues. You have not asked me what happened to Mary Francis."

"I say, what happened to Mary Francis?" asked Eddie.

"I am glad you asked, Mr. Grey. An orphan, she had no family to take her in. She was driven from place to place by folk suspicious of her involvement in the deaths, until at last she was taken in as a maid in a grand house not far from here. There she lived but a few years—and, it must be said, uncanny things took place in the house after her arrival. Some believe her ghost still haunts the gardens on summer nights."

"Do tell us, old boy," Eddie asked with a knowing smile, "what was the name of the grand house?"

"The name?" Colonel Andrews dropped his voice low. "Why, Pembrook Park, of course."

Charlotte and Miss Gardenside both gasped at once, then laughed at each other.

"But the house isn't old enough," said Charlotte.

"Oh, parts are old," said the colonel. "Parts are very old indeed. Is that not right, Mallery?"

He nodded. "Older than the trees."

"You're related to the Wattlesbrooks, aren't you?" asked Charlotte.

"Mr. Wattlesbrook's father and my grandfather were brothers," said Mr. Mallery. "Pembrook Park would have been my father's inheritance, but Grandfather lost it to his brother in a card game."

Silence followed this remark. Colonel Andrews cleared his throat.

"I propose we set about to uncover the mystery of Grey Cloaks Abbey. Pembrook's ball is in just under a fortnight. Before that occasion, let us solve once and for all the mystery of Mary Francis and her murdered sisters." He pulled a small leather book from his breast pocket. "I have uncovered this ancient text from the library of Pembrook Park. Each night let us read from it, learn more of the story, and follow the clues to the end . . . wherever they may take us."

home, last december

"JAMES SENT A PACKAGE HERE with a Christmas gift for you," Charlotte's mother said on the phone.

Lu and Beckett were gone to their father's for the holiday, and the house felt cavernous and unpleasant. Charlotte was packing for North Carolina, where she would spend Christmas with Mom, as if she were a childless college student again. Was life moving backward?

"He knows it's your first Christmas without him and the kids," said Mom. "Isn't he thoughtful?"

Charlotte considered other adjectives that might apply to James, but she had to agree: Sending a gift to her mother's house *was* thoughtful. She felt guilty now she hadn't sent him a thing.

"I'd rather not unwrap it in front of everyone," said Charlotte. "Would you open it now and just tell me what it is?"

There was a sound of ripping paper and her mother mumbling to herself.

"Hm . . . it's some kind of . . . oh! It's a vibrator."

The hairs on the back of Charlotte's neck stood up.

"What?" she said, remarkably calm.

"It's one of those vibrator things."

Charlotte took two very deep breaths, then said through clenched teeth, "Mom, I'll call you back later."

She phoned James. "How dare you! How dare you mock me like that, and in front of my mom?"

"Charlotte, nice of you to call. How are things?"

"Please don't insult me further by acting ignorant. I never thought . . . I didn't think you were so beyond—I'm speechless."

"You're going to have to explain," he said tiredly.

"The Christmas present, James. My mother opened it early and told me what it was."

"You're angry I got you a present. Duly noted. I try to be nice—"

"Don't pull that crap." Ooh, she'd never talked like this to him. She'd been conciliatory Charlotte, mending Charlotte, accommodating Charlotte. But it felt so good to fill up with righteous indignation! His "gift" had *so* crossed the line of politeness and trudged right on into vulgarity and maliciousness. Why hadn't she confronted and accused him for the ever-so-slight infraction of adultery and breaking marriage vows? Well, he'd had the "love" defense then. How could Charlotte, nice Charlotte, fight back? She couldn't blame him for not loving her anymore. She'd taken her part of the responsibility—she must have failed him somehow. A responsible adult takes responsibility even when it's disagreeable, right?

But the vibrator? Oh, now things were black and white. Now James was truly, grotesquely Evil. She could tell him so, and it felt great!

"What?" he asked, all innocence. "I put a lot of thought into that gift. I know I'm not around anymore to do that for you, so I thought—"

Charlotte gasped so hard her throat hurt. "You're serious? You weren't just mocking me? That would have been bad enough, but you actually thought that was a legitimate gift? That I would use that *thing* and maybe . . . maybe think of you? And you sent it to my mom's house, where I would open it in front of my parents! You disgusting—" Then followed a string of words that she would never speak in front of her children. They were neither original nor worth repeating, and she didn't regret a one. Yet.

"Hey, take it easy!" said James. "Return the stupid massager, I don't care."

There was a pause.

"Mass . . . massager?"

"A neck massager. What'd you think it was?"

"Mom said . . . Mom said it was a, uh, a vibrator."

"Oh. Oohh."

"Those are . . ." Charlotte tried to swallow, but her mouth was suddenly dry. "Those *are* two words my mother would mix up."

James snorted. "Yeah, she would."

At that point, Old James and Old Charlotte would have laughed. The universe seemed to expect that laugh, had created a space for it, a pause to be filled. Nothing filled it. Charlotte rubbed her forehead.

"Sorry," she said and hung up.

She pulled a pillow over her head and waited to die. When an hour passed and she still wasn't dead, she got up and pruned the rosebushes.

austenland, day 3, cont.

THE GENTLEMEN SPREAD PICNIC BLANKETS on the grass and servants appeared to serve a cold lunch among the scattered ruins. Charlotte kept looking at the rocks, expecting to see raw, white nun skeletons half-exposed in the dirt.

You're not going to run into a nun skeleton after all these years, she assured herself.

It's probably just a made-up story anyway, just like everything else around here, she reminded herself.

Then again, she told herself, unexplained deaths happen all the time. How can I say what's really real?

Chills took fingernail-thin steps up and down her back, and she shivered and smiled. This wasn't exactly the Austen-induced sensation she'd been hoping to re-create, but it was something, and she would enjoy it. At least, while it was still light out.

Mr. Mallery sat beside her and offered her punch in a crystal tumbler. She almost protested at his attention, but Eddie caught her eye and nodded, so she accepted the glass and sipped.

"Do you think Colonel Andrews is playing with us," she asked, "or is the story true?"

"I make it a habit never to speculate about what goes on inside our colonel's mind."

"Such a peek might be enough to drive one mad?" she guessed.

"Perhaps," he said.

"Or make one smile? In your case, that might be the same thing."

He looked at her and did smile, and though it wasn't very sincere, was even a little goofy, it helped.

Whew! She'd done it! Well, her comment wasn't incredibly witty, but it was something. After all, Mr. Mallery wasn't a blind date. Not *really*. He was an actor. She didn't have to give herself a headache trying to figure out if her date was uninterested and so she should skip dessert, or if there would be an exchange of numbers, a walk to the door, a goodnight kiss, an expectation of an invitation in. No worrying here. Her obligations had been thoroughly outlined by Mrs. Wattlesbrook: be Mrs. Charlotte Cordial, live by the house rules, and at the end of two weeks, go home.

Still, her mind would rather solve a problem than contemplate the way Mr. Mallery was looking at her, so she said, "Colonel, will you read some of that little book now?"

"Very well," he said, pulling it from his breast pocket. "I have perused the first few pages. It is a book of accounts kept by one Mrs. Kerchief, the housekeeper. She jotted down lists for shopping, laundry, and such, with the occasional note to herself. Here is the first mention of Mary Francis":

> Hired a scullery maid today, as Nell has got herself in trouble by the looks of things and headed home in the night. Mary seems young enough for hard work, and desperate too. Simon told me no one in town would take her in, as she was an initiate in the cursed abbey, but I say if she is willing to work I do not care where she lived before. Superstitious lot.

He flipped a few pages, then read again, this time his tone bending toward the ominous.

> Coal is running low. Seem to be burning more these past weeks, ever since Mary arrived. Simon said she brings the cold. Nonsense. Still, she sleeps in the room next to mine on the second floor, and many nights I hear noises what I never heard before. Wakes me up. It does make a body curious.

Colonel Andrews shut the book and put it away. "That is enough for now, I think. I despise rushing headlong into a mystery. Much more satisfying to dip in a toe, test the waters, ease in slowly before we start to swim."

"Or drown," Eddie added.

"The second floor," Miss Gardenside whispered.

"You think there's something still there?" asked Miss Charming.

"It might be worth investigating." Colonel Andrews looked at her significantly. "Mary Francis may have left a clue behind to tell the truth of the deaths."

A clue. Charlotte's shoulders vibrated with an exhale.

"This is fun," she whispered.

Mr. Mallery asked, "Because it feels dangerous?"

"It's better than sewing samplers."

"Ah, but perhaps one day the ability to sew a sampler could save your life."

She squinted at him. "In what possible scenario?"

"Well . . ." He paused. "If there was . . ." He smiled. "I have not the faintest idea."

"Let me know if you figure it out, and on that day I'll show you the most magnificent grouping of red and purple grapes on a field of white that you have ever dreamed of."

"I long for that day," he said.

When they finished lunch, Mr. Mallery helped Charlotte into the phaeton. By her hand. She was relieved—sort of. It'd been a long time since a man had picked her up. Or touched her much at all, to be honest.

And now Mr. Mallery in his top hat was driving her home to the manor house and its mystery on the second floor.

He won't ask for a goodnight kiss, she reminded herself. *Or a passionless tumble with the understanding there would be no follow-up date. That's not Regency appropriate. And there's no question of long-term compatibility, because we have two weeks to play and then that's that. So, relax.*

She realized they were going home a different route, the carriage no longer following them.

"This is a longer road, but I do not like the other," said Mr. Mallery. "Too much . . ."

Traffic, she thought. "So you're not kidnapping me and carrying me off to your secret lair?"

"Not today, Mrs. Cordial." He glanced at her then back at the road. "Would you like to take a turn driving?"

"Me? I don't know how."

"It is simple enough," he said, handing her the reins. "Keep to this lane, straight ahead. I will drive again when we come to the bend."

She gripped the reins, sitting so straight her back hurt.

"That is fine. Do not pull back unless you wish to stop. Give him a tap there, he is slowing. There, well done." He leaned against the bench, angling toward her. "Now I can get a look at you."

She tore her gaze from the road for the barest moment and saw that he was, indeed, looking at her, and in a way that made her hands sweat on the reins.

"Oh no, don't do that. Stop it."

"Why?"

"Because you make me nervous."

"So you said. It becomes imperative that I determine why you have that effect on me."

"Come on, I don't make anyone nervous."

"Apparently, I am not *anyone*."

She blew out her cheeks and tried to focus on driving. She could feel him staring at her, contemplating her, and it was such an unfamiliar sensation that she sprouted goose bumps as if she'd been tickled. Thoughts fled her head. Apparently they found the place too crazy to stick around.

"Hm . . ." he said.

Her heart beat harder. Had he noticed her brow wrinkle?

"What is it? What are you *hm*-ing about?"

"You have freckles." He ran a fingertip along her cheekbone. "A thing I had not noticed before. Yes, this has been productive."

"I don't think you're supposed to do that," she whispered, his finger still touching her face. She didn't mind so much, except for how hot her face felt.

"Mrs. Cordial," he said gently, "you are the one with the alluring freckles. I simply observe." But he removed his hand.

At last the bend appeared, and she stuffed the reins into his hands, leaning back to sigh.

"And what would you do if I stared at *you* now?" she asked.

"The same as you, I suppose—grit my teeth and look elsewhere. Preferable to be the gazer than the gazed upon, is it not?"

She did look him over since she could. His profile was significant, as if it belonged on legal tender. His jaw was delightful to contemplate, and his long hair pulled back beneath that top hat was just so manly.

Really? her Inner Thoughts said. Are you sure ponytail plus top hat equals manly?

You tell me, Charlotte challenged.

Her Inner Thoughts shut up after that, probably too distracted by Mr. Mallery's manliness to taunt her anymore.

"If you must look at me so," he said, "I wish that you at least would speak."

"I don't know what to say."

"Speak aloud one of your thoughts."

"I . . . I think your profile belongs on a dollar bill."

"That sentence will keep me wondering late into the night."

She could see the roof of Pembrook Park in the distance, but closer still was a cottage. Some country dweller's home? She flinched, thinking she might have to be seen again by the denimed and T-shirted variety. But as they pulled alongside, she noticed the air of abandonment.

"What's this house?"

"Pembrook Cottage."

"It's a sweet little house," she said.

He nodded. "Pembrook Cottage has belonged to the same people who own the Park for centuries. But it is to be sold soon."

His tone edged with bitterness, and Charlotte recalled that the big house and the cottage would have been his. Or his character's, anyway. She tucked that information away in case it might prove helpful later.

The carriage was already at the big house when they pulled up.

"I feel fine," Miss Gardenside was telling Mrs. Hatchet, but she did look gray and wilty and eventually gave in to her nurse's injunction that she nap before dinner. Eddie took her arm and walked her inside.

Mr. Mallery insisted on caring for the horse himself and drove off to the stables, so Charlotte took Miss Charming's arm.

"Come help me look for the clue on the second floor. Though I don't know where he wants us to look—inside our bedrooms?"

"Our bedrooms aren't on the second floor. Don't you speak British?" Miss Charming asked. "They call the first floor the 'ground floor.' 'Second floor' is what they call the third floor. And 'booty' is what they call a car trunk."

"There's a third floor?"

The ground floor housed dining room, morning room, drawing room, and such. The first contained bedchambers for guests and actors. What was on the second? She supposed she'd noticed a third story of windows from outside, but she'd never seen a way up. Miss Charming, veteran Pembrook Parker, led her to a hidden, spiral staircase on the west side.

"This goes directly from the kitchen to the servants' rooms," said Miss Charming. "You know, so noble guests don't run into servants on the main stairway. Don't know why it mattered. Maybe way back when the servants smelled bad?"

They sneaked upstairs, giggling and scurrying away from servants. There was no need for the furtiveness, Charlotte thought, but it did make it more fun.

It was darker upstairs, with only a small window on the far end of the corridor to bring in daylight. Charlotte didn't let go of Miss Charming's arm.

"What exactly are we looking for?" Miss Charming whispered loudly.

"Something to do with Mary Francis the scullery maid and the murders at the abbey."

A single table with an empty vase stood against the wall. Above it was a painting depicting a man with a Friar Tuck haircut talking to a wolf. All the doors were shut.

"Do we open them?" Miss Charming asked.

"I don't know."

"Well, I will." She marched up to one of the doors and opened it wide. A girl inside was changing her shirt. She screamed and covered herself up.

"Sorry!" Miss Charming yelled as she shut the door and ran for the stairs. "That wasn't the ghost of Mary Francis, was it?"

"I'm pretty sure that was one of the maids," said Charlotte, running down the stairs after her.

"Good, because I don't believe in ghosts."

"Neither do I," Charlotte said, still running.

home, before

CHARLOTTE HAD ALWAYS HAD A thing for plants. Her yard was a laboratory where she constantly planted and replanted, moved things around, played with dirt and perennials like a child with candy-colored clay. It was just that—play. A hobby. Nothing to take seriously.

Sometimes she'd help neighbors design their landscaping for fun. And just as soon as she'd really get to know all the best plants for that climate, James's job would change and away they'd go. They were living in their fourth state since their marriage when Charlotte first got the idea: a Web site for residential landscape architecture. There didn't seem to be one out there. She built a site with free information about the best plants for different climates and basic design strategies. Her Web site grew. Her readership e-mailed, wanting specific help with their own yards.

Inexpensive custom landscape design? She could do that. She just needed to create a detailed questionnaire for the clients and a template she could reuse with each new request, cutting down on the time she'd have to spend. Her designs weren't as grand or detailed as those from a professional landscape architect who'd visited the property in person, but they also cost a tenth as much. People loved it. She had to hire employees to help her create hundreds of designs each week. Ad revenue from her site also began to add up.

It's just a hobby, she told herself. Nothing serious.

She had to adjust that opinion after she made her first million.

austenland, days 3–5

THAT NIGHT AT DINNER, CHARLOTTE worked at turning off her rapid, crazed thoughts. She tried to stop watching herself, wondering how everyone saw her. Instead, she watched the others. Better to be the gazer, as Mr. Mallery had said. Why not give it a try when she was not Charlotte at all but the mysterious and not-yet-defined Mrs. Cordial?

Colonel Andrews was serving Miss Charming from various dishes.

"Ooh, I know you fancy these, my dumpling," said the colonel, serving her dumplings.

She blushed and speared one through the heart. "You know everything I love, pip-pip."

Yes, it did indeed seem that Colonel Andrews was Miss Charming's Romantic Interest.

Miss Gardenside was eating very little. Her eyes sparkled, yet so did her forehead. How much pain was she in?

Charlotte wondered at Miss Gardenside's character choice. This girl bore little resemblance to the brassy, street-smart persona Alisha exuded in interviews. Why was she so deep in this character? Then again, maybe Lydia Gardenside really was her and Alisha was the character.

Eddie was *aware* of Miss Gardenside. Even when speaking with Miss Charming or Mrs. Wattlesbrook, he noticed as soon as she fidgeted or coughed. He didn't fuss like Mrs. Hatchet, but he seemed ready to receive her smallest command. Charlotte approved. If her brother was Miss Gardenside's Romantic Interest, then he should be so kind.

And Mr. Mallery (Charlotte glanced at him then away again) was aware of *her*. She took a breath and met his gaze. He subtly lifted his glass to her.

"May I propose a toast?" she said, surprising herself.

A brief silence was followed by Mrs. Wattlesbrook's polite "Of course."

Charlotte lifted her glass. "To my brother Eddie, who gave me some great advice today. It's really nice to have you here, *old boy*."

Eddie winked at her.

"Ooh, I want to toast Colonel Andrews," said Miss Charming. "Can I?"

"Of course," Mrs. Wattlesbrook said again.

Miss Charming's face became serious, her brow wrinkled, and she said unselfconsciously, "To Colonel Andrews and his tight britches."

Mrs. Wattlesbrook frowned, but Miss Charming didn't notice. She smiled lovingly at the colonel, who lifted his glass in return.

"Well, someone should toast poor Mr. Mallery," said Miss Gardenside.

"That is unnecessary," he said.

"Sidestepping will only provoke me," Miss Gardenside said with a smile. "You know me, sir, and once I have an idea in this brain, it will not be dislodged. I may put myself forward amazingly, but that is the way I was made, formed from clay all unseemly and irreverent."

She began to stand, wobbled, sat back down, but raised her glass all the same.

"To—"

Neville the butler hurried into the room and ran to Mrs. Wattlesbrook. To be honest, he was not a man who *should* run. In fast motion, he looked like a poorly made flip book, stick-figure limbs flailing.

"Madam—"

He had only gotten as far as "madam" when the dining room doors opened. Both of them. A man stood framed in their gaping maw. He wore a gray suit with a loosened tie. Iron-creased pants. Patent leather shoes. The semblance of fantasy snapped. Snapped not so much like a stick as like a turtle. Charlotte squirmed in her corset. This suited man with his bloodshot eyes and wild hair reminded her that she wasn't in 1816, that she was playing dress-up, and not even very well.

"Dinnertime, is it?" he said in a British accent thickened considerably with alcohol.

Mrs. Wattlesbrook slammed down her fork. "John!"

"Pickled quails eggs on the menu? You know how I enjoy a good pickled egg." He leaned over the colonel, picked a quail egg off a plate, and plopped it into his mouth.

Mrs. Wattlesbrook shoved her chair back and stormed down the long room. She hooked the man's arm and pulled him into the hall. Neville followed and shut the doors behind them.

Colonel Andrews cleared his throat. "Mr. Wattlesbrook has been . . . unwell. Poor fellow. Not to worry, Neville will have him fixed up shipshape in no time."

So that was their hostess's husband. There was a real story

there, thought Charlotte, watching the doorway as she bit down on a pickled quail egg. Vinegar and eggs. It was a combo that reminded her of Easter. She liked Lu and Beckett to dye dozens of eggs, hard-boiled and raw, so each time she opened the fridge door she was greeted with the garish colors—and as a side effect, the odor of tangy vinegar and sulfurous eggs.

"It's so confusing," Miss Charming whispered to Charlotte. "The first time I was here, he was Sir John Templeton, and now he's Mr. Wattlesbrook. I wish they'd all keep the same names."

"You mean, sometimes the cast plays other characters?" Charlotte whispered back.

Miss Charming nodded. "I've met a dozen different guys who are sometimes Mr. So-and-So and other times Lord or Captain Whatever. Mr. Mallery is always Mr. Mallery, and lately my colonel keeps his same character whenever I'm here. I don't know about Mr. Grey—he's pretty new."

Charlotte felt a thrill getting a peak at the underskirts of this place.

"What about Mrs. Wattlesbrook?"

"When there were three estates, she lived at the inn and other ladies played hostess at Pembrook. But I'm not supposed to talk about any of this. Don't tell."

They withdrew from their whispers to discover no other conversation occupying the dinner table. The gentlemen's attention was hardly on the food and certainly not on the women.

"Colonel Andrews? Colonel Andrews, did you hear me?" asked Miss Charming.

"Sorry?" He looked away from the dining room doors and back at the woman at his side.

"I was saying that we couldn't find a clue on the second floor. You should give us a hint."

"Should I?" His gaze flicked to the closed doors again, then back to Miss Charming. "Yes, I suppose I should. And I will. Sorry, I find myself a bit distracted tonight. Perhaps Mr. Mallery—"

"Do not pull me into this, Andrews," Mr. Mallery said in a low voice. He did not look up from his plate, glowering as if he could break the china with a look. "I am not in the mood for your schemes."

"I can lend a hand, old boy," said Eddie. He took a bite of mutton and smiled while he chewed.

"Capital," said Colonel Andrews, but he didn't sound as if he meant it. His attention returned to the closed dining room doors.

The gloomy mood sloshed over into the drawing room as well, and after an absentminded game of whist, everyone called it a night. Mr. and Mrs. Wattlesbrook never reappeared.

Charlotte went to bed but couldn't fall asleep. All the questions she'd set astir nagged at her, keeping her awake like an unproductive cough. Mary Francis, Mr. Mallery, Mr. Wattlesbrook, Miss Gardenside . . . She'd just begun to contemplate the way the house seemed to breathe audibly in the night when she heard sirens.

She threw a robe over her nightgown, put on her slippers, and ran into the hall. Miss Charming was there, still in her evening dress. Mrs. Hatchet seemed to have just woken up, and she ran bleary-eyed into Miss Gardenside's room. Soon the group converged downstairs on the front steps. It did not appear Pembrook Park itself was in danger, but a fire truck was camped outside. The night sky nearby was mossy with smoke.

"Something happening at Pembrook Cottage?" Charlotte asked.

"Nothing ever happens there," said Miss Charming. "Sometimes people stay there instead of here. I never knew why. Looked boring to me."

"It was a lovely little house." Eddie was beside them, his

gaze on the smoke in the distance. He was still dressed in his evening clothes, his jacket removed.

"Is it ruined?" Charlotte asked.

He nodded.

"Shame that, right-o," said Miss Charming, shimmying back into her accent now that a man was present.

Charlotte, Eddie, and Miss Charming walked closer to the action, past another fire truck with spinning lights and Mrs. Wattlesbrook in severe conversation with one of the firefighters. He wrote down what she said, and what she said gave her no pleasure.

The fire was already out. In the dark, Charlotte could just make out a house with a collapsed roof, the lurid lights of the fire truck running over the ruins again and again. Mr. Wattlesbrook sat on the ground nearby, a blanket around his shoulders. His face and nostrils were gray with ash.

"Mr. Wattlesbrook," Eddie said coolly.

"Not my fault," he muttered. "She *would* have all the finest things, all authentic, nothing flame-resistant, mind you. Bloody rug took up the flame too fast."

"The flame from your pipe?" said Eddie.

"A man can smoke, can't he?" The older man glared.

"You mean you were here the whole time?" Charlotte asked. "If you saw the fire start, why didn't you put it out?"

"I tried," Mr. Wattlesbrook said.

"Tried with a glass of port, I shouldn't wonder," said Eddie.

"That was very badly done," said Charlotte. This man had burned down a house! And he showed no remorse! She wished she could give him a spanking, but he'd probably enjoy it. "You should be ashamed."

"Sod off," said the man.

Charlotte could see Mrs. Wattlesbrook illuminated by the

headlights, how she wrung her hands, how she kept glancing fretfully at Charlotte and Miss Charming.

Charlotte took Miss Charming's arm. "I think Mrs. Wattlesbrook would rather her guests didn't witness this. I'm going back to bed."

"Okay," said Miss Charming. "Yo ho, Colonel Andrews! I say, rawther, was the fire ghastly big?" She hurried off to her colonel.

Charlotte was about to leave when she noticed Mr. Mallery. He was standing by the fallen house, his back to her. A bucket lay beside his feet, and his clothes were damp and filthy. He must have been trying to put out the blaze before the fire trucks arrived, she thought.

She almost went to him. Then she noticed the rock-hard set of his shoulders, the touch-me-and-die cramping of his back, and his hands formed into fists as if, even though he was perfectly still, he were in the midst of a fight.

Never creep up on Mr. Mallery, she advised herself.

Alone now, Charlotte thought the walk back to the big house seemed longer. She felt half in the world and half out, like she had a cold, or at least was doped up on cold medicine. A fire burned down a house. It was such a real thing to happen in this pretend place.

Miss Gardenside waited on a settee in the front hall, wrapped up in a large shawl. Mrs. Hatchet sat beside her, back stiff.

"What happened?" Miss Gardenside asked.

"Pembrook Cottage, a house nearby, caught fire. Mr. Wattlesbrook's careless pipe, I guess. The fire's out and no one's hurt, but the house was destroyed."

Mrs. Hatchet crossed herself.

"Such a shame," Miss Gardenside said. "Such a shocking

shame, is it not?" Her voice trembled as she spoke, and she wrapped the shawl around her tighter, visibly shaking.

"Now you know," said Mrs. Hatchet. "Back to bed."

"Miss Gardenside, you do not look well," said Charlotte. "At least let me get you something hot to drink. I bet there's someone in the kitchen still, given all the commotion."

"Don't baby her," said Mrs. Hatchet. "She got herself into this mess." She pulled Miss Gardenside to her feet and shooed her toward the stairs.

For just a scrap of a moment, the girl looked at her nurse with an expression full of loathing, anger, and hurt. Then she shut her eyes, and she transformed back into calm, happy Miss Lydia Gardenside.

"Goodnight, Charlotte dear," she said through chattering teeth.

It felt very late when Charlotte fell into bed. Buried-alive late, caffeine-is-useless-at-this-point late. She found it easier to fall asleep now that it was well past midnight in Austenland. It's hard to keep questions spinning in your brain when thoughts are even heavier than eyelids. Even stories need a chance to sleep.

THE NEXT MORNING, THE MAID Mary brought Charlotte tea and a light breakfast on a tray, saying that no one would be convening for breakfast in the dining room. Charlotte ate alone, staring out the window. She couldn't see any smoke left in the sky.

After dressing, she spent some time on the second floor. She didn't open doors but walked the hallway carefully, examining corners and windows, looking for a stray bit of paper that might have a message or for an out-of-place item that could be a clue to the mystery. She examined the lone vase and turned a painting around. Nothing.

After a rousing game of croquet, the gentlemen went "hunting" for the rest of the afternoon—or as Charlotte suspected, took a break. Miss Gardenside was ill, Miss Charming was charmingly petulant, and Charlotte couldn't stop thinking of her children. She'd never gone five days without talking to them. Maybe they were going crazy missing her! The thought pierced her right through her corset.

In the yellow blaze of afternoon, she put on her bonnet and made the ten-minute walk to the inn beyond Pembrook's gates. Mrs. Wattlesbrook wasn't there, but Patience the maid knew of the arrangement and admitted Charlotte into Mrs. Wattlesbrook's study, where she produced Charlotte's purse from a locked cabinet and left her in privacy.

Charlotte pulled out her cell phone and dialed James's number. Lu answered. Oh good! Charlotte knew that Alisha's presence at Pembrook was supposed to be a secret, but Lu didn't know exactly where her mom was—just that she was on vacation somewhere in England—so it wouldn't really be telling if she shared that juicy gossip. And besides, there were no rules when it came to a mother earning points with her teenage daughter.

"Lu! I'm so happy to hear your voice. You're never going to believe who else is here."

"Mom, Aunt Shelby told me you hired a private detective to follow Pete."

A pause.

"Did you hire some guy with a camera to follow Pete?"

Another pause.

"Um . . ." Charlotte said cleverly.

"Mom!"

Aunt Shelby! Sisters-in-law were supposed to be trustworthy. Well, she no longer felt guilty for never hanging up Shelby's rainbow-and-smiling-sun cross-stitch.

"Honey, listen, I was worried. I just wanted to make sure he was safe . . . that he was worthy of—"

"I'm done with you."

Sounds of the phone being passed along, then Beckett's voice said, "Hello?"

Charlotte cleared her throat and tried to sound unrattled. "Hi, baby. How are you doing?"

"Fine," he said.

"What have you been doing for fun?"

"Nothing."

Okay. "So, tell me the favorite thing you've done in the past week."

"Sleep."

Mm-hm. "Do you sleep on the pullout couch?"

"Yep."

"I'm having a pretty weird time. I'll have to tell you all about it when I get home."

"K bye."

"Wait—I love you, Beck, and I miss you lots. Can you put your father on before you hang up?"

Sound of phone switching hands.

"Charlotte!"

This was not James. This was Justice, a.k.a. the Other Woman. Charlotte's stomach seemed to withdraw into her body like a snail into its shell.

"Charlotte, I just want to tell you how *darling* the kids are. *So* cute. I thought you'd like to know. *SO* cute."

"Thanks, Justice. I think so too."

"No, I mean *now.* This week. I'm sure they've never been *so* cute as they are this week. I mean, *SO* cute."

"I'm glad it's all going well."

"The best! Just the best! I could eat them up! Do you know, Beckett called me 'Mom'?"

Now Charlotte's stomach dissolved into nothing. "He did?"

"Mm-hm! Isn't that great?"

"Yeah."

"It's healthy for them, right? To accept me as another mom, right? Not *Mom* like you, of course, but another mom, right? So, are you having a fun time playing in England?"

"Yes, I am, thanks."

Justice's voice dipped low and suggestive. "Meet any men?"

Charlotte's face made an expression that belonged on Mrs. Wattlesbrook's face. "May I speak with James, please?"

"Sure thing. Just don't try romancing him. I'm watching you two!" She laughed pleasantly.

Charlotte stayed silent.

Sound of phone switching hands.

"Hello."

Now *that* was James. His "hello" sounded more like "be concise."

"Hi, James. It's Charlotte. The kids were a little nonverbal, so I just wanted to check that everything was okay."

"Yep, it's all okay. Having the time of their lives."

"Okay then. Thanks for watching them."

"Sure, bye."

Charlotte pushed End and sat back. *Deep breath and exhale those toxins*, she could hear her yoga instructor say. Charlotte made herself light-headed trying to purge out the toxins. They weren't budging. Stupid, stubborn, lead-butted toxins.

Why had she thanked James for watching them? He was their father, not a babysitter. Get a spine, girl. And how could she just take all that from Justice? But maybe she deserved it . . . Stop that, Charlotte! It'd been good to hear Lu's and Beckett's voices at least. Would have been nicer had their words been different.

The phone's battery was low, so she dug through her bag, found the recharger and adapter, and plugged it into the wall. She looked around the desk for a magazine or something else to read while she waited so she wouldn't replay the conversation in her mind again and again. She moved aside a folder.

The one beneath was labeled "Windy Nook." It really was an appealing name. Charlotte flipped the folder open, hoping to find a photo that would match the lovely image of it that she had in her head. First she found a stack of legal papers: lists of debts, back taxes, threat of foreclosure, then a lease to a third party.

Okay, now she was just straight-up snooping.

Underneath the stack was a series of group photographs from the past ten years labeled "Windy Nook Cast." Several gentlemen, servants, and an older-looking married couple (possibly the host and hostess?) posed in front of a grand house. Pembrook Park looked as happy as Cinderella's castle by comparison. Windy Nook was decidedly Gothic—narrow windows, toothy battlements, and a tower with a single window watching over all. Mary, Charlotte's maid, was present in the last three photos, looking her usual pale-to-transparent self. Neville apparently had been the butler there for several years. Mr. Mallery was in every single photo.

A folder beneath, labeled "Bertram Hall," contained similar documents—debts, taxes, and this time a sale, though the sale price barely covered the debts and taxes owed. There was a floor plan of Bertram Hall, which, though not as large as Pembrook Park, was a very grand house, and she had to believe it was worth more than the sale price, especially if it was kept up as nicely as Pembrook. Mrs. Wattlesbrook did not seem like a careless businesswoman, but apparently she'd dropped the ball on this one.

Then Charlotte noticed the signature on the bill of sale: John Wattlesbrook.

The cast photos showed Bertram Hall to be cheerier than Windy Nook, with a yellow stone facade and an exuberantly flowering garden. A younger Colonel Andrews made an appearance in two of the cast photos for Bertram Hall. Charlotte couldn't find Eddie in the casts for either house, and she remembered Miss Charming's whispering that he was new to Pembrook Park. What had he been up to before?

The door opened. Charlotte stood up hastily, knocking the stack of folders to the floor. Mrs. Wattlesbrook was in the threshold, eyes narrowed.

"Mrs. Wattlesbrook! Sorry, you startled me. I couldn't find you this morning so I came alone to make my call. You remember, I'd talked to you about having to call my kids regularly. So I just did. And now the phone is recharging . . ."

She felt her face heat up, and she crouched behind the desk, hurriedly stuffing the loose papers back in their folders.

"Sorry. I startle easily, I guess, and I've messed up your tidy folders."

"I can take care of that, Mrs. Cordial," she said, stooping over to retrieve the papers.

Charlotte stood. "Okay. Sorry. Thanks."

Her heart was thumping, unused to artifice. Just how had James managed to have an affair and not show it? The hassle of furtiveness would have done her in. Maybe it had been exciting for him, in some sick way. Maybe the heart-pounding and face-flushing he'd felt whenever he'd lied to Charlotte or almost got caught made him euphoric, not sick in the stomach.

"Sorry," Charlotte said again before returning her phone and bag to the cabinet and leaving. She didn't know who she was apologizing to. Maybe everyone in the whole world.

She walked slowly back to Pembrook Park, feeling the threads of that phone call clinging to her like cobwebs on a wandering phantasm. Lu and Beckett were okay. They were fine. Great without her, actually. That should be good news, right? She could get back to her vacation and not worry that they were pining away for their mother, that she was doing them harm that could only be remedied by years of therapy.

So shake it off, Charlotte. Shake it off, Mrs. Cordial. Your fantasy awaits.

She'd just passed through the gates when the clouds scraped, tore, and dropped lower, releasing enough rain to make one want to board an ark. She played a mental game, thinking of the rain as a kind of ritual, cleansing her of all those toxins, remaking her into Mrs. Charlotte Cordial, a woman who astounds dinner guests with her wit, relaxes in a corset as if it were made of flannel, solves ancient mysteries, and doesn't care that her eleven-year-old son called his father's mistress-cum-wife "Mom."

The baptism, as it were, was quite thorough. By the time she reached the house, her bonnet hung limp on her head and her dress clung to her legs. She sloshed into the main hall, making a puddle on the marble floor while Neville rushed around her, removing her soggy bonnet, squeezing her skirts with a towel.

"Sorry," she said. It seemed to be the word of the day.

It rained all day, then it rained all night. By morning, the world seemed resigned to rain. The spongy grass soaked it in, the trees held bucketsful teetering on thin leaves. The windows streaked and ran like those on a submarine just surfacing.

After breakfast Colonel Andrews organized games of charades and taught a new card game that involved shouting and running around the room. But after lunch the men absconded. Charlotte wondered if they were in their rooms napping or if there was a secret actors' lounge tucked in the back of the house where they played video games.

The ladies sat in the morning room, sewing samplers in the halfhearted gray light trickling through the windows.

Neville hustled in for Mrs. Wattlesbrook. She didn't ask questions and followed him out.

"I wonder what that was about," said Charlotte.

"Yeah." Miss Charming yawned. "I haven't seen Neville book it like that since Mr. Wattlesbrook showed up three sheets to the wind."

"That's true." Charlotte frowned at the door.

Miss Gardenside began a violent coughing fit and excused herself to her room, leaving Charlotte and Miss Charming alone with their samplers.

A few minutes later, Miss Charming gasped. But then, Miss Charming gasped a lot. She gasped when someone shut a door too loudly; she gasped when there were sausages for breakfast. She sometimes gasped and then coughed, as if she'd meant to cough from the beginning and gotten the two confused.

Charlotte enjoyed cataloging the provocateurs of Miss Charming's gasps, so she followed her shocked gaze to the door of the morning room.

"Hullo, what's here?" Mr. Wattlesbrook leaned against the threshold, wearing brown pants and a plain T-shirt. His smile showed an unlikely series of yellow, twisted teeth. "I know one of you. Or two, rather."

He smiled at Miss Charming's chest. She made a small whimpering sound.

"But you're new." He looked now at Charlotte.

"We met before," said Charlotte, "though at the time you were wearing a fire brigade blanket and coughing up smoke."

That seemed a little rude, so she finished it off by offering a small curtsy.

"None of the bobbing for me, thanks," he said. "I'm way past that. And so are all of you, soon as I'm finished. Things burn too easily. Best to sell them while you can."

He ambled in, his hands in his trouser pockets, and looked about, appraising the room. "Fit out quite well, isn't it? Looks nice, looks presentable." He tripped on a corner of a rug and took two sloppy steps to the side before regaining his balance. "First thing that goes," he said, glaring at the rug.

Mrs. Wattlesbrook poked her head in and groaned when she saw her husband. "John, come with me."

"That rug is your fault," he said, then turned his smile back at Miss Charming.

Miss Gardenside reentered, her eyes feverish. She hesitated when she noticed Mr. Wattlesbrook.

"Wait a minute . . ." He peered at Miss Gardenside. She turned away, her cheeks dark, her lips pressed together, and sat on a sofa with her back to him.

Mrs. Wattlesbrook pulled on his arm, but he shrugged her off and went closer. Suddenly he laughed.

"So that's who this is! What a joke. I know all about you, miss," he said, jabbing a finger into Miss Gardenside's shoulder. "Oh yes, all about it."

Miss Gardenside sat straight, her face impassive, but after a moment her hand rose to her forehead and a visible chill passed through her body.

She looked in genuine pain. Charlotte hadn't expected Alisha to react so strongly to being recognized. She hadn't squirmed when Charlotte had been so stupid with her that first day. Why now? Still, no need to make her unhappy.

"Sir," said Charlotte, "Miss Gardenside isn't well. Consumption, you know."

"Ha!" he said, and poured himself a drink from the crystal decanter in the corner.

"John, I insist you come with me," his wife tried again, hands on her hips.

He ignored her, turning to Charlotte as he drank. She was pretty sure that sip of alcohol would encounter an ocean of friends in his bloodstream.

"This is my house," he said. "You are my guests. I decide what I'll do with you."

The gentlemen arrived and stood behind Mrs. Wattlesbrook. Mr. Mallery wore no jacket, and Eddie's shirt was untucked, as if they had indeed been lounging somewhere. Colonel Andrews looked as immaculate as ever, and it was he who stepped forward.

"If you will come with us, sir," he said. "No need to distress the ladies."

"I'll do as I please!" Mr. Wattlesbrook shouted, throwing his glass on the rug. Red port bled out into the yellow fibers.

"All right, gents," Colonel Andrews said.

They grabbed Mr. Wattlesbrook and hauled him out of the room, while he hollered and kicked. Mrs. Wattlesbrook shut the door against the noise and turned to the ladies, dabbing at her forehead with a handkerchief.

"I—" She looked at the ceiling. She seemed to have no words. "My husband . . ."

Miss Gardenside patted the woman's arm. "The drink is the devil, Mrs. Wattlesbrook. And that is all we need to say."

Mrs. Wattlesbrook nodded. She dabbed at her forehead again and left the room.

"Wow," Miss Charming said under her breath. "Haven't seen that plot twist before."

Charlotte stood by the door but couldn't hear any more noise. Perhaps it *was* a plot twist. Perhaps Mr. Wattlesbrook was playing a part, creating a conflict that would need to be resolved by the end of the two weeks.

A maid rushed in with a cloth and began to soak up the spilled port.

But Mrs. Wattlesbrook's story world wouldn't be this messy, thought Charlotte.

Outside, the wind picked up behind the rain, lashing it against the windows. Clouds thickened and sunk low, and it seemed to be evening in the morning room.

"Anyone for tennis?" Charlotte asked.

home, twenty-nine years before

CHARLOTTE'S BIRTHDAY PARTY. SIX LITTLE girls in pajamas were lying atop their sleeping bags in the basement. A neat circle, faces in the center.

Her eleven-year-old brother emerged from the stairway, hands in pockets. The presence of the Boy elicited muted gasps and a general clambering for the cover of sleeping bags.

"Wanna play hide-and-go-seek?" he asked with a disquieting grin on his face. "I'll be It."

Charlotte's friends squealed happily at the idea. Because Tommy proposed it. And Tommy was cute and older and a boy, and therefore, *cool.* Charlotte didn't argue, even though he was hijacking her party. Her friends wanted to, and so, as a good friend and hostess, she should comply.

Everyone hid.

Then the lights went out and the screaming began.

What Charlotte found out later was that Tommy had waited to propose the game until their mother had run next door for a moment and no parent was supervising the house. While he counted, his friend Sam snuck into the basement and turned off the breakers. Then they both donned gorilla masks and went hunting.

Charlotte was the one doing most of the screaming. The pantry had been a very, very bad place to hide. A being with a gorilla face pounced on her from the darkness, and there was no exit—just endless boxes of macaroni and cheese knocked by her flailing arms, hitting the tile with sounds like shotgun blasts. When she finally got free, there was a second creepy-faced psycho blocking the hall. Hello therapy.

Charlotte's mother heard the screams from next door. She unmasked the villains, turned the lights back on, and sent Sam home and Tommy to his room. Tommy laughed all the way there.

At school on Monday, her friends summed up the event as "*So* fun. I was so scared. Tommy is *so* cool!" The terror forgotten, the girls swooned into the arms of sublime crush.

And Charlotte thought, Why are girls stupid?

Charlotte didn't answer herself, and she didn't forget. She'll never forget.

austenland, day 5, cont.

DINNER ENTERTAINED THE USUAL SUSPECTS, with no Mr. Wattlesbrook to be seen. Mrs. Wattlesbrook gripped her knife and fork a bit too tightly and startled at sounds like the clatter of cutlery or distant thunder.

She expects him to return any moment, Charlotte thought.

But he didn't, and the gentlemen covered up the bleak mood with plenty of conversation.

As per after-dinner custom, the women retired to the drawing room while the men stayed in the dining room, ostensibly to drink and smoke out of sight of the ladies. Tonight they stayed away a little longer than normal, and when they joined the ladies—first Colonel Andrews, then Mr. Mallery, followed a few minutes later by Eddie—only the colonel smelled of smoke, and none of them wafted alcohol breath, though Mr. Mallery and Colonel Andrews usually partook of a postprandial port. Eddie, she realized, always passed up the alcohol, as did Miss Gardenside.

Miss Gardenside seemed perkier than usual, sitting up straight and even rising to walk about. She sat at the piano and began to play, drawing a liquid song from the keys, but stopped abruptly and moved to the window. Lightning turned the night briefly silver, throbbing in and out before going dark again, and thunder groaned not far behind.

"Read some of the book, please, Colonel Andrews," said Charlotte.

"Quite right, Mrs. Cordial," he said, pulling the book from his breast pocket. "Excellent suggestion. There is much to learn of Mary Francis, I believe, and this weather creates the perfect ambience. Now, let's see, where were we?

> I hear sounds in the girl Mary's room at nights, my own chamber beside hers. Pacing or scraping. It is unnerving, but whenever I mean to ask her about it come morning, she looks so sad and tired I hold my tongue. The girl Betsy what used to board with her ran off one night and never come back to collect her wages. Cook tells me she feels a cold wind around the girl Mary and to get rid of her. Even if—

Colonel Andrews stopped reading as the electric lights in the room crackled and flashed, then went dark. Only the glow from the candles and a few kerosene lamps remained, their trembling flares making pockets of uncertain light. Charlotte stood from the couch and instinctively went closer to Eddie. He put a hand on her back.

"Lights out, Mallery?" he asked.

Mr. Mallery checked the electric lamps, clicking them on and off without effect. He stepped out and was gone a few minutes. Probably checking a breaker, Charlotte thought with an eerie feeling of déjà vu. He returned, a candle in hand, and shook his head. At least he hadn't donned a gorilla mask.

"Quite a storm," he said. "It has stripped us of all but firelight tonight, I think."

Charlotte took several steps closer to Mr. Mallery and his candle. The rain clawed at the window as if looking for a way in. The night storm seemed much closer now that the electric lights didn't blaze it back. No one spoke for a few moments. It seemed unlikely that anyone was ready for sleep. Charlotte's own mood was zigging and zapping her pulse.

"Now what on earth can we do in the dark to pass the time?" Colonel Andrews said, his voice velvety.

Miss Charming giggled.

"Indeed," said Mrs. Wattlesbrook with an offended sniff.

"I have it!" The colonel's voice brightened. "Let us play Bloody Murder."

"Ooh, the name alone gives one the shivers," said Miss Gardenside.

"Bloody Murder," Mrs. Wattlesbrook said. "That is most certainly not my cup of tea."

"Now, Missus—" Colonel Andrews began.

"I will retire," she interrupted. "Do not let the 'murderer' take refuge in my chamber, and keep things proper, sir, and you young creatures may have your merriment. Good night."

Charlotte watched Mrs. Wattlesbrook leave, a candle in hand, and wished she could go too. Which was ridiculous. She was a grown woman, and however ominous the game sounded, it was just a game.

"How do you play Bloody Murder?" Charlotte asked casually.

Colonel Andrews smiled. "I approve of your eagerness, Mrs. Cordial! And I shall not leave you in suspense. First we put out all the lights in the house."

Colonel Andrews picked up a brass extinguisher and capped three candles on the mantelpiece, then turned off the kerosene lamps. He nodded at Eddie, who licked his fingertips and quenched the candlewicks on the sideboard.

The room seemed to put on a shawl against the chill of the night. Miss Charming squealed in delighted terror.

"One of us will be the murderer," said Colonel Andrews, lifting the last remaining lit candle closer to his face, pushing the shadows up.

"The murderer hides somewhere in the dark house," he continued. "After a count of fifty, the rest of us hunt him out—each of us alone, mind you. The first to discover the murderer wherever he hides gives a shout of 'bloody murder!' and all the hunters flee for the drawing room. With the shout, you see, the murderer is loosed from his hiding place and can pursue."

"And what happens if he catches us?" Miss Gardenside asked, her tone playful.

"If the murderer touches you, you are dead and fall where you stand. The murderer tries to touch everyone before they can get to the safety of the drawing room. The last one touched will be the next murderer."

A hand grabbed Charlotte's shoulder. She screamed. It was Eddie.

"Upon my word, Charlotte," said her brother, "you are providing this game the perfect music."

Charlotte took some comfort in the fact that surely no one

could see her blush in the dim light. Only Colonel Andrews's face was strictly visible, though it was flickering like the flame.

"I don't really understand," Charlotte said shyly. "If there were a murderer hiding somewhere in the house, why would we all split up and hunt him out? I mean, wouldn't we want to stay away? Or together at least."

Colonel Andrews clicked his tongue. "You are delightfully practical, Mrs. Cordial. We hunt for the glory of discovering the culprit!"

"And because it's fun," said Miss Gardenside.

Theoretically, thought Charlotte.

There was a cracking noise in the dark. Eddie stepped into the circle of candlelight, six matches in his fist.

"Whoever draws the short stick is the murderer," he said.

Charlotte drew first, relieved her match was long. It was the solitude she feared most, going out into that dark house, waiting alone. She would make a horrible murderer, more afraid of her victims than they were of her, a feeble spider trembling on her web. *Stay away, flies! Please, stay away!*

The other two ladies likewise drew long sticks. The colonel offered his fist to Mr. Mallery, who hesitated before drawing. His match was half the size of the others.

"Mr. Mallery is the murderer!" Miss Gardenside shrieked.

Later Charlotte wondered if she misread his expression, because the gentleman's face seemed momentarily alarmed—more, even a little frightened. Was it possible that he too hated the dark, the solitude, the waiting? She almost took pity on him and volunteered to be his partner. But he so quickly recovered that she didn't trust her memory.

"Very well, then," said Mr. Mallery. "I suggest you all prepare yourself for a speedy death."

Miss Gardenside giggled. Charlotte shivered as if icy fingers were tickling her ribs.

"A right jolly fright I've got," Miss Charming said with glee.

"I'll warn the servants to stay in their chambers or in the kitchen," said Colonel Andrews. "We shall limit our playground to rooms with open doors, all right?"

He left, taking the only candle with him.

"Colonel, the candle—" Mr. Mallery began, but Andrews was already gone, leaving them in darkness. "What a dolt."

There was silence. The room was absolutely dark after the departure of that single light. Charlotte didn't dare move for fear of touching people unexpectedly, and maybe in unexpected places, which would so not be Regency appropriate.

"Should we sit down?" Miss Gardenside whispered.

"I fear I would sit on you rather than the sofa," Eddie whispered back.

"Why are we whispering?" Miss Charming whispered.

"Well, we *are* in a dark room with a murderer," said Charlotte. "No need to alert him to our presence."

"Ho hum, poor me," Mr. Mallery said somewhere to her left. "A murderer, all alone, and no one to murder. If only a potential victim would speak up and alert me to her presence."

Miss Gardenside giggled.

"Got you!" Eddie said suddenly, seizing the lady's arm.

Miss Gardenside screamed. So did Charlotte. Stupid brothers.

"What? Wait! Do not start without me," Colonel Andrews said, rushing back in, the candle flame bobbing. He placed the candle in a holder on the mantel. "We are safe. The servants absconded, and the house is ours. Go on, Mallery. We will give you till fifty."

Charlotte stood close to the candle and watched their elected murderer leave the room, his expression decidedly sneaky. Charlotte put her arm through Miss Charming's.

"Want to be hiding buddies?" she whispered.

"Don't be silly," Miss Charming whispered back. "If we're together, it makes cornering a gentleman and accidentally kissing him on the mouth a lot harder."

"Oh. Right, of course . . ."

Colonel Andrews took care of the counting. "Fifty" came quickly. Charlotte could see the indistinct figures of Miss Charming and Miss Gardenside bobbing with excitement as they ventured off into the inky house. The colonel and Eddie both wore dark jackets, and the blackness swallowed them up at once.

Stop it, Charlotte. This is just a children's game. And you aren't a child. You're fine.

Her heart beat like a fleeing rabbit's, but she left the safety of the drawing room and its single spark of light. She could hear the creak of steps and hurried breaths of the others, and she tried to make for the sounds, hoping for any companion in the dark. She thought she was on the trail of Colonel Andrews, but when she caught up with him, instead she found her own face in a mirror guarding the dining room.

"Hello?" she whispered in the black. "Hello? Anyone there?"

A rustle from the corner. Was it Mr. Mallery? He wasn't really a murderer, of course. Nothing to fear. And if it was Mr. Mallery, she could yell "bloody murder" and get this game over with.

She reached out, feeling cloth. Her breath caught. His jacket? No, it felt like velvet. The drapes.

The sound of running feet upstairs sent her spinning, looking for danger. The drawing room and the safety of its candle felt way too far away. She started to run and slammed her leg into a chair. A cry escaped her lips, and she might have fallen, but hands caught her. She couldn't scream—her breath was already gone. But the hands were warm and righted her, one holding her hand, one steadying her back.

"Are you hurt?" Mr. Mallery whispered. She could hear his distinct tone in that whisper, even if she couldn't make out his face. "Your heart is thumping like a beast."

She wasn't surprised he could feel her heartbeat through her back. She could feel it in her fingernails and eyelashes.

"You scared me," she said.

"Isn't that the purpose of the game?" he asked. "Truly, I am not certain, so perhaps you could enlighten me."

"I'm as much in the dark as you are," she said, then laughed.

He didn't laugh, but his hand moved on her back, a comforting kind of pat. It was so small a gesture but felt like fire on her skin, and instead of calming, the pounding of her chest magnified. A man was holding her in the dark. She sighed at her own pathetic heart.

"I believe you are obliged to yell 'bloody murder,'" he said.

"I don't really want to." She wanted to stay still. For the briefest moment, the dark felt like a good place to be.

"Mrs. Cordial . . ." His hands fell away.

She took a deep breath and yelled, "Bloody murder!" Then she dropped to the floor. Mr. Mallery rushed off.

From the carpet in the dining room, she heard the screams and laughs, the pounding footfalls and shouts of warning. When the sounds died out, she stood and moved carefully through the dining room, knowing that Mr. Mallery had left minutes ago but feeling that he was still there, watching her. It was not a comfortable sensation, not as it had been when he'd held her.

All the players had returned to the drawing room and were recounting their various hiding spots and moments of terror with breathless excitement.

"There is our murderer!" said Colonel Andrews, smiling at Charlotte.

"What? I'm the only one he touched?" she said.

"I missed them all," Mr. Mallery said. "I was clumsy."

Miss Charming giggled. "Right-o! The bloke nearly broke the stairs with his head."

Colonel Andrews was smiling at Charlotte, though in the traitorous shadowing of candlelight, the smile seemed full of malice. "Very well then, Mrs. Cordial. You have till the count of fifty."

"But—"

"One, two, three . . ." Miss Gardenside began.

Chanting numbers prodded Charlotte from the room, and before she could lose her nerve, she ran into the dark.

She'd meant to hide somewhere close to the drawing room and get it over with, but as soon as she was alone, she just kept running, passing up dozens of hiding places: the dining room with its voluminous drapes and vast under-table territory; the morning room with its concealing chairs and settees, its windows curtained from the occasional buzz of lightning; the ballroom, large as the moon and echoey as a seashell.

Up the stairs she went, counting along in her head—thirty-one, thirty-two, thirty-three—past the gallery and its creepy staring portraits. Charlotte didn't know she had a plan until she was on the spiral staircase leading to the servants' rooms, which she found in the dark by memory. The second floor.

The far window was like a glint of gray water at the bottom of a well. Charlotte could hear distant thumping, feet running. The count was over. They were on the hunt. She pressed her back to the wall and walked along it, her hands running over the wood paneling, her eyes alert to the shifts in the dark, shapes that could be a person, watching.

Her breath got louder in her own ears. She hated this. She

wanted to be wrapped in velvet drapes like Mr. Mallery, not standing naked as a skeleton in the middle of a hall. Hide, hide, hide . . .

There was a creak to her right. Her breath startled out of her. She pressed her back harder to the wall, kept moving, her hands sliding over the wainscoting.

She felt a notch. Her fingers investigated it. And suddenly the wall at her back wasn't there anymore. She gasped and fell backward, landing on her rear. Something clicked shut.

Charlotte scrambled to her feet, and her shoulders hit a wall. Where was she? Had she entered one of the upstairs rooms? But she hadn't turned a doorknob.

There was a bare window, and the room was filled with murky gray light, thick as oatmeal. This was definitely not the hallway. She pressed her hands to her pounding chest and looked around. There must be a door. Of course there had to be a door. How else did she get in?

She could not walk without bumping into things. This chamber was filled with objects—a storage room perhaps? She put her hands out, feeling her way around, trying to work toward the window and its pale invitation of light. From there she could find the other walls and search for a door.

Her fingers drifted over dusty wood, crates, cardboard boxes, glass vases, fringed pillows. Then something cool and fleshy. She paused.

That is not what it felt like, she told herself.

Of course not. What a ridiculous notion! She'd just take a closer look then laugh at herself and her prickly imagination. She moved aside what appeared to be a heavy velvet curtain from atop a sofa and peered in the half-light at what lay underneath.

Lightning filled the window, piercing the room with an

X-ray flash. And she saw. It seemed to be . . . it couldn't be but it sure looked like . . . a hand. A cold, dead hand. And in her experience, hands tend to be attached to bodies.

She saw for just a splinter of a second. The room went post-lightning dark, but still Charlotte stared. She stared for the count of three, waiting for her mind to come up with an alternate possibility.

It didn't.

Charlotte screamed. She screamed as if her voice could shatter windows. She screamed as she threw herself back the way she thought she'd come, fingers scrambling at the wall, searching for a way out, an escape. Something clicked, a piece of the wall lurched open as if on springs. She was knocked back. She crawled out the opening and kept screaming.

The scream lasted as she went down the spiral stairs, down the main staircase, and zipped into the drawing room, though by then it was breathy and restless, a scream that wouldn't stay put in her throat but kept slipping down into her middle or floating out harmlessly on an exhale.

The candlelight was a bronze haze hanging in the room, earthy and solid-seeming. The five others were staring at her. Colonel Andrews and Mr. Mallery seemed a little winded, as if they'd only just run into the room themselves.

"I didn't hear anyone shout 'bloody murder,'" said Miss Gardenside.

"Who found you?" asked Colonel Andrews. "Did you touch someone?"

"I . . . no," said Charlotte. Except a dead hand. But she felt supremely silly now that she was back among living people in the security of candlelight. Sure, she thought she'd found a dead body on the second floor, but why couldn't she be clinical about it? Simply shout, "Hello everyone! There's a dead body here. Come take a look, please, and someone perhaps should ring the coroner." But no. Thanks to her brother in a mask, she was a quivering ball of feminine terror.

"You know you were screaming?" Eddie came up to her, holding the candle. "You do look a bit mad. I suppose that is the point of this game though, eh, Andrews?"

"There was something, I touched something . . ." Charlotte looked at Mr. Mallery as she spoke. His eyes were hooded in the dim light, strong arms ill at ease in this setting. They were arms fit for *doing*, not playing children's games. The danger of him made her trust him now. A dead body on the second floor was something Mr. Mallery could handle.

"You are frightened," he said.

She nodded. "I think there was a body . . ."

Miss Charming gasped. Miss Gardenside tittered nervously.

Mr. Mallery didn't respond for a few moments. Then he offered his arm and said, "Mrs. Cordial, if you would, show us what you found."

She took his arm and immediately felt safe. Whatever might lurk upstairs, it couldn't be more dangerous than the man on her arm.

I'd like Mr. Mallery to rescue me, Charlotte suddenly thought.

That's a weird thought, said her Inner Thoughts. You'd never catch me thinking stupid thoughts like that.

Charlotte didn't lash back, because it was, frankly, a stupid thought. She didn't need saving. And why would a woman fantasize about being rescued at all?

With Mr. Mallery beside her and a lit candle in her hand, Charlotte led the way up the main staircase, down the hall to the spiral stairs, and up to the mysterious second floor. She took the candle from Colonel Andrews and examined the hall.

"There was a door here. I remember going past the table . . ." She shoved her shoulder against the wall. Nothing.

A door across the hallway opened. Mary peered out, her pallid skin and hair absorbing the tint of the dark, making her seem a ghostly blue.

"Mary, is this your bedchamber?" asked Mr. Mallery.

Mary nodded. Her large, unblinking eyes didn't leave his face.

"Good. Mrs. Cordial is a bit upset. Can you tell us if there is a room on this floor that is . . ."

He looked to Charlotte for more information.

"It's filled with furniture," said Charlotte. "And boxes and stuff."

Mary pointed to the other doors. "That's Kitty's and Tillie's room, there's Edgar's and Hamilton's—"

"Not a bedroom," said Charlotte. "Like a storage room."

Mary shook her head. She still hadn't looked away from Mr. Mallery.

"Thank you, Mary," he said.

She offered him a brief, hopeful smile then slowly shut her door.

Colonel Andrews yawned. "Well, good jest, Mrs. Cordial. I think our game has beat me. I am off for some shut-eye. You all go on without me."

"No!" said Charlotte too loudly. She checked herself. "I mean, I'm tired too."

"As am I," said Mr. Mallery.

They all agreed and made their way downstairs, Charlotte and Mr. Mallery going a bit slower than the rest.

"Sorry," she said. "I don't know what I was . . . I don't know."

"Mrs. Cordial, I do not care to hear an apology from you. You are the one coerced into running blind through an unfamiliar house. In the dining room, I should have realized that you were genuinely agitated. I should have put a stop to this before it went too far."

He thinks I'm crazy, she thought. He thinks I was so terrified of the game that I imagined a dead body in a disappearing room.

And perhaps, in fact, she had.

Mr. Mallery stopped on the landing and put a gentle hand on her shoulder. "Are you all right?"

"I feel like an idiot, but I'm fine."

"Get some sleep. And I promise you a more peaceful day tomorrow."

He took her arm, walked her to her chamber door, bowed, and left.

Colonel Andrews lingered at Miss Charming's door, whispering. He kissed her hand before departing to his room. Miss Charming placed a hand on her bosom and sighed.

"'Night, Mrs. Cordial."

"Goodnight." Charlotte stayed where she was. Outside her circle of candlelight, the house was excessively dark, and in the wind it creaked like a ship. Charlotte pictured the night as an ocean, and imagined that she alone was floating in that vastness. Lost at sea in the midst of a storm.

Miss Charming popped her head back out her door. "Hey, Charlotte?"

"Hm?" Charlotte took a few steps closer, only too glad to stall in the presence of another human.

"Do I look pale to you? Kind of sickly, like I've been half-choked or something?"

"No . . . why?"

"Because you do, and I wondered if everyone looks like that in candlelight."

Charlotte laughed. "I really, really spooked myself tonight."

Miss Charming gestured for Charlotte to follow. "Come on, honey lamb. There's room for two in my bed. Nothing hokey—I don't swing, thanks. You just look like a sad little puppy tonight."

"You don't mind?" Charlotte ran back to her room, shivering as she entered the darkness, as if she'd passed through a cold, wet veil. She grabbed her nightgown from a hook in her bathroom and was back in Miss Charming's room in a flash.

"My kids . . ." Charlotte stopped, knowing she wasn't supposed to speak about the real world. She chose her words carefully, so that she might have been speaking as Mrs. Cordial. "My children are of sturdier stuff than I am. When she was little, my girl loved thunderstorms, and I'd pretend to as well so that I wouldn't scare her. But sometimes I wished she was a little scared so she'd snuggle in bed with me at night."

Miss Charming sniffed. "I'm not offering a snuggle."

Charlotte smiled. "I accept all the same."

"You sleep left or right?"

James had slept on the right, Charlotte cramped up on the left, afraid to move and disturb his fragile sleep. "You point to a spot, and I'll sleep there all night without so much as a snort or rustle."

Miss Charming put her hands on her hips. "Is that right?"

"If I have one superpower, Miss Charming, it's silent, motionless sleep. You'd almost think me dead."

"Well, if we're going to sleep together, Mrs. Cordial, you'd better call me 'Lizzy.'"

They took turns helping each other out of dress and corset and jumped into bed. Charlotte pulled the covers up to her chin. A giggle started in her belly and tickled up her throat.

"What's funny?" Miss Charming asked, giggling too, as if she couldn't help herself.

"I haven't had a sleepover in . . . I don't know, almost thirty years." Had her brother-in-mask birthday party been the last? In retrospect, it had felt ominously final.

"Me too. Or in ten years anyway. Since I'm only twenty-eight."

"Oh," said Charlotte. She hadn't realized they could fudge their age as well as their name. Age seemed like such an indisputable thing, something branded into the wrinkle between her eyes. If she was in a place where a woman of fifty could just say, "I'm twenty-eight," then what else was possible?

They said goodnight, and Miss Charming blew out her candle. Charlotte rolled onto her side, and the good feeling the laugh had traced through her dissolved into the dark behind her lids. She saw again the handlike image flashing in the pop of lightning. A gray hand irradiated by moonlight, mysterious, neither feminine nor masculine. A hand was unmistakably human.

Had she been mistaken? No. Impossible. But then, where had the storage room gone? The uncertainty made her want to pace. She hugged the blanket to her chest.

All through the night, each time her thoughts peeked into consciousness, she saw again the hand, felt it in memory, and opened her eyes, sure she would see a ghostly figure in the room, watching her. Sometimes the figure wore a monk's robe, like in the painting on the second floor. Sometimes it was missing a hand.

It's hard to get much sleep when you're checking for a menacing presence every twenty to thirty minutes. It's also hard to sleep next to Miss Charming when she's on her back. Either her snores or the wind rattled the window. Then, as Charlotte lay awake trying to paint the darkness in happy sunshine and rainbows, she heard a thud from outside. She slid carefully from the bed and tiptoed to the window.

The rain had stopped, but the night was wet and cloudy,

with no moonlight to glint on the puddles and shaking leaves. She stared, trying to determine the source of the noise. It hadn't been a sharp sound, like a falling roof tile. It hadn't been flat, like a slamming door. It was a thud, like something heavy but not breakable dropping onto the front walk below. But she couldn't make out anything in the dark and gave up, returning restlessly to Miss Charming's bed.

Around five in the morning, gray light replaced black, and Charlotte found she could keep her eyes shut and sleep.

I didn't know I was so scared of the dark, she thought as she began to drift. I didn't know I still believed in monsters.

home, ten months before

CHARLOTTE SAT ON A love seat in her family room, the mail strewn around her, and stared at the wedding announcement. James's mistress-soon-to-be-wife was named Justice. The glazed ivory card stock and cursive raised lettering slapped so much dignity on the name that it seemed to mock it.

Emotional responses aside, let's be careful not to vilify Justice. Just because she had a prolonged sexual affair with another woman's husband doesn't mean she was rotten to the core. Here's a woman who donated all her discarded clothing to the Salvation Army—why, she even boxed up her old, stained Tupperware and empty egg cartons in case schoolchildren wanted them for crafts projects. She knit scarves. She drove slowly through duck crossings. She observed Yom Kippur even though she wasn't technically Jewish.

As a general rule, Charlotte loved her fellow human being. So in a gesture of acceptance, Charlotte pinned the announcement to the corkboard. Then Charlotte pinned a flyer from a yoga studio over it. Thank goodness she was still numb.

Justice . . .

austenland, day 6

IF THERE HAD BEEN A body, then whose was it?

Charlotte sat at her vanity as Mary did her hair. Mary's movements were skittery, and yet her eyes were always wide open, looking around. Little happened that she would miss.

"Will all the guests be at breakfast today?"

"I believe so, ma'am." Mary had a high voice. It scraped the ceiling.

"And what of the staff . . ."

"Ma'am?" Her expression was smooth, but her voice remained suspiciously squeaky.

"It just seems like someone is missing. For some reason. Did anyone . . . leave the manor recently?" Or get offed and stuffed in a disappearing room?

"Not that I know of, ma'am."

Mary caught Charlotte watching her in the mirror and looked away.

Dressed and fitted up, Charlotte started to head down the stairs for breakfast in the dining room. But then, looking back to make sure no one observed her, she hurried to the spiral stairs instead.

Truth is rarely more horrible than imagination, she told herself.

Then she started imagining scenarios where the truth really was more horrible. That's a thought cycle that never ends well.

The second-floor corridor seemed narrower in the daylight. It was the darkness itself that had made the corridor seem cavernous, filled with frights from her own overactive brain.

Pipe down, brain, Charlotte commanded. I blame mystery novels for your bad manners.

As she left the safety of the stairs, goose bumps prickled her arms. She took silent, careful steps down the hall, passing the table with the empty vase. The entrance to the room would be between the table and the next bedroom. The wainscoting created panels about the height of a door. She pushed against a panel, then the next, the next—

"Skulking back to the scene of the crime?"

Charlotte spun around. Eddie was coming up the stairs. Even his slight, surprised-looking smile brought out those dimples. He had such a harmless face.

"Eddie," she breathed. "Don't do that."

"You look positively criminal, Charlotte. Are you sneaking sweets? Have you drawn on the walls or perhaps spilled your juice on the carpet?"

Charlotte let her shoulders relax. "If I did, would I get a spanking?"

Eddie raised a single eyebrow.

"Whoa!" said Charlotte, feeling a blush come on. "That's not what I meant. I was trying to keep with your naughty-child theme, not add another kind of naughty something or other. Sorry, brother of mine."

She giggled, then covered her mouth, not sure if she should appear more penitent.

Eddie narrowed his eyes. "What are you up to?"

She glanced up the hallway. The far window seemed to sink back even farther, the light barely shuffling down the hall.

"Come with me. I'd rather not do this alone."

He approached slowly, his feet reluctant. "I don't know if I should encourage this fancy of yours."

"It's already encouraged. It's beyond encouraged. Just help me resolve it, if you would be so kind."

She continued pushing on the wall as she went, feeling for

give. "It can't have been a normal door. There must be a disguised door here somewhere."

"A *secret* door? Charlotte—"

"I know you all thought I was crazy, and I was ready to believe you. But by daylight, I don't feel crazy. There's got to be—aha! Here, push," she said, taking his hands and placing them on one wall panel.

"See how it feels kind of . . . loose? A little bit?"

She stood with her back against the wall and slid along it, as she had been doing the night before, feeling for a lever or switch. He laughed.

"I wanted you here so you could *help*."

"Actually, I believe you wanted me to protect you from the Pembrook Phantom."

"Maybe." She tried to sound cheeky, but truthfully she really didn't appreciate him throwing around words like "phantom" while she was in a dim corridor looking for a secret passageway. Her goose bumps were getting goose bumps.

Then she felt it—a kind of knob, hidden in the wainscot. She flicked it with her finger. The wall at her back swung in.

She almost fell back again, but Eddie grabbed her arm and pulled her upright. His wide eyes took in the room behind her.

"See? See? I'm not completely crazy."

"Not completely," he whispered and went in, his hands together as if he were entering a holy sanctum, or perhaps Willy Wonka's Chocolate Factory. Charlotte followed. The door shut behind them, making them both jump.

"It does that," said Charlotte. "But I don't like it that it does that. In fact, I wish that it wouldn't do that. I really wish that it—" She shut herself up because she realized she was rambling, and she realized she was rambling because the secret room did in fact exist. Which also meant . . .

Charlotte met eyes with the sofa. That is, if the sofa had eyes, she would have met eyes with it. As it was, she just had the creepy sensation that it *knew* she was looking at it. Which of course it didn't. It was just a sofa, after all. A sofa that seemed to have eyes, and if it did have eyes, it would be glaring—kind of smugly. A smug kind of glare.

She was still rambling, even in her thoughts.

Shut up, Charlotte, she told herself.

She pointed at the sofa. "It was there."

Eddie didn't speak. Perhaps if he had, he would have rambled too. Instead, he approached the sofa cautiously (almost as if the sofa had eyes and Eddie didn't like the way it was smugly glaring) and lifted the velvet coverlet.

Nobody. No body at all. Not even a severed hand.

Charlotte's relief was chased from her chest by an aggressive stampede of disappointment and confusion.

"But . . . there was . . . I swear . . ."

Eddie looked around. "I don't know that we should be here. This is a bit of an underbelly, isn't it? Like seeing backstage."

"But it's real, Eddie. Everyone thought I was crazy, but the room is *real*."

He nodded, eyeing the wobbly stacks of chairs and old sofas with ripped covers. He knelt at a box and pulled out a fencing foil with stubbed tip.

"Ooh," he said.

Charlotte examined the velvet coverlet and what wasn't underneath it. She shut her eyes and saw again the hand, lit up silver by the well-timed lightning. It had been real, just like the room. Right? There was nothing on the sofa now but the coverlet, and its fringe could hardly imitate five fingers and a palm.

"I'm sure I saw . . . I touched it." Her stomach squelched. "Oops. Excuse me."

Eddie put back the foil. "Come along, Charlotte darling, I will escort you to breakfast. Breakfast should always come before sleuthing." He went to the door . . . or what was an outline of a door. There was no knob.

"How exactly do we extract ourselves from the belly of the beast?"

"I'm not sure." She studied the wall. "It was dark. And I think I was, well, flailing around."

The wainscot was carved. She pressed it until she found a rounded bit that gave way under her hand, and the door swung in.

"Look out—that is alarming each time," said Eddie.

The door clicked shut behind them. They'd just taken a step toward the stairs when a non-secret door opened and Mary peered out. She saw them, and her face turned very red.

"Hello, Mary," said Charlotte.

"I'm . . . I'm in my room," she said and shut herself back in.

"She's perpetually jumpy," Charlotte whispered.

"Let us keep the secret room a secret, shall we, Charlotte?" said Eddie, taking her arm and walking to the stairs. "Mrs. Wattlesbrook does not like guests to see anything dusty or untidy."

"But . . . we should call the police. The secret room is real! So that must mean the body was real too."

He took her hand and looked at her with concern.

He has brown eyes, she thought. So does my real brother. But Eddie's have more honey in them.

"Are you certain, Charlotte? Are you absolutely certain you encountered a murdered human being last night?"

Yes! She was! They'd been playing Bloody Murder in a dark and creepy old house and she'd fallen into a secret room and naturally there'd been a dead body. Well, she'd only seen the hand. Now that she thought about it, the hand had felt odd. Not that she'd ever encountered a real corpse before, but did they all feel so . . . so rubbery? It had seemed to be attached to something, and she'd assumed it had been a body, and again had assumed that the deceased person had been murdered and hidden away. Wow, she *had* assumed quite a bit. But if it hadn't been real, then why was it gone? Why would someone put a prop corpse on a couch in a secret room and then move it between midnight and morning?

"I . . . think so."

"Mrs. Wattlesbrook is sensitive. If you call the police, and they come search the house and find nothing, well, it will be disruptive and very hard on her. I just want you to be certain."

"I'll think about it," she said. "Maybe I should just talk to her first."

He nodded and, seeing she intended to go about her business immediately, went to the dining room alone.

Charlotte found Mrs. Wattlesbrook working at a desk in the morning room.

"Mrs. Wattlesbrook, do you have a moment?" she asked.

The woman gestured to a seat and put on a patient face. An impatient sort of patient face, like an impatient face dressing up as a patient one for Halloween. Charlotte decided to speak quickly.

"Last night while we were . . . um, playing . . . Bloody Murder . . ." Charlotte almost whispered the last two words. For some reason, they filled her with shame. "Well, I was alone and I stumbled into a room without a real door on the second floor, and I just wanted to make sure you were aware of its existence."

"Of course I am aware. This house has been a part of my husband's family for generations. The Wattlesbrooks have always been eccentric. Some ancestor probably had the room's door disguised as a good joke. I use it for storage." She sniffed. "I assure you that the rest of the house is kept properly and am sorry you were exposed to our less-than-regal side."

"No, it's fine, really. I mean, I'm not a stickler for well-ordered drawers." She tried to smile companionably, but the woman didn't return it. "Oh, I meant 'drawers' as in the things you open, not, like, underwear, because clean and tidy underwear is a passion of mine!" Really, Charlotte? she thought. Is it really? Is that a statement you want defining you? Charlotte cleared her throat and looked down, begging herself to shut up. This ghost-hand business really had her flustered. "Have you been there recently?"

"Not in a month at least, I should think. Why?"

"It's just, when Mr. Grey and I went in this morning—"

"You should not be alone with any gentleman in a closed room."

"But he's my brother."

Mrs. Wattlesbrook sniffed. "Quite."

"So . . . so when we were there, I realized that something wasn't there anymore." What could she say? I wonder, Mrs. Wattlesbrook, if you find yourself missing a corpse this morning? Do you perhaps know if someone was recently murdered and stashed in your storage room? Perhaps you could count heads and take pulses amongst your staff and see if anyone happens to be dead?

She met Mrs. Wattlesbrook's eyes and said boldly, "I can't be sure, but I might have seen a dead body in there last night."

Mrs. Wattlesbrook's look turned white hot. Charlotte cringed. Then, even worse, Mrs. Wattlesbrook tried to smile through her rage. It was like watching an alligator make a kissy face.

"I let Colonel Andrews indulge in his games because my guests seem to find them amusing," she said slowly. "But let me be frank: I prefer not to take part."

No concern over the implication of a murder in her house? The woman was often severe, but this morning she seemed beyond. As Beckett would say, Who peed in her Cheerios?

"Mrs. Wattlesbrook, are you all right?"

Mrs. Wattlesbrook's forehead creased, but she looked back at her papers. "Quite so." She began to write.

Charlotte felt invisible. She whispered something that might have been "thank you" or "I'll just go now," or possibly "Moses supposes his toeses are roses." She curtsied as she left, though no one saw.

The gentlemen and ladies were in the dining room, chatting over breakfast. Mr. Mallery watched her enter, his expression unreadable. Charlotte smiled and hurried to the sideboard, looking for something without grease. Her stomach couldn't take it today.

"You gave us all a fright last night, Mrs. Cordial," said Colonel Andrews. "With your dead body and screams fit to wake it. I say, you put a twist on old Bloody Murder. Well done."

Charlotte smiled politely. He glanced around, as if to check that no one was observing him, and then winked at Charlotte. Winked as if they were in on the same joke, and gave her a little conspiratorial nod to boot.

Charlotte sat as realization descended on her like an alien's tractor beam. Of course. How could she be such a doofus? It had been part of the mystery of Mary Francis! Mrs. Wattlesbrook said it was the colonel's game and she didn't want to take part. Colonel Andrews had hinted about clues on the second floor. She had discovered the room. There would be clues inside. The rubbery hand had been part of a fake corpse, and he'd carried it off before she could examine it by light of day and see just how phony it was.

But it'd been a fleshy dead body, not a skeleton, so Colonel Andrews hadn't intended for her to believe it was the corpse of Mary Francis centuries later. This was an entirely new mystery perhaps.

Whose body was it supposed to be?

None of the players, of course. Mallery, Andrews, Eddie, Miss Charming, and Miss Gardenside had all been in the drawing room when she went upstairs. And Mrs. Wattlesbrook was accounted for this morning.

"Is Mr. Wattlesbrook still around?" Charlotte asked.

Someone at the other end of the table clattered a dish. Charlotte looked up but couldn't tell if it had been Mr. Mallery, Mr. Grey, or Miss Gardenside.

"No," Colonel Andrews said, frowning. "I have not seen him. Have you, Grey?"

"Not since yesterday," Eddie said a little stiffly. "Perhaps he went to town."

"Nothing to keep him here." Mr. Mallery was busy with his bread and butter. "He was as useless for society in the drawing room as he was for fetching game in the hunting field."

"Unlike you, old boy, right?" Eddie said. "A fair *prince* of the drawing room, conversation to dazzle and delight."

"Lydia, you're looking well," said Charlotte.

"Thank you. I am feeling on the mend."

"Perhaps your nurse, Mrs. Hatchet, is to be praised?" Charlotte asked slyly. "I haven't seen her since yesterday morning."

Silence hung over the table, stronger than the aroma of the just-cooked sausages still sizzling on the sideboard.

Miss Gardenside did not look up as she said, "Mrs. Hatchet is no longer with us."

Charlotte gasped. "What?"

Now all eyes were on Charlotte. Perhaps she'd voiced her shock a little dramatically.

"I sent her home," said Miss Gardenside. "Since I was feeling better."

"Oh. Right."

After breakfast they put on boots and went outside, sloshing through the swampy grass and along the muddied path, breathing in the wet air. As it turned out, the sky *is* blue in England, from time to time. The rain-scented air, the sunshine, Mr. Mallery on her arm—there was a deliciousness to the moment she could almost appreciate.

"I can see your freckles," said Mr. Mallery, staring straight ahead.

"You cannot," she said.

"You taunt me with them constantly." He snapped a rosebud off a bush. "Come riding with me today. Just the two of us."

"Um . . ." Danger, danger! She couldn't be alone with this man. She'd have to let go and figure out what to feel and think and wasn't there something she needed to do? "There's something I need to do."

As the group meandered through the rose garden, Charlotte made her way over to Eddie.

"The hidden room is part of Colonel Andrew's mystery," she said.

"Is it?"

"Yes—it's his clue on the second floor. The body was a fake, and I wouldn't wonder if this second mystery will tie into the Mary Francis story somehow. Did he tell you who was supposed to be the new murder victim?"

"I would not tell you if he had," said Eddie. "That would spoil the fun."

"I think it's Mrs. Hatchet or Mr. Wattlesbrook. Colonel Andrews would pick someone obvious. I need to figure out if they've really gone or disappeared under mysterious circumstances, that sort of thing."

"Have you been reading Gothic novels, Charlotte? You know what Mother would say. Women should not indulge in dark fantasies. It disrupts the proper workings of the womb."

Charlotte snorted and coughed at once, she was so surprised. "The proper workings of the *womb*?"

Eddie was trying very hard not to laugh. "Indeed."

"Never fear, protecting my womb from Gothic novels is my first priority."

"I am much relieved."

"So, how do you propose we figure out if Mrs. Hatchet or Mr. Wattlesbrook was done in?"

"You are morbid. I never knew. Well, the eyes of Pembrook Park belong to Neville the butler."

Charlotte gave Eddie a scheming smile and headed back to the house. Mr. Mallery's gaze followed her, and she almost regretted her quick departure, but Colonel Andrews was going to be so impressed when she solved his mystery!

She found Neville in the dining room, setting the grand table for dinner. She peered through the inch of open door, observing how carefully he placed the utensils, measuring the distance between each fork. As carefully as if he were building a bomb.

"Excuse me," she said as she entered.

"Oh! Is something the matter with Mrs. Wattlesbrook?" he asked.

"No, um, not that I'm aware of. She didn't send me. I just wanted to ask you something."

He straightened up, his hands held behind his back as he waited for her to speak. His whole attention seemed directed toward her, but a slight fidget made her wonder if he wasn't dying to get back to his table. Maybe he lived for a neat place setting, she considered. Maybe if she gave tidy tableware a fair shot, her life would be complete.

"I understand Mrs. Hatchet has left Pembrook Park?" Charlotte hesitated before speaking on, but reminded herself that lying wasn't really lying here. "I lent her my handkerchief one day, and I never got it back. She probably didn't realize it was my grandmother's and has sentimental value. Do you know if she took all her things with her?"

"I believe so, madam."

"Oh." Charlotte fiddled with a fork at the nearest place setting before catching herself. Neville sniffed almost imperceptibly. He'd have to remeasure that one now.

"Sorry, I didn't mean to mess up your work."

"You may do as you please, madam."

"Well, I might just check her room, in case she left it for me."

"I will send Mary to look for you."

"Don't bother. I can go. Um, where was she staying?" she asked innocently.

"Just west of Miss Gardenside's chamber," he said with some reluctance.

"Thanks. And thanks for making my stay so nice here. It's a really beautiful house, and you all keep it up so well."

"It is my pleasure to do so," said Neville, sounding as if he meant it.

She paused before the doorway and asked, as if it were no more than an afterthought, "Do you expect Mr. Wattlesbrook to come back?"

Now Neville's cool exterior cracked. The slightest emotion dominated his face, just as any action above a slow walk made his skinny frame look like a crazed marionette.

He composed himself, but not before Charlotte understood Neville's opinion of the man Wattlesbrook.

"I never expect him to return, Mrs. Cordial," he said. "Yet he always does."

Well. "Did you see him leave?" asked Charlotte.

"I did not."

"So you don't know what time he left yesterday or if he stayed the night?"

"I do not believe he stayed the night. When Mr. Wattlesbrook is in the house, he generally makes himself known."

Neville's voice was becoming strained. He was going to bottle up. Charlotte decided to apply some well-timed truth.

"I was just wondering because . . . well, he makes me uncomfortable."

This Neville could easily believe. "Mrs. Wattlesbrook would want to know of any discomfort you have during your stay, madam."

"I know, but I don't want to complain. I worry she has enough to juggle."

"Mrs. Wattlesbrook is a very capable woman."

Aha! His face lit up, his hands clasping earnestly in front of his body. Oh yes, Neville felt quite the opposite about the woman Wattlesbrook.

"She's the best," said Charlotte, dangling the hook.

"I am happy you see her truly, madam."

She smiled at the butler and made again to leave, but asked on her way out, "Oh, by the way, how did Mr. Wattlesbrook arrive here?"

"He generally comes in his own . . . vehicle."

Of course he would drive a car. This was not a man who cared about keeping up Regency appearances. "And is that 'vehicle' still around? I just don't want to see it, if you know what I mean. I'm trying to be immersive!" she added gamely.

"I noticed it gone, madam. That is why I am certain the gentleman is gone as well."

Charlotte thanked him and went upstairs to investigate Mrs. Hatchet's room. The drawers and wardrobes were empty, but there was an ominous-looking trunk at the foot of the bed.

A dead body could fit inside there, she thought.

But it was empty too. She wished Colonel Andrews would be more obvious with his mystery. She left the room just as Miss Gardenside was entering her own.

"Charlotte! What were you doing in my—in Mrs. Hatchet's room?"

"I was looking for clues to Colonel Andrews's mystery."

"The Mary Francis affair? In Mrs. Hatchet's room?"

"Yes. Well, Mrs. Hatchet did disappear, and I thought maybe it was just a hoax."

Complete bafflement registered on Miss Gardenside's face.

"She went home," Miss Gardenside said.

"Okay. I guess I just got carried away." Charlotte made her halfhearted smile.

"Why would you think my mother would be involved?

"Mother?"

"Did I say 'mother'? Odd, I don't know what I meant."

Miss Gardenside shrugged prettily and went through her door.

Charlotte remembered her mentioning that her mother bore scars on her knuckles from nuns' rulers, which must mean she'd attended a Catholic school. And once she'd seen Mrs. Hatchet cross herself—forehead, heart, shoulder, shoulder—an unconscious gesture, the reflex of a lifelong Catholic. Mrs. Hatchet was pale and blonde, but Miss Gardenside could have a dark-skinned father or be adopted. So, Mrs. Hatchet was her mother. And she had sent her away. Or something.

In the safety of her own room, Charlotte started to dress for dinner, but the excitement of the mystery made her too antsy to do up the hooks, and she didn't want to ring for Mary. Mary—she had the same name as Mary Francis. Maybe that was a clue?

Stop it, Charlotte! She lay on her bed and tried to thrust the crumbling abbey and Mr. Wattlesbrook's car from her thoughts.

Obviously she was getting way more into this than Miss Gardenside and Miss Charming were.

You're doing that thing you do whenever you're supposed to relax, she told herself. Hunting out any old problem just so you can solve it.

Yeah, you totally do that, added her Inner Thoughts. So why didn't you figure out the million clues pointing to James's affair? How can you be so hawkeyed and yet so dense?

Her Inner Thoughts could be a real downer. Charlotte put her arm over her eyes. No more unraveling just to avoid leisure. She exhaled slowly and cleansed her mind of this Gothic mystery. Done.

Other thoughts promptly swooshed in to take their place:

Lu: "I'm done with you."

Justice: "Beckett called me 'Mom'!"

Charlotte opened her eyes and welcomed the all-consuming mystery to take back her brain. It really wasn't such a bad preoccupation when compared with others.

home, eleven months before

"I'M WORRIED ABOUT WHAT THIS is doing to the kids," Charlotte confessed to James when he stopped by the house to pick up Lu and Beckett for the weekend. She peered out the kitchen—the kids were in the living room watching television. She lowered her voice. "Beckett hasn't been sleeping well. He's anxious . . . about you. About us."

It was weird talking to James about the kids after everything they'd been through. They'd spent thousands of hours speaking as partners in the past, but now . . . well, it was like trying to eat amazingly realistic rubber food. But who else could she talk to?

"I don't know," said James. "They seem fine to me. And it's not as if divorce is uncommon. Over fifty percent of all marriages end in divorce. I'm sure at school they're just one of the crowd."

Could that statistic really be true? Among Charlotte's acquaintances, about 10 percent of the marrieds had divorced. Before James had left, divorce had seemed distant and improbable. Besides, statistics felt as irrelevant as a nice wool blanket in the vacuum of space. Let's look at a mother who is standing in a hospital waiting room, a doctor telling her that her child has died from a rare disease. Is it a comfort for her to hear that only one in five million children contract it?

Some postdivorce statistics:

- James saw the children 75 percent less than before.
- He missed 85 percent of their afterschool woes.
- He was absent for 99 percent of their family dinners.

Screw statistics. One hundred percent of Charlotte's marriage had ended in divorce, and for her, that was the only number that meant anything at all.

austenland, day 6, cont.

CHARLOTTE REACHED BEHIND HER AND tried to do up twenty-seven buttons. This mad world. It had all been very real for Austen, for her characters. Their clothes, their manners, their marriages—all absolute survival. But for Charlotte, in the twenty-first century, it was like eating Alice's mushroom and shrinking a couple of centuries.

She was playing dress-up, playing pretend, playing hide-and-seek and chase and kissing tag. Does play belong exclusively to children? How does one be an adult in a child's world? Well, for one thing, she would dress in her fine pink silk. Her hair still looked decent, so she stuck in some pearl clips and called it good. She got up and headed to the hallway, but she saw Mr. Mallery rounding the stairs and hurried back into her room.

Why was it that just thinking of that man made her aware of

every cell in her body? And the state of her lipstick. She wasn't proud of this fact, but when Mr. Mallery was around, she became increasingly concerned with the general appearance of her lips.

There was a knock, and Mary entered with some towels. She curtsied when she saw Charlotte in the bathroom reapplying lipstick and then went about her business. Charlotte felt the lack of a "Do Not Disturb" sign. She forgot her lips and started downstairs.

Another maid passed her in the hall, pausing to curtsy. Another maid dusted in the morning room. Was there nowhere in the house she could be alone? Even the gazes of the portraits seemed to follow her.

She was early to the drawing room. Empty, it seemed as stiff and forbidden as a roped-off museum display.

Outside, the summer evening still burned, the sun getting in all the dazzle it could before English rain took over again. Violent wind belied the blue sky, tangling her hair and skirts, warning of coming changes. She meant to just stand on the steps, appreciate the wind and soak in some vitamin D, but her brain was in full mystery mode and skipped from Miss Gardenside's disappearing mother to Mr. Wattlesbrook's vehicle. Where did he park it last night? She would have noticed a car out front.

The wind pushed at her, nudging and restless, and she caught its mood. She left her perch and walked around the side of the house, looking for a likely garage. There were outbuildings—stables, a separate servants quarters—but none had a large door that looked like it would fit a car. Had he left it out in the open? Perhaps around the side.

There! A tire track. His tire must have dug into the mud underneath the gravel, now drying in the sun. Up ahead was another tire mark. Why had he driven this way? He hadn't seemed concerned about hiding his modern clothing whenever he barged in, so it seemed unlikely he would park his car so far from the house entrance just to keep it out of sight of the guests. She knew from her phaeton trip with Mr. Mallery that there was no road outlet from that side of the estate, only dirt paths that would have been treacherous for a car during the heavy rain. He would have had to exit back through the main gate, and yet here were signs he'd driven in the opposite direction.

She spotted another tire mark and followed it, the wind encouraging her into the wooded area near the stables and the pond.

The countryside was molded for wind. Her hotel in London had overlooked a stone square. While sitting on her balcony, she'd noticed that the only sign the wind was blowing was the intemperate pieces of garbage tumbling about; the city itself was still, unmoved by the storm. The country, on the other hand, was teeming with breeze teasers—grass and shrubs, trees and pond, everything tossed and upset by the wind. The massive oaks boiled with it, shaking their tops, bending their branches to keep from breaking. The pond waters thrashed into white, mocking the idea that water is transparent. Wind made everything opaque—wind made everything move.

Charlotte moved too, as agitated as the pond. She approached it cautiously, the banks sloppy with mud. Did that look like another set of tire tracks over there? She tiptoed nearer to the shore, stepping on tangles of grass and dried crusts of mud.

Yes, right at the rim of the pond, almost as if a car had driven out of the water—those looked an awful lot like tire marks. But they stopped suddenly, as if stamped out and smoothed over. Seemed like an odd detail for Colonel Andrews to create, but then again, perhaps she was off track and this had nothing to do with the mystery. She took another step, caught her toes on her skirt, and stepped down hard.

"No . . ." She lifted her hem. Gray mud soaked through her silk dress.

Charlotte scolded herself right back into the house and upstairs to change, passing the drawing room quickly, before the gathered gentlemen could notice her dress.

Mary was just then emerging from Charlotte's room. She kept her face down after seeing Charlotte. Was she embarrassed or had pale-as-bone Mary started wearing blush? If so, she'd put it on like a novice, pinking from cheekbone to jaw.

"I was outside," said Charlotte, "and I got my dress dirty. Do you think it's salvageable?"

Mary squatted and examined the stain. "I will try, ma'am, but that pond mud is desperately hard to get out of cloth."

Hm. "It *is* pond mud. How did you know?"

Mary stood upright, as startled as a pheasant. "I . . . I've seen that mud on clothes before."

Other guests must have slipped in mud in the past, Charlotte thought, and Mary may have experience trying to draw the viscous stuff out of cloth. But if it was such a regular occurrence, why did she seem agitated by the question?

Mary helped her change into a new dress, and Charlotte rushed downstairs, the last to arrive for dinner.

"There is our fine summer breeze!" Colonel Andrews said as she entered.

Mrs. Wattlesbrook was on her feet at once and organized everyone into the order of precedence for the walk across the hall and into the dining room. Mr. Mallery took the hostess's arm, followed by Miss Charming with Colonel Andrews. Charlotte wasn't sure it was completely Regency appropriate, but Eddie took both Miss Gardenside's and Charlotte's arms so no one walked alone.

"If Mr. Wattlesbrook were here, would he escort his wife?" she asked.

"I believe so," said Eddie.

"Then everyone would have a partner."

"Now, you do not mind sharing, do you, ladies? Plenty of Grey to go around, I assure you."

Still, it seemed a slight imperfection to Charlotte, one that a woman like Mrs. Wattlesbrook must detest. If her husband were present, and behaving, he would make all the numbers even.

And Charlotte would be on Mr. Mallery's arm . . .

Oh my word! That's what's bothering you, her Inner Thoughts accused. You have a crush on Mr. Mallery and want his attention constantly!

I do not, she thought back. That's silly. He's just an actor.

Mm-hm, and how often do you watch a movie and get a crush on an actor? Like, all the time?

Charlotte pondered for a moment why her Inner Thoughts tended to sound like a teenage girl.

Fine, that's true, she thought, but I never expect an actor on the screen to fall in love with me.

That's your prob, isn't it, Charlotte? You never expect anything! You're, like, paying actors a lot of money to make you feel all swoony and romantic, and you still don't *expect* it. For a "nice" girl, you're totally a pessimist.

I am not! I'm optimistic a lot of the time, like when . . . when . . .

"Er, Charlotte? Are you all right?" asked Eddie.

"Hm?" She looked up from her empty plate. Everyone else's was loaded with food, and everyone's attention was directed at her. Even her Inner Thoughts cringed.

"Fine! Fine. Looks great," she said, dishing herself some kind of salad. "I keep thinking about your mystery, Colonel Andrews. Maybe you could give us more clues tonight?"

He banged on the table happily. "Yes indeed, Mrs. Cordial, yes indeed. I knew you for a confederate, I did, and I have new entries to add to the story that will tickle your spine and make you cry out in terror for your mummy."

"Or at least for Mr. Mallery," Eddie said into his drink.

Charlotte gave him a subtle kick under the table, but he just smiled.

See, even Eddie noticed, said her Inner Thoughts.

After dinner in the drawing room, Colonel Andrews didn't wait for another invitation. He pulled out his book and began to read more of the housekeeper's account.

> Mary and I were shelling peas this morning in the garden. She has been here now three months and still does not seem to settle down. It does make one uneasy. I asked her just as prim as you please about the deaths at the abbey. She shook her head. You best tell me what you know so you can get it out, says I. And Mary says there are things a body can talk about and things no one should. And that is all she will say. Her silence does not help her much. She has made one friend here, the girl Greta, who is German and perhaps does not understand much anyhow. But most do not take to Mary. I see how the kitchen hands stare her down, knock her with a shoulder as they pass by. They are getting rougher. Mary does not answer back. And on Sundays she is on her knees, looking heavenward, praying mightily. I guess maybe for her own soul, I do not know. I guess maybe she did something right horrible. A body has to wonder.

"Did she do it?" Miss Gardenside asked. "Did Mary Francis kill those poor nuns?"

"Would you know the ending before it is time?" asked Colonel Andrews, shutting the book.

"If I can. I always read the last page of a book first."

"You do?" Charlotte said. "How can you stand it?"

"How can you stand the suspense?" said Miss Gardenside. "You know me of old, Charlotte dear. I am not a girl of much patience. Sad endings simply throw me into agonies, and if the story will not end well, then why should I waste my time?"

"But how do you know if the ending is truly good for the characters unless you've traveled with them through every page?"

"Oh, it is simple enough—happiness, marriage, prosperity," said Miss Gardenside. "That is how all stories should end. Otherwise, I have no use for them."

"What about you, Eddie?" Charlotte asked. "Do you take a peek at the last page?"

"Never. I cover the right page while I read the left, lest I accidentally read ahead. I am a slave to a story. So long as a book is not trying to be useful or pontificate at me tirelessly, I am its willing servant."

"And you, Mr. Mallery?"

"I do not spare time for novels, I am afraid," he said.

"I didn't used to," said Charlotte. "Not much. But recently I discovered a new author and now I find books . . . wonderfully, I don't know, rejuvenating."

"All stories?" asked Miss Gardenside. "Or just the happy ones?"

"The happier the better. I'll be curious to see how Mary Francis's story ends."

"We shall uncover it together!" said the colonel. "While Miss Gardenside hopes for happiness, let me be the devil's advocate and hope for horror most hair-raising."

"Miss Gardenside, play a song for us," said Eddie. "You revealed yourself as a pianist the other day, so do not deign to profess shyness nor inexperience."

"I am not comfortable performing for others," she said.

Charlotte believed Lydia Gardenside. But surely Alisha loved a stage. Which was the real girl?

"Come now," said Eddie. "I will not have you go to your room this evening and write in your journal, 'Alas, none appreciate the depth of my talent. I am a light under a bushel.' "

Miss Charming choked on her glass of sherry. She leaned over to Charlotte. "What on earth is a bushel? Sounds naughty."

"I think it's a big basket used for fruit and stuff," Charlotte whispered.

"Oh, okay," Miss Charming whispered back. "That makes sense. I guess."

"Mr. Grey, you are meddlesome!" Miss Gardenside was saying. "You know I would rather sit quietly and observe, but you provoke me out of my shell."

"What does 'shell' mean?" Miss Charming whispered.

"Just . . . like a shell, like what a hermit crab crawls into," Charlotte whispered back.

"That's what I thought, but sometimes I think I'm missing something."

Miss Gardenside sat at the piano and began a tune that was pleasant and compatible in that setting. After a few moments, she sang.

Miss Gardenside didn't have a grand performing voice—it was less opera and more boutique, but agile and perfectly pitched. She sounded a little raw, perhaps from her illness, but that only added to its character. Charlotte doubted the girl had ever given a better performance.

Charlotte rarely sat anywhere just to listen, to appreciate a moment. The mood was otherworldly. She folded her hands in her lap and bade them be content not doing anything. In its idleness, her mind started spinning, searching for a productive occupation. First it worried about her kids.

Stop that, they're fine, she told herself.

So the wheels spun in the direction of the mystery.

Not now, let it lie, she admonished her thoughts.

She felt Mr. Mallery's gaze on her, and she turned and met his eyes, contemplating him in return. It wasn't a staring contest or a smoldering flirtation. The music just buffered the usual social awkwardness of gazing at another adult. It was easy for the moment, just as it was easy to stare at a small child or a dog. Not that Mr. Mallery was a dog. Quite the opposite.

Goodness, that corset felt tight.

After a time, Miss Gardenside stopped singing and just played, smoothing over the roughness in the room, making everything feel all soft and cozy.

Charlotte drifted by the piano and whispered to Miss Gardenside, "I don't think I've ever enjoyed a performance so much. You are wonderful."

Miss Gardenside blushed.

The guests and actors didn't bother with card games but instead spoke in small relaxed groups. Soon enough, Charlotte found herself with Colonel Andrews on a settee. Charlotte had never used that word before—"settee." But in Austenland, settees were prolific. There seemed to be a virtual herd of them in the house, reproducing like bunnies.

"You really are a gem," she said. "You put people at ease, and your mystery games are splendid."

"Why, thank you, Mrs. Cordial." He seemed touched.

"Do you . . . stay often at Pembrook Park?"

"Most summers. I love the Park. I used to visit other homes nearby, but . . ."

"Like Bertram Hall?"

"You have heard of it? Yes, the Wattlesbrooks used to keep up other houses besides Pembrook Park—the sadly fallen Pembrook

Cottage, of course, but Windy Nook and Bertram Hall as well. But times are hard." Colonel Andrews blinked, as if adjusting his thoughts to the proper time period. "The Napoleonic Wars. War takes men from home, incomes are spent overseas. Bertram Hall was sold, Windy Nook was let, and Pembrook Cottage . . ."

She nodded.

"At least we still have the beauty of the Park to console our bones." He gestured to the grandeur of the drawing room. It was a gorgeous chamber, with wide double doors, hanging candelabras, sets of furniture to create several spaces within the room. The ceiling itself was worth gazing upon, with scenes of Cupid with a bow, ribbons and arrows worked into the molding. She felt queenly just sitting there, though she couldn't imagine living in the house. What kind of a person would desire this full-time?

Mrs. Wattlesbrook must, though her husband, apparently, did not. Miss Charming had of late. And Charlotte could not imagine Mr. Mallery outside this world.

She could picture Eddie in casual clothes—maybe a gray sweater or peacoat, some jeans, a five o'clock shadow. Why not? And Colonel Andrews too—though she imagined him in a bit more color. A shiny lime green shirt came to mind.

But Mr. Mallery in jeans? Her imagination failed her. He seemed carved from this time period, molded for breeches and riding cloaks. He didn't even look silly in a top hat.

Miss Charming and Miss Gardenside sat together in the corner, visually the opposites of each other, both giggling over a book. The piano bench empty, Mr. Mallery sat and began playing. It took Charlotte a few moments to absorb the melody and realize it was beautiful. He played softly, unobtrusively, with a gentleness that surprised her.

Usually the women in Austen played the pianoforte. Men were too busy being men—getting money from farmers who lived on their land, hunting game birds, and visiting relations, where they sat around in drawing rooms not playing the piano.

But Mr. Mallery seemed to *do* things. She wished she knew what he did when he was out of sight. The musician in him seemed but a hint.

She sat beside him.

"What were you thinking of while Miss Gardenside played? When you looked at me?" he asked, his eyes on his hands moving over the keys.

He was direct, wasn't he? In Austenland, men and women usually played and teased in conversation. Forthrightness came in rare outbursts that either separated couples or brought them together. They were rare and dangerous events, but apparently Mr. Mallery didn't play by all the rules.

"I was thinking that you are a handsome man," she said.

He didn't react.

"And I was wondering if you would still make me nervous if you weren't. How much of your effect on me has to do with how you look and how much is just your presence, your demeanor?"

He kept playing. "And what did you decide?"

"I'm not sure how to separate all the parts of you. I'm not sure about a lot of things."

He stopped playing and looked at her hand resting on the edge of the piano. He spoke softly, for her ears only.

"Sometimes I curse the bonds of propriety. Sometimes I long to just reach out and hold you."

Charlotte's mouth opened, her bosom rose up with a deep breath, and she felt as if her heart were trying to escape that cage. Not a part of her remained numb.

"Charlotte!" said Miss Charming. "Charlotte, come see the illustration in this old book. We can't tell if it's supposed to be a dog or a rat."

In a haze, Charlotte went to Miss Charming and Miss Gardenside, put in her vote for rat, and then turned to see that Mr. Mallery had disappeared.

She went to her room that night half expecting him to knock at her door. He didn't.

home, before

CHARLOTTE'S TEEN YEARS FELT AS long as a lifetime. Her true self, her glassed-in helpless self, mouthed silent warnings while teenage Charlotte blundered ahead, making mistake after mistake (e.g., Robbie, Howie, the guy at the fish fry, Pep Club, stirrup pants . . .).

Each year older was a victory, but by age twenty, she didn't yet feel cleansed of immaturity. The confidence wasn't there, and the way from her mind to her tongue was still a dangerous path.

Finding James had been such a relief! He was levelheaded, marriageable, and had a calming presence that helped her feel less dunderheaded. She married impatiently at twenty-three and seized on an early pregnancy as a way to finally rid herself of her youth. A mother is mature. A mother *must* be mature. Now that she was grown and married, all her troubles would be over.

austenland, day 7

CHARLOTTE DIDN'T GO TO BREAKFAST the next morning. She was likely to see Mr. Mallery, and after his declaration last night at the piano bench, what could she say? And how would she feel? Austen's book-induced sensations had felt safe, at least. The Mallery-induced sensations most definitely did not. She wanted it—and she didn't. She was determined to let herself fall in pretend-love, but not just yet. Too fast! Too scary!

So what now? She was standing in the hallway looking at the ceiling when Eddie came up the stairs.

"What does this determined expression on your face mean?" he asked.

"I was psyching myself to go back up to the secret room."

"I see. Have you always been so tenacious?"

"No."

"Well then, little sister, I am honored to witness this unexpected growth spurt. But I think I ought to be with you whenever you engage yourself in these diabolical investigations. You may need my protection from phantasms and assassins."

The secret chamber was not an easy place to look for clues, heaped as it was with furniture and boxes and stacks of things. She combed the sofa, looking for any telltale hair or ripped cloth, drops of blood or hidden daggers, maybe a convenient letter of confession from the pretend killer. But there was nothing obvious. Why did Colonel Andrews make things so hard?

"Are you sure Andrews meant for you to investigate this room?" Eddie asked, playing with the fencing foil again behind a tower of chairs. He scooted back and forth in lunge position.

"Wow, you look deadly," said Charlotte.

"Really?" He wore a hopeful smile.

She snorted. Eddie was more friendly dog than ravenous wolf.

"Laugh at me, but someday I will be the world's greatest swordsman, and you will come to me in tears. 'Dear brother, forgive the insolence of my youth! I see now that you are indeed a deadly and formidable man, and I was so wrong to scoff.'"

"I bet you haven't changed much in the past twenty years," she said.

"So you have forgiven and forgotten my dastardly, selfish youth? Wonderful news. But truly, what do you expect to find here?"

"I don't know." She was examining various dust collectors on a small table. A black Chinese vase with a lid seemed to scream, I HOLD A CLUE! but it proved empty. "Colonel Andrews hinted to look on the second floor, and after I discovered this room, he confirmed that a key to his mystery is in here."

"He said that?"

"Yeah, I think so." She couldn't remember now his exact words, but she'd had a very strong impression. "Why else would he lead me here?"

Eddie shrugged and made a few more thrusts and parries. "Never can tell with Andrews."

"Well, he's written—or rather, he's *discovered*—a detailed mystery surrounding Mary Francis. I don't see him as a sloppy guy."

"He does dress with care."

"Surely the secret room and the body are part of that mystery, and uncovering clues to one will help solve the other, all neat and tidy. I think he's being so secretive, though, because he used this room without Mrs. Wattlesbrook's permission and he doesn't want to upset her. But really," she said, gesturing to the mess, "he could be just a teeny, tiny bit less opaque. I can't find the needle for all this hay."

She briefly thought, Well, maybe the body *was* real, but then scoffed the thought right out of her head. Dead bodies don't show up then disappear; murders don't cross her path in real life. Of course this was all part of the game—just as was Mr. Mallery's amorous confession from the night before. She would not get unduly sucked in. She would not allow her fancy to run wild, imagining murders in the dark and handsome actors genuinely falling for her. She was never the type of child to jump off the garage roof believing that a costume cape could make her fly.

"Perhaps the fake dead body was the only intended clue in this chamber?" said Eddie, slightly out of breath from ducking under his imaginary opponent's swing.

"Maybe. But he went to all the trouble of stowing the corpse in a secret room. Once a secret room is introduced in a mystery story, it always comes back into play. Besides, I don't know where else to look for clues."

Eddie rested the tip of the foil on the ground. "Why does this matter so much to you?"

She shrugged, then laughed. "I came to get lost in a story, I guess, and ironically the make-believe mystery and murder story seems safer than . . . than whatever I'm supposed to accomplish with Mr. Mallery, and a lot more hopeful than the news from back home."

"Are your children all right?" he asked.

"Oh yes. They seem to be great, actually. Now that I'm . . ." She slumped down on the bodyless sofa. "Never mind."

"Ah, but you need never 'never mind' me, Charlotte dear. You may always tell me anything."

Charlotte's eyes were on the floor. Was there something peeking from beneath the sofa? She got on her hands and reached under, pulling out a yellow rubber glove, like the kind one wore when washing dishes. She shook her head.

"Found the corpse, did you?" Eddie asked.

Was this what she had seen? No, the hand had been gray for one thing. Then again, night and lightning would drain the yellow into gray. But she couldn't have confused a rubber glove for a fleshy corpse hand. Could she? Well, she had been pretty freaked out.

"I give up." She dropped the glove on the floor.

"Ha-ha!" said Eddie, bounding forward, his foil raised. "You surrender to my skill with sword and derring-do. Very well, I accept."

He presented her the foil, handle first. It was amazing how much more confident she felt with a weapon in her hand—even a useless, blunt-tipped play sword. Eddie took its partner from the box, and they dueled badly until lunch.

TABLES AND SHADE WERE SET up on the lawn, refreshments sparkling in glass pitchers and silver trays. The day was radiant, the sky blaring the news that it was summer and to please take notice and act accordingly. Everyone was dressed in clothing as bright as the garden flowers. Mr. Mallery gazed at Charlotte, an invitation to come hither and fall in love. It was as idyllic a scene as artist or poet could e'er express! And yet Charlotte's thoughts wandered a dark alley.

The glove/hand thing confused her, so she set it aside and seized instead on the question of the murderer. Neville the butler and Mary the maid seemed like juicy suspects, but she'd never seen Miss Gardenside or Miss Charming speak to Neville, and Mary was Charlotte's personal maid. Surely Colonel Andrews would design a game not just for Charlotte but for all the lady guests and so would choose one of the central characters to be the villain.

It's a universal truth that nothing spoils a postlunch game of croquet like suspecting the other players of murder.

That evening in the drawing room, Mrs. Wattlesbrook

brought out large pieces of paper and charcoal. They dimmed all the lights except one hooded shade pointed at the wall and took turns drawing each other's silhouettes. Charlotte proved the best for the task, and soon all were sitting for her, Miss Gardenside's piano music providing the soundtrack for the evening.

She enjoyed tracing the mounds of Miss Charming's hair, the sleek line of Colonel Andrews's nose, the brave forehead of Miss Gardenside, that wonderful chin Eddie bore so well. There was an intimacy in the process, and she fumbled as she traced Mr. Mallery's lips.

"What I said last night . . . I made you uncomfortable," he whispered.

"Don't speak," she said. "I mean, you move when you talk. You have to hold still."

She didn't want him to say anything to make her heart all frantic like that again. It was much more intense in person than in a book, even if this was a game. She dragged the charcoal over the shadow of his bottom lip, plumper than its twin, and caught herself contemplating what it would be like to nibble on it.

"Ha," she said.

"What?" he asked.

"Nothing, just thinking about you."

It was an odd exercise. While she worked, he was free to gaze upon her, but she could only observe his shadow. She supposed that was always true—he saw her, the real Charlotte, while all she knew of him was the shadow of himself, this character he played. The thought gave her a shiver.

She traced his jaw and neck and thought, He's not an easy person. He seems to cherish his own opinions better than anyone else's, and sometimes he plain isn't nice. Remember the tourists with the camera?

But then, maybe nice was overrated. Besides, she wasn't really dating Mr. Mallery. She was just playing, and of course she expected nothing real would come of it. Right? So why be so afraid?

After filling in the outline with solid black, she displayed it to the room.

"I say, Mallery," said Eddie, "you are not a bad-looking fellow when you are sitting still like that and not pounding one with your glare."

Charlotte dusted off her hands and looked over her work. Mr. Mallery's shadow certainly looked the most lifelike of all those she'd drawn. Did that say more about him or about her? She taped it to the wall beside the others—six profiles displayed like Wanted posters.

That's a weird comparison to make, accused her Inner Thoughts.

Charlotte didn't sleep well that night. It may have been the dry thunderstorm that crackled outside and the periodic booming of unproductive thunder. Or it may have been the electric storm in her brain, her buzzing synapses using nighttime to piece together the colonel's mystery.

It did seem odd that Colonel Andrews would lead her to a body then provide no other clues, except perhaps that kitchen glove, which really told her nothing. And honestly, how could a recent murder tie into his ancient tale of dead nuns? What if . . . (stop it, Charlotte) . . . but what if it really . . . (you'll make a fool of yourself) . . . really was . . . (oh, go ahead—it's safe to think it in the darkness, where we're free to explore our most foolish imaginations) . . . What if it really was real? What if she'd discovered a genuine murder victim, and the murderer had returned in the night and hidden away the body? Then the murderer was someone at Pembrook Park, most likely someone who had been up playing Bloody Murder and who would know that Charlotte discovered the crime scene: one of the lady guests, gentleman actors, or perhaps Mary. Everyone else had been in bed. But then who was the victim? Should she go to the police with a half-baked suspicion? Here, after midnight in her room, she couldn't believe her discovered corpse had been nothing more than a rubber glove. But without a body, how could she prove it?

It turns out that it's not always safe to think things alone to oneself, even at midnight.

After forming that needling dread into a thought, Charlotte had to get up a few (or twelve) times to peek outside her door and make sure there wasn't a murderer lurking in the hallway, preparing to come in and kill her in her sleep. No murderer would find her sleeping, by golly! If a murderer wanted her dead, he/she would have to face her like a man/woman and just go ahead and kill her to her face! Because that's a much nicer way to die. Awake and aware, so you can really experience the whole nauseating horror of it.

Oh, go back to bed, Charlotte.

home, before

MORE THAN ANYTHING, CHARLOTTE WANTED not to take up space. She longed to sit in a corner of the world, inconspicuous, being harmless and pleasant. Cheery. People could come to her when they needed a hand or a friend or a loan, but otherwise not trip over her in passing. Nice Charlotte. Clever Charlotte. Out-of-the-way Charlotte.

austenland, days 8–9

CHARLOTTE PUSHED HER BREAKFAST AROUND on her plate, thinking of the many poisons Agatha Christie's murderers employed. There might be arsenic in her eggs, strychnine in her sausages, or cyanide in her cider. (Her glass actually held orange juice, but "cider" was alliterative.) Why couldn't she let this go? Did she *want* there to be a murder? Didn't her brain have anything better to do, like, say, contemplate Mr. Mallery's lower lip again?

She looked around the table. Who's a murderer? Who drew the short stick?

After breakfast she paced the gallery upstairs, thinking about rubber gloves and real bodies, British police and the fears that crawled over her through the night.

That's when she saw it. A painting of a girl in a dark hallway holding a candle, opening a door, her eyes wide with fear. The title plate on the frame read, "Catherine Morland."

It took her a moment to place the name—Catherine Morland is the heroine of Austen's *Northanger Abbey*, who is so carried away in the horrific pleasures of Gothic novels that she imagines murder where there is none.

"I am Catherine Morland," Charlotte whispered.

Charlotte looked at herself in the corridor window and laughed. When the laugh faded, she didn't look away. Her reflection was that of a stranger. This was not the woman who had discovered a brow wrinkle in the bathroom mirror at home. This was a woman of stature. Her height, which at times in her life had proved awkward, now seemed designed for these long gowns. Wearing her hair up changed her face—her blue eyes seemed brighter, her lips fuller. She felt descended from Amazons, from Greek goddesses. Why, she was practically formidable.

Beyond the pane, one spot in the sky had cleared to a misty blue. Mr. Mallery crossed the lawn alone toward the stables. Charlotte put on a riding frock and boots and ran to meet him. She was breathing hard when she caught up.

"I'd like to take that ride with you now, if you don't mind."

Mr. Mallery smiled.

She was not going to be the haunted waif in this story. She was going to take pretend romance by the horns and wrestle it into submission. She was going to be noticed.

"You have been absent of late," Mr. Mallery said, ducking

under a wet branch as they rode their horses into the trees. "Even when you are here, you are not completely here."

"You're right. I was getting caught up in what wasn't real to escape what was real—or wasn't technically really real but was *more* real. That makes no sense. Anyway, I'm determined to live the story. Now I'm undead. Or alive. Or back, anyway."

Why couldn't she speak like a human being with this man? It was easier when she wasn't looking at him. His gaze made her feel naked.

Mr. Mallery pulled his horse short. "Look," he said, pointing.

A red fox sat on a fallen tree. It stared back, its tail swished once, then it turned and loped off.

"Do you hunt them?" Charlotte asked.

"It is a gentleman's sport. If left alone, foxes breed like rabbits and make their own use of chickens."

"But they look so smart. How can you kill something that looks as if it knows you and what you want to do?"

"My conscience is clear. Ridding the countryside of foxes is a boon to the Wattlesbrooks' tenant farmers."

He probably didn't really kill foxes. He probably was just speaking as Mr. Mallery the character. She told herself this but didn't believe it, because she couldn't imagine that Mr. Mallery was anyone but who he seemed.

"You bewitch me when you go silent, Mrs. Cordial," he said.

Even when he said stuff like that? And looked at her like that?

"Is it too much? Am I too forward to desire an intimacy with your thoughts?" he said. "I wish you would speak, and jealously, I wish you would speak only to me."

"I don't think my thoughts are interesting enough to repeat."

The corner of his mouth ticked up. "I doubt that."

"Well, I was wondering who you really are."

"I am as you see me. I am not a man given to artifice. I am Thomas Mallery."

"Nephew of the Wattlesbrooks."

He inclined his head. "Though my estate is in Sussex, this land is a second home to me. I spent many holidays here, exploring the grounds, the house. I know Pembrook Park better than any, I believe. No matter that my grandfather lost the deed to his brother. In ways the law cannot understand, she belongs to me."

There was such conviction in his voice that Charlotte wondered if he sincerely felt that way, but about Windy Nook. From the photos she'd seen at the inn, he'd been in that cast for ten years.

"I wonder about you as well, Mrs. Cordial. Sometimes at night, I do not sleep for wondering."

Why did this make her blush? How could she have a genuine, uncontrollable physical reaction to a line from an actor? She laughed at herself, and at him too.

"Clearly we're thinking too much about each other! But now you must ask me what you're wondering about."

His lips held a slight smile. "I dare not ask, or you would call me no gentleman. Yet I do not mind the mystery. I will enjoy uncovering you, layer by layer."

Again with the blushing. Even if her head knew she was really Charlotte Constance Kinder playing dress-up, her cheeks bought into the whole deal. Naughty cheeks.

Mr. Mallery looked over the scene. "Dismount and come sit with me."

"I think I'd rather keep riding."

He raised an eyebrow as if curious why but nicked his mount with his heel and moved forward.

Why was she still afraid? Come on, Charlotte, it wasn't like he was going to murder her or threaten her maidenhead here in this sequestered, dark, fox-infested wood. He was an actor, and there were Regency rules of etiquette to be adhered to, my lady!

But she rode on. And briefly imagined what might have happened if they'd stopped. Briefly.

They traveled to the inn, where Charlotte dismounted.

"I have some business here. Could you take my horse back, please?"

She reached up, handing him the reins. He took them, holding her fingers for a moment.

"I am your servant in all things."

She watched him ride away before sighing and going inside. She retrieved her phone, a nervous flutter nudging her stomach. Charlotte had called the kids at James's house yesterday at the appointed time. There'd been no answer.

Message #1: "Hi guys, it's Mom . . . um, Charlotte. I just wanted to check in, see how you are. Maybe you're all still asleep? It's not raining at the moment, which is my big news. Anyway, I miss you all. I'll call again later."

She'd come back a few hours later to try again.

Message #2: "Hey, it's me. I'm so disappointed to get voice mail. Beck and Lu, I really want to hear your voices. Hope that everything's okay. I miss you tons. I'll call back tomorrow."

She e-mailed both of her kids as well, typing brief inquiries and I-love-yous from her phone. There were no messages from them of either the voice or the electronic variety. What if they were all hurt or hospitalized with the swine flu, or had fallen into comas after a random dirigible accident? Or what if James didn't have carbon monoxide alarms in his house and in the night they'd been put under by the silent killer? Dead suddenly like the Grey Cloak nuns? What if there were four corpses snug in their beds?

The third call rang and rang and rang. She'd thought riding

with Mr. Mallery made her anxious. It was nothing compared with the pit in her middle when she got voice mail again.

Message #3: "James Kinder, I will return tomorrow morning to check for messages, and I'd like to hear one from you along the lines of 'We're not dead, just happen to all be out whenever you call.' And if I don't hear from you, I'll be calling the local police to come check your house for bodies. Please, please call."

The next morning there was a message.

James: "Nope, not dead. We must've left the phones off the rechargers for too long. Just realized you called a few times. Everything's fine."

Left the phones off the rechargers? If Charlotte had the power of laser vision, red-hot beams would have shot out of her eyes and burned anything she looked at. As it was, she just glared harmlessly at the houseplant in Mrs. Wattlesbrook's office. It didn't even have the good grace to drop a leaf in shame.

Because of the time difference, it was too early to call back, so Charlotte had to comfort herself with the hope that her kids hadn't been killed in the few hours since James had left the message.

On the way back to the house, Charlotte passed Colonel Andrews, his face glum.

His face did not respond well to glumness. She had to toss a spark on this bundle of sticks.

"Colonel Andrews! I've been meaning to tell you, I'm completely caught up in your mystery."

He turned a generous smile on her. "Indeed! I had thought none of our fine guests had taken a shine to it."

"I can't believe Mary Francis killed all her sister nuns. But if not, then who did? And how? I wish you'd read more of it tonight."

"Your wish is granted, Mrs. Cordial. I am your fairy godmother tonight."

Andrews ran off, his steps full of spring, his eyes sparkling anew.

She turned and discovered Eddie alone on a bench, contemplating her.

"You made his day."

"Did I? I hope so. But I wasn't being flippant. His mystery's been a kind of lifeline for me here. Something to think about besides . . . other stuff."

He patted the seat beside him and she joined him, sighing as she sat.

"How are your children doing, Charlotte?"

"I was just thinking about them."

"I thought so. You're worried?"

"They're . . . not very good correspondents. And I can't turn my mind off. I keep imagining—"

"All the various ways they might have been killed?"

"How did you know?"

"I *am* your brother," he said smugly. "And, as my sister, of course you know that I am a parent as well. Julia's mother has been gone these fourteen years. Her grandparents raise her, and I go to London as often as I can. But when I am away too long and no letters come, I get that mark too." He scowled with mock worry, revealing a wrinkle deep in his brow. "But tell me about yours. It feels like . . . *forever* since I saw them last."

She smiled. "Beckett is eleven now and so smart. He doesn't talk to me much, but, you know . . . Lucinda's fourteen, and she, well, she hates me—"

That's when Charlotte started to cry. The word "hate" triggered a hormonal reaction that demanded an outpouring of tears, and there was no stopping it.

"Ignore me, please," she said, putting a hand over her eyes. "I'm so stupid. Just ignore me."

She felt an arm go around her shoulder, and Eddie pulled her into him. She rested her head on his chest, covering her eyes with her hands.

Maybe you should ask him to get you some warm milk and Nilla Wafers, her Inner Thoughts said.

Stuff it, said Charlotte.

"It's my fault. I don't give her breathing room. I don't show her I trust her, because maybe I don't. Because she's my daughter, and I made mistakes and I don't want her to make any, and I know it's pointless, but I can't help trying, can I? Oh shut up, Charlotte, you're on vacation, not in group therapy."

Eddie didn't let go. His hand rested on her upper arm.

"Julia's fifteen," he said.

"How often do you see her?"

"A few times a year."

Charlotte frowned. "As in, three or four? That is pathetic, Eddie. A daughter needs her father. I've read all about it."

"Her guardians do not approve of me. I suppose I let them chase me away."

"You? Ha! I've seen you in a secret room of a possibly haunted house using a practice foil in an extremely menacing manner. I think you're capable of standing your ground."

He clenched his teeth, his jaw firming, and nodded his head. "You're right. I should see Julia more. Upon my word, Charlotte, I really should. I will stand my ground. I swear it."

"I shouldn't be so hard on Lu. I need to trust her and let her make mistakes."

"Perhaps it is never amiss, as a parent, to improve just a tad. What say you, Charlotte? Let us show those girls the sheer glory of our parental prowess."

"Eddie, I'm so glad you're my brother."

She felt him kiss the top of her head. She closed her eyes and exhaled slowly, letting herself be held for the moment. This was nice. This was all she needed. She was not going to analyze it, wonder if Mr. Edmund Grey had a fifteen-year-old daughter or if the actor did, or how much he knew about her and James (just what was in Mrs. Wattlesbrook's file?), and if she should be embarrassed for so clearly breaking character. She was just going to let herself be held for a moment. Men were nice. She liked nice men.

What would Jane Austen do now?

Charlotte straightened up. "Let's write them letters. I haven't written my kids letters in . . . I don't know. Which is odd, of course, since it's 1816 and letter writing is practically a daily occupation for women."

"Along with swooning, fanning oneself, and consuming cold cow tongue," Eddie added.

"I haven't done any of those things yet today. I'm behind."

She marched into the morning room, found paper and ink in the desk, and honest-to-goodness quill pens. "Look, you can actually write with feathers!"

She and Eddie sat side by side, dipped their quills in the ink, and started to write. The flow of ink changed her handwriting, made it elegant and unexpected, thick and thin lines, blots and drops and whiskers of ink. She loved it. Till the tip got dull and she had no idea what to do. Eddie was struggling too.

"Mr. Mallery," Charlotte called when he passed by the room. "Sir, would you be our hero? Are you well versed in the art of feathers?"

Mr. Mallery leaned against the threshold. "I will of course help the lady. If you want for my aid as well, Grey, I suggest you don a skirt and bonnet."

Eddie, sans skirt and bonnet, peered over Charlotte's shoulder for Mr. Mallery's Quill and Ink 101. Things went more smoothly after that.

Charlotte didn't mention James or Justice, stalking Lu's boyfriend, or the dead batteries in the phones. She just talked to her children, sharing favorite memories, listing their traits she admired, telling about Colonel Andrews's mystery and how scared she'd been playing Bloody Murder (leaving out mention of the was-there-wasn't-there corpse).

Mr. Mallery sat on the sofa and watched as she wrote. She was getting used to this. She didn't even look up.

Eddie's missive was three pages long. Whether or not Julia was real, she was getting quite a letter.

Charlotte sealed up her letters, addressed them, and asked Mr. Mallery to take them to Mrs. Wattlesbrook to mail that day.

"Is there such a thing as 'post haste'?" Charlotte asked. "Because that's what I want. Post haste, if you please!"

Mr. Mallery bowed. "I will do anything you ask, Mrs. Cordial, but perhaps next time your favor will not require me to leave your presence."

As soon as he left, a panicked hiccup escaped Charlotte's throat.

"What are you thinking?" Eddie asked, resting the side of his head lightly on his hand while he studied her.

"He's so different from . . . what I left behind. And I know I'm supposed to get wooed and all. That's how Mrs. Wattlesbrook designed this. But I get scared. I don't want to disappoint him."

"Still worried about Mallery? Come, Charlotte, you need to enjoy yourself more. Do you ever allow yourself that? You do not have many hobbies, do you?"

"I work, I take care of my children . . ." She shrugged.

"Well, in our world, at the very least, you should learn to dance. My—" He caught himself. "Our mother, as you recall, was a dance instructor, and naturally, as her only son, I was often employed as a demonstration partner. Odd that you somehow escaped dance lessons."

"Yes, that is odd."

They smiled at each other.

"You learned the country dances from Mrs. Wattlesbrook?" he asked, taking her hand and drawing her to her feet.

"I don't remember them very well, and the ball is in four days."

"The steps are repetitive, and you're clever. You will be fine."

He went to a carved wooden box in a corner, turned a key several times, and lifted the lid. A tinny song squeaked out.

"There is a new dance that is just being admitted into civilized society, in this, the year of our Lord 1816: the waltz."

He pulled her into his arms and began to move—one, two, three, one, two, three. His hand was tight on her back, their middles almost touching. She felt featherlight and a little giddy.

"You are a natural," he said. "Flows in the Grey blood, I shouldn't wonder."

Was she being frivolous? Shouldn't she be doing something productive, like . . . um . . . She briefly wished the murder had been real so she could get back to work investigating. All this vacationing was proving to be a mental strain.

You're such an idiot, said her Inner Thoughts. Don't you know how to relax?

She looked at Eddie. It was easier to relax with Eddie there.

"Having fun?" he asked.

She nodded, and her feet skipped a little, adding an extra hitch to the step.

"Ooh, you saucy thing," he said. "Next time I will teach you the polka."

"Post haste it is." Mr. Mallery was leaning against the threshold.

Charlotte stopped, feeling guilty. His confidence seemed to fill the room, leaving no place for hers.

Mr. Mallery approached and bowed deeply. "Mind if I cut in?"

Eddie bowed in return and left them.

It was different dancing with Mr. Mallery. His hands held her in the same places, and yet his touch felt hotter, more intimate. She had to wonder, Did people really waltz in 1816? Why, it was almost scandalous! She wasn't certain it was bringing her deeper into Austenland, but waltzing with Mr. Mallery did feel wonderful and a little bit naughty.

For the rest of the day, Mrs. Cordial let Mr. Mallery court her thoroughly. They went for a walk around the gardens, skipped stones in the pond, talked about clouds and history and other topics that were time-period neutral.

He maintained a gentleman's distance, but he never hesitated to offer his arm and take her hand when they walked over uneven ground. When the sun was dallying with the horizon, they stopped to watch the clouds take up the yellow and orange, colors bright and hot like a house fire.

"I abhor the thought of going inside tonight," he said. "The tedium of the drawing room, all those people. I would rather just listen to you."

"Really? I don't think I've said anything that interesting."

"*You* are interesting."

"Mrs. Cordial!" Colonel Andrews spied them through the open door. "There you are. Mrs. Wattlesbrook is anxious to start dinner, as am I, if you must know. I have a deliriously wild passage to read to you all tonight, and you must attend me or I will be quite put out."

He made a pouting expression and scampered off.

Mr. Mallery kissed Charlotte's hand, subtly inhaling through his nose as if enjoying her scent. Wow. If she wasn't careful, this man would eat her alive. Hm, maybe she shouldn't be *too* careful.

"We . . . we should probably go in," she said.

All through dinner, Colonel Andrews was especially anxious, his mouth more full of secret smiles than of food. He drank vibrantly and sometimes giggled to himself.

"You are up to something, my bonny wee cream puff," Miss Charming said.

"Only enchanted by your company and much looking forward to our diversions this evening. The story of Mary Francis progresses, yes it does."

After dessert and Madeira, the evening hushed into night. The players gathered across the hall on the prolific settees, and the colonel read from his little leather-bound book. He'd begun to adopt a cockney accent for the housekeeper, which required Charlotte to concentrate on his every word.

> The kitchen lads provoke Mary, I can see that. Anyone could. I told them to stop teasing her, but I cannot be responsible for the girl, not when she refuses to talk about the abbey. People are curious, and afraid too, as am I. But I never expected what happened. We was in the kitchen cleaning up, and Mary was quiet on her stool, and all were working hard, but maybe some of them was teasing her again. They got a little chant they whisper at her, What do you know of our Mary? Twenty-one nuns she did bury!
>
> So we was working and then there is a howl that makes Cook drop a bowl and we look outside and see something in the kitchen garden. I say it is a ghost, for it is white and filmy and moves around like it is floating, and it howls and says all screeching and horrible with a right odd voice, Leave innocent Mary alone! It says the nuns cannot rest when folk stain

Mary's name with lies. I tell you we all turned white as the ghost and shut up the door and covered our ears. All except Mary. She did not seem afraid. Worried, sure enough, but not afraid. She just went on washing pots and frowned.

And I am writing this by candle, which I should not waste, but I cannot sleep so I write it out and I will say my prayers again. And I will make those lads behave for I do not want to see another ghost my whole life, I do not.

Colonel Andrews shut the book.

"Wow," said Miss Charming. "A real ghost. And it was protecting her, right-o. So maybe she's not guilty."

"Or she is," said Miss Gardenside, "and her dark deeds gained her unholy friendship with wraiths."

The group was quiet. Charlotte heard a distant howl.

What a coincidence, she thought. There's some animal out there howling just after we read about a howling ghost.

She heard it again.

"What is that?" Miss Gardenside was on her feet.

Colonel Andrews rushed to the window, looking around madly. "Why, I believe there is something in the garden!"

"I can't see a blawsted thing," Miss Charming said, peering beside him.

Colonel Andrews turned off the electric lamps and blew out some candles, dimming the room. "There. In the shrubs."

Miss Charming gasped. Charlotte hurried to the window along with the others.

The sky was a watery black, evening stars and a low moon breathing a little color into pale shapes: the fountain, the gray-stoned drive, and the figure moving in the garden. Double take—yes, Charlotte did see someone out there, not plodding along like a creature with two feet, but, well . . . floating. Flitting in a mournful way. She could not see a face, only white robes and a headdress.

"It's Mary Francis," Miss Gardenside whispered.

Colonel Andrews opened the window, and a high, raspy wail came in on the cool night air.

"Perhaps she wishes to communicate," said the colonel.

The figure stopped and its eyeless face turned toward the window, a pointed finger raised.

Charlotte startled away from the window. She had felt as if Mary Francis were pointing directly at her.

"Let's chase her," said Miss Gardenside, hastening out of the room.

"Wait!" said Colonel Andrews.

Off they both ran. Miss Charming and Charlotte hesitated before joining the chase.

Miss Gardenside, followed closely by Colonel Andrews, was cruising over the gravel drive and toward the garden. The ghost was still sliding along, though there was nothing haunting about its gestures now. In fact, they reflected the very human emotion of panic.

"Caution!" the colonel was yelling. "Not so hasty, Miss Gardenside. The spirit could be dangerous."

"We're not afraid of you!" Miss Gardenside shouted.

The ghost bent down to pick something up and then moved as if fleeing for its life—that is, if it weren't already dead. The flowing headdress caught on a bush and the ghost tore it free.

"Wait!" shouted Miss Gardenside. "What are the secrets of death? Who really killed those nuns? What's heaven like?"

Near the stables, the ghost disappeared.

"Where'd it go?" Miss Gardenside asked, out of breath.

"Dissolved . . . back into the ether . . . from whence all spirits come," Colonel Andrews said, resting his hands on his knees while he slurped in air.

Charlotte and Miss Charming had reached the spot where the ghost had first appeared.

"Come look," said Charlotte. "There are marks in the ground. See there? Long indentations, almost as if something with wheels rolled back and forth."

A skateboard, Charlotte guessed silently. Our ghost was out here gleaming the cube.

"I did not know ghosts had invented the wheel," Eddie said, ambling up from the house with Mr. Mallery. "They seem so Stone Age, wouldn't you say?"

"'There are more things in heaven and earth, Horatio, than are dreamt of in your philosophy,'" quoted Mr. Mallery.

Eddie pretended to look concerned. "Mallery, it is I, Edmund Grey. I say, Andrews, there Mallery goes calling me 'Horatio' again. Perhaps he would benefit from a brace of brandy. Or is that the problem?"

"What can these marks mean, Colonel?" asked Charlotte, as he and Miss Gardenside joined them.

Colonel Andrews lifted his hands. "Generally speaking, people do not chase after spirits. Generally speaking, people stay safe in drawing rooms and observe them from a distance and make frightened noises and might, for example, hide behind draperies and beg brave gentlemen to protect them from the frights of the night. Generally speaking."

"Sorry," said Miss Gardenside.

"Indeed, Miss Gardenside," Eddie said, posing with one foot up on a bench. "If you had not run so boldly into the night, seeking adventure and questioning a phantasm from beyond the grave, I should have stood between you and the window whilst you quaked with fear. I should have said, Fear not, gentle maiden! And I should have closed the casement with nary the slightest tremble in my hand. Then I should have served you biscuits and let you win at whist even if I had been dealt the cards of a god!"

"You are, indeed, the best of men," Miss Gardenside said, taking his arm.

"Aha! And I did not have to feed you that line. How spontaneous and sincere it sounded sprouting from your own lips."

"It was sincere," she said.

He put his hand over hers. "And you, Miss Gardenside, are the bravest and best of your sex."

They smiled. And wow, their fondness for each other seemed real. Charlotte looked away. Miss Charming was beside Colonel Andrews, patting his back in a consoling way while making googoo faces to get him to smile. Mr. Mallery stood aside, hands in his jacket pockets. He was probably looking at her, though she couldn't tell for certain in the darkness. Did Miss Gardenside ever observe Charlotte and Mallery and think, Wow, their affection seems so genuine!

The night was as warm as a breath on the cheek, and the couples took arms and strode through the garden, calling out for the ghost to attend them and grant them wishes.

"Yoo-hoo!" shouted Miss Charming. "Come back and make me the prettiest lassie at the ball!"

"I am not certain this particular specter was of the fairy godmother variety," said Eddie.

"Well, you never know unless you try," she said.

"By Hamlet's father," said Colonel Andrews with mock shock. "The wish has already been granted. You are stunning!"

Mr. Mallery was humming some tune under his breath.

"You seem content this evening," Charlotte said.

"You know, I think I am."

"You thrive out here where ghosts wander?"

"That is an intriguing place to inhabit." He placed his hand atop hers, where it rested on his arm. His hand was cold. "Or perhaps I am just content to be with you."

She sighed. And decided it was okay to let her heart flit and flutter around, and for her breath to get caught in her chest like the ghost's flowing headdress on a shrub. It was okay to fall in love inside books and stories, and where was she if not inside a story? And wasn't this why she'd come, after all? She felt certain she would be able to withdraw herself intact when the time came. She felt certain she was not in too much danger.

home, the previous two years

ABOUT A YEAR BEFORE THE divorce, James remarked to Charlotte that they ought to put their various bank accounts, investments, and Charlotte's business in both of their names.

"For tax reasons," he said.

"Really? Since we file jointly, I didn't think that would make a difference."

James frowned. "It's almost as if you don't trust me. It's almost as if you are trying to keep separate from me."

The next day, Charlotte added his name to everything of hers—except the business. That turned out to be a little more complicated, and so she put it off until after her Web site redesign. But by then James had revealed the affair and asked for a divorce. There would be no alimony—Charlotte was the real breadwinner, and James's infidelity prevented his asking for payments. Despite her lawyer's advice, Charlotte didn't want to make a fuss and agreed to a fifty-fifty split of their joint assets. Which now included her bank accounts and investments. Everything but her business.

Despite the financial severing, over the next few months her income boomed. The harder she worked, the easier it became not to feel.

austenland, days 10–11

THE NEXT MORNING, CHARLOTTE DRAGGED Miss Gardenside and Miss Charming to the second floor.

The night before in the garden, the colonel had told them, "Dear ladies, there is still a clue on the second floor. And, I mean to say, in the corridor. No need to open doors and disturb the maids in their chambers."

But what about the secret room? Charlotte thought. She was sure Colonel Andrews would bring that back into the story at some point and she would finally understand what she'd seen the night of Bloody Murder, but apparently it was not time yet.

"I need fresh eyes, ladies," said Charlotte. "What are we missing?"

Miss Charming hunched over, examining the carpet.

"It is quite bare, is it not?" said Miss Gardenside. "Nothing in the corridor but that table, vase, and the painting of Saint Francis."

Charlotte whirled around. "Did you say 'Saint Francis'?"

"Yes, that painting there. It depicts the story of Saint Francis speaking to the wolf."

"'Francis' as in *Mary* Francis?" Charlotte said.

"Oh, I see!" Miss Gardenside clapped her hands. "We discovered the clue! But what does it mean?"

Charlotte took the painting off the wall. The back was covered in brown paper, stapled all around, but something shifted inside.

"Tear it open," Miss Gardenside said.

Charlotte hesitated. Mrs. Wattlesbrook would not be pleased if she tore the backing off a priceless work of art.

"Go ahead," said Miss Charming. "It's not real."

"How can you tell?"

"I'm really good at spotting fakes." She gave her chest a gentle shake. "It's a genetic gift. I grew 'em real—and how—and as a bonus, I'm gifted with a radar for detecting frauds of any kind."

As much as Charlotte wanted to believe that Miss Charming's abnormally large authentic bosoms granted her a superpowered ability to detect fake paintings, it seemed just a tad far-fetched.

Miss Charming turned the painting over. "See the even texture? This was one of those spray-on jobs, mass-produced duplicates. Not even a good one. Tear it up, darlin'."

Charlotte ripped open a corner of the brown paper. Out slid a parchment, folded in thirds.

They opened it up breathlessly. The page was blank.

"Is this a joke?" Charlotte asked.

"Naw, it's just Andrews," Miss Charming said with a fond smile. "He loves prolonging the climax."

She examined the paper at arm's length, squinting, then ran downstairs. "Come on!"

Miss Gardenside and Charlotte followed.

They stood on the front steps, holding the paper up to the sun. Charlotte thought she could detect faint markings.

"Lemon juice!" she said. "My son used lemon juice as ink for a school science project once. We need heat."

They hurried back inside, giggling and jostling and generally resembling a flock of busy geese. One lit candle later, they held the paper close to the flame and watched as marks painted in lemon juice darkened to brown.

Among dusty tomes stands
The work of the saint
And one girl's confessions
Penned without constraint

"Another clue. He does play with one," Miss Gardenside said.

Miss Charming laughed. "Oh, you don't know the half."

Charlotte led the women to the library. On the shelves of nonfiction was *Francis of Assisi: Patron Saint of Animals.*

Miss Gardenside and Miss Charming gathered in as she flipped through the pages. The end papers were covered in handwriting, made with the unmistakable strokes of a quill pen.

"I, Mary Francis, write this in my own hand—" Charlotte began to read.

"Aah!" all three screamed.

"We found it!" Charlotte yelled, as they ran back through the house. "We found it, we found it!"

Eddie, Mr. Mallery, and Colonel Andrews came from separate directions, converging in the front hall. Miss Charming was hopping up and down, her bosom nearly rising to slap her own forehead.

"We found the clue, Colonel Andrews! We found Mary's own words!"

Colonel Andrews clasped his hands together, his face aglow. Charlotte was so elated by his happiness that she wanted to squeeze his cheeks. His face cheeks, that is. Not that he didn't look great in breeches, but she didn't dwell on it.

The group rushed into the morning room and gathered around Charlotte. She opened the book, then thinking that Miss Gardenside might enjoy it more than she, gave it over to the girl to read. Miss Gardenside smiled and cleared her throat.

I, Mary Francis, write this in my own hand. I have just heard tale of the passing of the good abbess and now my tongue is loosed to speak. God alone will judge the abbess, for I will not and would not speak of the matter while she lived. Truth is a sword, and though it be good, it cuts. I will not wound anyone if I can help it. I have seen enough death. My parents of the fever. My brother in the fields. And then at the abbey . . .

I know the villagers think I killed my sister nuns, and if they could have claimed how, they would have hanged me at the moment. God knows my hands are clean. And none else believe me but Greta, the good cook's helper at the big house. She did not like how the others treated me. She could see how tortured I was, how I could not sleep for the nightmares, how I paced my room at night to keep from screaming. She meant well, but I did not think it wise for her to pretend to be a Spirit of Vengeance, warning them away. Though she was clever, putting on the muslin and balancing on that butter board to appear to float, and the others did leave me alone after that. Still I fear the lie in the thing and asked Greta to stop.

Now I will write the truth of that night, and pray to God that he take me home soon so I can rest. For some time the abbess had been doing poorly. Her hands shook, and her thoughts often muddled. That night she made the tea for supper, and, wishing to brighten the sisters' spirits, made it extra sweet with honey. The exertion tired her, and she took to rest. Poor abbess. She was mother to me, the kindest woman, a saint. I feared for her health and so was fasting that night in earnest prayer that she be made well.

The sisters sat to eat. I, fasting, served them, pouring their tea after the meal.

When tea was drunk, we retired to the chapel for compline prayers. But before we could start, some of the sisters began to moan, clutching their bellies. One fell to the earth, then another. I ran around, frantic, trying to help, but their faces convulsed horribly. Some screamed. In minutes, all lay dead. In confusion, I feared the Devil and his army were attacking and I hid beneath a pew, praying to the Almighty most fervently. Soon the abbess came in and saw the death. She fainted and I carried her to bed.

There was naught to be done. I laid out the bodies of my sisters and covered them in blankets. Come morn, I would go to the village and fetch help to bury the dead. In the meantime, I cleaned up the dishes from the last supper, thinking it was the only service I could offer my poor sisters. When I emptied the tea cauldron, I discovered something strange. The abbess had not boiled the usual dried herbs we had grown from our garden. I thought at first she had boiled fresh pine needles, as we sometimes did in winter, but the smell was wrong. Then I realized—the abbess in her confusion had mistaken the yew hedge for the pine trees. I have seen yew kill a horse. My dear sisters drank yew tea, well-sweetened.

I am consoled that the abbess will never know, and I pray God pardon her, for her heart was pure.

Miss Gardenside shut the book and looked around. "Well, I would like Mary Francis pleading for me at the final judgment."

"Amen," said Eddie.

Charlotte was silent, imagining Mary pacing in her room each night, haunted by the faces of the dying sisters.

Then Colonel Andrews began to laugh. He rocked back and forth, holding his knees. "Well done! Well done indeed. I say, what a right splendid way to end it all. I hereby declare the mystery solved!"

Miss Charming and Miss Gardenside hurrahed and clapped.

"Solved?" said Charlotte. "But what about the rest?"

"What rest?" the Colonel asked.

She sat beside him, speaking low so the others didn't overhear. "The fake body on the second floor. Or was it just a hand? Was there more than the rubber glove? I already guessed it was supposed to be Mr. Wattlesbrook or Mrs. Hatchet."

Colonel Andrews's eyes widened. In amazement, no doubt! He hadn't realized she'd gotten so far into the mystery on her own.

"They were the only main characters who disappeared," she explained. "And mysteriously too. No one seems to have witnessed Mr. Wattlesbrook's departure, and Miss Gardenside said she dismissed her nurse herself. It was the last night of the storm, and I looked around the next day. That's when I found the tracks from Mr. Wattlesbrook's—"

Car. She was about to say "car." That was not a Regency word. That was an off-limits word.

Oh no. Oh dear. She'd gotten this so wrong. Colonel Andrews would never involve a car in his Regency mystery. He was a purist. What was she saying? This had nothing to do with Mary Francis.

"Never mind. I just . . . never mind. I was thinking about another story line." She trailed off and joined the others, who were gathered around the tea trolley.

Eddie sniffed his cup. "Does this brew smell a bit yew-ish?"

That night, Charlotte lay in bed and stared at the ceiling. Sometimes instinct isn't fancy. Sometimes when you think you've touched a corpse's hand, you actually have, and sometimes when you suspect there's a murderer lurking in a big strange house, there really is, and you should figure out who it is before they come for you.

She tried to sleep, but the noise of her fears grated in her head, loud as a siren, and she might as well have been trying to sleep atop a wailing fire truck. She dozed when she could, just trying to make it till dawn. She didn't dare venture out in the dark.

What do you think will happen? asked her Inner Thoughts. The bogeyman will bite you?

Basically I'm afraid of murder most foul, Charlotte answered.

Duh, people are killed at noon just as often as midnight, her Inner Thoughts replied.

Not helpful, Charlotte thought forcefully.

Well past midnight and between bouts of unconsciousness, Charlotte began to wonder if the house itself was the real assassin. It groused and soughed as if it had a voice and something to say. Perhaps someone had crossed the house, and it had seized the threat in its gullet and consumed it entirely. Charlotte had discovered the victim's body mid-digestion, finding only a hand, and by morning the house had absorbed the rest.

"Nice house," she said, patting the wall. "Good house. Charlotte is friend."

It couldn't hurt.

As soon as paleness filtered the black of the sky, Charlotte slipped on a robe, creaked her door open, and tiptoed to the second-floor secret room. She didn't really believe that the house had killed someone and swallowed the body. Not now that it was morning, anyway.

Charlotte lifted the lid of the black Chinese vase again, just because it seemed like something that should hold a clue. But it was still empty. In the unfinished light of dawn, the stack of broken chairs did resemble a dragon, but that wasn't particularly helpful. Even in her sleepy half-madness, Charlotte didn't believe in dragons.

Charlotte sat on an abandoned settee, slumping in the absence of a corset. A body had lain right over there on the couch.

She couldn't talk herself out of it anymore. No way had she mistaken a glove for a fleshy dead hand.

To keep calm, she tried to reason it out logically.

1. Murderer approached victim. Lured up to this room? With intent to kill? Not likely. Must have been an unplanned crime or else a stupid criminal. The top floor of an occupied house was not an ideal location for a murder.

2. Victim killed in secret room, and body abandoned on sofa. Until more convenient time? Murderer lay velvet coverlet partially over the body. Possible sign of regret? Also a disregard for the value of a velvet coverlet.

3. Charlotte found body in room. The hand was cold, but she didn't remember any stench, so most likely the body was fresh. (Ugh, what a horrible adjective to apply to a body, as if it were meat, which, she supposed, it kind of was.) Killed recently? Same week? Same day?

4. Charlotte announced find to gentlemen and two ladies, none of whom claimed to know of the secret room. And Mary the maid had come out of her room, learning of Charlotte's find as well. Other servants could have heard of it after that, possibly via Mary. But it'd been very late. Unlikely any servants but those on the second floor would have found out that night, and besides Mary, the others had probably been asleep.

5. Next morning the body was gone.

Wait! A point to add—stick it in as 4.1. Charlotte had heard a thud outside during the night. She visualized the location of Miss Charming's room, and sure enough, it was below the secret room. The murderer must have returned in the night, thrown the body out the window, rather than drag it down two flights of stairs, and then retrieved it outside and disposed of it somewhere.

Charlotte went to the window. It was wide enough to fit a body through. She didn't see any telltale shards of ripped clothing or flesh (shudder). If only she had some proof to take to the police. Charlotte hadn't heard a car or wagon move after the thud. The murderer most likely didn't have an accomplice. Alone in the middle of the night, he or she must have gone downstairs and out the front door, then carried/dragged the body nearby to some kind of vehicle.

Like Mr. Wattlesbrook's car.

Charlotte crept back downstairs, a ghost in her white robe haunting the spiral staircase. It felt nice to think of herself as the ghost; it offered a kind of armor to her jumpy fear. Ghosts can't get re-killed. She tiptoed past the dead eyes of the wall portraits and the shut doors, known to no one but the house itself, her companion in the creeping.

I'm sorry I didn't like you at first, she thought at the house. And I'm sorry I thought for a minute that you might be an evil monstrosity. Let's be friends?

Sleepy and alone at dawn, the thought didn't feel ridiculous.

She opened her door and heard a creak behind her. She whipped around. Nothing.

"Someone there?" she whispered.

Old houses creak, she told herself.

And sometimes, said her Inner Thoughts, people make them creak by sneaking around. Maybe with a knife in hand. Ha ha . . .

Charlotte ordered her Inner Thoughts to take a hike. She closed her door and wished, not for the first time, that it locked.

home, over a year before

THERE WERE THE LATE NIGHTS, the unexpected trips out of state, the irregular laundry patterns. There were the phone calls from unlisted numbers, the caller hanging up if Charlotte answered. There was the odd way James touched her now, or didn't touch her at all, the curtness in his tone, with no explanation of what she'd done wrong. Things escalated, as they tend to do: a neighbor saying she'd run into James downtown when he was supposed to be in New York on business; a local hotel calling to say James had left behind a phone charger; finding the wrapped lingerie in his closet and assuming he'd forgotten to give it to her on their anniversary—and forgotten her size.

It is much easier to solve someone else's mystery than to take a step back to survey the one haunting your own home. Charlotte had the gall to be blindsided by James's confession. Perhaps, Charlotte thought later, she was not so clever. Perhaps she was in the habit of seeing only what she hoped to see.

austenland, day 11

EVERYWHERE CHARLOTTE LOOKED, SHE SAW signs of murder. The eerie, knowing expressions on the portraits' faces, the silence in the hallway, the clatter of a plate in the dining room, the emptiness in Mrs. Hatchet's room.

Charlotte had bathed and dressed after her daybreak snooping and was just about to descend the stairs to breakfast when she heard voices on the landing. She peeked one eye around the corner. Mrs. Hatchet and Miss Gardenside.

"I came to check on you," said the mother/nurse.

"I'm doing better," said Miss Gardenside. "A lot better. In fact, I've never felt so good."

"Good. That's good. You have three more days to go?"

Miss Gardenside nodded.

"Good. That's good," Mrs. Hatchet repeated. "So, do you need anything?"

"No, I'm fine. I'm good."

"Good."

They both looked out the window.

"You got all dressed up," Miss Gardenside said, gesturing to Mrs. Hatchet's navy blue dress. "Are you staying?"

"I just wanted to check on you. But I can stay if you aren't handling things well on your own."

"I'm handling things just fine."

"Well. I will see you next week. Behave yourself."

"I am," Miss Gardenside said through clenched teeth.

Mrs. Hatchet nodded and left. Miss Gardenside remained alone on the landing, still staring out the window.

"Riveting," said a voice beside Charlotte's ear.

She startled back.

"Eddie. You love to sneak."

He peeked back at Miss Gardenside, who sighed and then headed downstairs. "I do hope Miss Gardenside was providing better entertainment before I interrupted you, or I might suggest more interesting avenues for spying. Such as through Mr. Mallery's keyhole. I have not spied that out myself, but perhaps Miss Charming could give you a review. Or Colonel Andrews."

"Mrs. Hatchet was here," Charlotte said, ignoring him. She didn't want to talk about Mr. Mallery with Eddie. "That's the interesting part. Because she isn't dead."

"That is a relief, though I wasted an afternoon drafting a damn fine eulogy. Wait—how did Mrs. Hatchet die again?"

"In the conservatory, by Colonel Mustard, with her own name," Charlotte said, pretending she was joking too, so that she wouldn't have to mention dead bodies again. After all, anyone could be the murderer. Even Eddie.

Eddie offered his arm. "No more mystery for you or your womb, sister dear. Breakfast trumps all."

And for that matter, if the murder was real and not part of Colonel Andrews's game, then the victim could have been anyone as well. Still, now that Mrs. Hatchet was confirmed alive, Mr. Wattlesbrook's disappearance the day of Bloody Murder put him at the top of Charlotte's Probably Dead list.

"What did you gentlemen do with Mr. Wattlesbrook that day he showed up drunk?" Charlotte asked Eddie and Colonel Andrews over breakfast. The others had already dined and departed.

"I was for tossing him out the front door," Colonel Andrews said. "But driving . . . a carriage in his condition did seem a mite dangerous. Grey feared for his life."

"Or the lives of others," said Eddie.

"So he proposed we lock him up till he sobered up."

"On the second floor?" Charlotte asked.

Eddie nodded. "In an uninhabited bedroom. But in the morning the door was unlocked and he was gone."

"Don't take it personally, Grey," said Colonel Andrews. "Perhaps he did not particularly enjoy that jab to the jaw."

Eddie rubbed his face.

The colonel laughed and said, "The old man would not shut up, speaking nastily about his wife, and your brother, here, decided a fist to the face was just the remedy."

"Did any of you stay with him?" she asked.

"No," said Eddie, looking at her curiously. "We locked him up and left. There was a bed in the room and a pitcher of water—"

"And a chamber pot," the colonel added.

"So how did he get out of the room?"

Colonel Andrews shrugged. "I suppose Mrs. Wattlesbrook let him out. Why? Have you seen the gentleman about?"

"No," she said significantly. "Is that strange?"

The colonel shrugged again, and Eddie did not answer.

Neville entered and began to clean up.

The butler's got a thing for the missus, Charlotte thought. But enough to motivate him to murder her husband? He didn't *seem* guilty.

Then again, neither had James.

Charlotte joined the gentlemen and ladies for a walk around the gardens and wondered who else might want Mr. Wattlesbrook dead. He'd signed away Windy Nook and Bertram Hall and burned down Pembrook Cottage. Perhaps someone feared Pembrook Park was next.

"What a lovely day!" Miss Charming declared, her face strained, as if desperate for it to be true.

Why so desperate? Charlotte observed her all morning. Between the "halloos" and "what-whats," before the giggles and after the gusty sighs, Charlotte detected fear.

She followed Miss Charming to her room before lunch and sat on her bed, waiting till she emerged from her bathroom.

"Charlotte! You made me jump out of my skin."

"Lizzy, I've noticed that you seem to be . . . well, afraid. Of something."

Miss Charming began to blink rapidly. She looked behind her at the open door, as if checking for eavesdroppers.

"It's all right, Lizzy," Charlotte whispered, patting the bed beside her, an invitation. "You can tell me."

Miss Charming sat, squeezed her eyes shut, and nodded. She whispered wetly, "It's my Bobby."

"I'm sorry, what?"

"My Bobby. And that toothpick."

Charlotte wasn't sure how a toothpick was involved—as a murder weapon?

Miss Charming began to talk like an erupting volcano. "Bobby and me'd been together since grade school. We were king and queen of the prom! And then thirty—er, a few years later, I catch him on a mattress sample with that toothpick of a girl. We sold mattresses, you know. Thousands of them. Eighteen stores in the tristate area, best bargains east of the Mississippi. 'The Mattress Shack has got your back!'" she sang. "I came up with that jingle. I was the brains, he was the brawn, till I found him on a mattress sample with an assistant salesclerk named Heather. What kind of name is 'Heather' anyway? Sounds like a disease."

This was not the course Charlotte had been expecting.

"So, you were afraid?" Charlotte prompted.

"I took the alimony and ran—cruises and resorts, till I found Pembrook Park. And I don't want to leave, ever. 'Cause back home I'll be the fat girl Bobby Murdock dumped, and our stores aren't mine anymore, and at least here no one can dump me again."

A burbling sound started inside Miss Charming that soon changed into sobs.

"You've been a guest at Pembrook Park for how long?" asked Charlotte.

"Well . . . I started on last fall, but they close up for December and January, and so I went on a cruise to the Mediterranean. And Greece is snazzy, honey lamb, and the food in Italy was *bushel baskets* better than here, but I got lonely. I came back again in March, and now everything's great!" She smiled with big, white teeth, her cheeks trembling a little to hold it.

"How can you afford to just stay here, session after session?"

"Oh, I got loads." She blew her nose. "I guess that's all I got."

Charlotte rubbed Miss Charming's arm. She knew from experience how little such a gesture could do to relieve that stabbing heart pain.

So she said, "My husband left me for a woman named 'Justice.'"

"Seriously? 'Justice'? That's worse than 'Heather'!" Miss Charming put her arms around Charlotte and squeezed her like a favorite teddy bear. "I'm so glad you've been dumped too."

Charlotte guessed that wasn't exactly what Miss Charming meant, so she hugged her back.

"We're not supposed to talk about our other lives," Miss Charming whispered.

"I won't tell. Were you serious before, when you said you can tell fakes from real?"

"Lifelong talent. I should've seen Bobby's affair from a mile off, but it's hard to get a good look at someone when he's breathing in your ear."

"Don't I know it. What do you think about the other Pembrook folk. Fake or real?"

"Lemme see . . . Colonel Andrews is real in a way, but just

because his phoniness really *is* him. Mr. Grey seems real, but I'm not sure. Miss Gardenside is as fake as they come. Mr. Mallery and Mrs. Wattlesbrook are real as real."

"And me?"

"You're solid gold, weighed and minted." Miss Charming gave Charlotte a big wet kiss on the cheek, sniffed deeply, and smiled despite her red eyes.

Charlotte left feeling determined. Miss Charming was not the murderer, but someone was. Charlotte wanted to cross a line, ford the Rubicon, commit herself to solving this whodunit so she could put it behind her and get ready to fall in love with Mr. Mallery at the ball. Her vacation was almost over, and there hadn't been enough vacationing going on.

She marched downstairs, peeking into rooms until she found Eddie in the library. He'd asked her to include him in her investigations, after all. And he really had the most innocent face.

"Off on an adventure?" he asked.

"Yeah. Will you come with me?"

Caesar wasn't alone as he waded into the waters of the Rubicon. When Charlotte solved a violent, shocking murder, it would be nice to have a friend beside her. Because when she thought about what she was about to do, she felt a buzzing in her fingers warning that her hands were most likely shaking. She gripped Eddie's arm harder to try to keep them still.

"And where are we going?" he asked, placing one of his hands over hers.

"The pond."

THE POND LAY DULL AND gray between the trees, no breeze to finger its surface into uneasy ripples. The sky was clogged with clouds, preventing reflected sunlight from winking mischievously on the waves, as one might expect if the waters did indeed hide a secret. But the pond resisted all personification, neither begging for inspection nor warning of horrors best left alone. It just lay there, uninterested.

Which was really irritating. Charlotte would have appreciated some seductive shore lapping, ripples beckoning like a curved finger, that sort of thing. But no. Thanks a lot for nothing, pond. So Charlotte did her best to supply the scene with the necessary exaggerations to provoke her to action.

See there, how that cloud's reflection was shaped like a hand?

My, but wasn't there a great looming shadow in the water's depths?

Hark, but didn't the twittering of birds in the trees seem to sort of imply that the wildlife was all aflutter about something horrid and unnatural that took place here, such as, oh, I don't know, *murder most foul*?!

Eddie and Charlotte stood on the banks of the pond. Staring at it. At least one of them wishing it looked more intriguing.

"So here we are," said Eddie. "At the pond. I certainly hope this vapid gaping does not qualify as an adventure, or I might have to take aggressive action and save you from the continued dullness of country life."

"Nope. I'm just gearing up to take a swim."

She started stripping down before he could reply.

"Er . . . several responses are coming to mind," he said, holding his head as if it hurt. "Hard . . . to choose . . . between them all."

"Just like we used to do back home," she said. That sort of logic usually worked with Eddie. Besides, there was no view of the house or any of its outbuildings from the pond. It was unlikely that Mr. Mallery or one of the others would come along. And her corset, chemise, and bloomers were far more modest than twenty-first century bathing fare, even if they did qualify as weird underwear.

"If you'd rather not, I'll go it alone. I'm just . . . uh, dying in this blazing sun."

Eddie squinted suspiciously at the overcast sky.

"Right. Blazing. You always were impetuous. Weren't you?"

"Always," she confirmed. Not really, but it was nice to imagine a brother who thought of her that way—wild Charlotte, unpredictable Charlotte, dive-into-unknown-waters-in-search-of-clues Charlotte. She could be that—for a little while, anyway.

"Yes, I remember well. So. It would appear my brotherly duty is to stand guard, because I am not climbing into that cesspool."

"Spoilsport," she said and jumped in.

Chilly. Oh yes, most definitely chilly. But she swam around, warming up her muscles, and the exercise felt great, as long as she avoided the shallower parts and the greedy little pond plants that reached up to tangle her ankles. *Way* creepy sensation in a pond where a murderer might have dumped a body.

She didn't want Eddie to know what she was really doing. Because, honestly, what on earth was she doing?

Charlotte flipped her hips up and dove underwater, swimming with her eyes open. It was deeper than she'd thought, and the water wasn't exactly country club clear. She came up for a breath.

"Doing your mermaid impersonation?" Eddie called from the shore.

"Come on in, the water's fine!" she called.

"So sings the siren before pulling the unsuspecting sailor down to Davy Jones's locker. I am no water nymph. And I do not like . . . fish." He shivered.

"What, you're afraid of teeny little pond fishies nibbling on your toes?"

He grimaced.

"Fish!" Charlotte screamed and went underwater as if pulled from below.

"Charlotte!" Eddie shouted, standing.

She popped back up with a wet grin. He glared and threw a chunk of grass at her.

She dodged and went underwater again, swimming toward the middle. Something was there. Something was really there. Her heart beat harder, making it difficult to hold her breath. She came up, breathing in deeply, and floated on her back, looking up at the sky. Once her breath slowed, she dove straight down.

Straight down to the roof of a car. Despite the murkiness, there was no mistaking it. She could see the silver glint of a BMW decal on the hood. Those *had* been tire marks on the edge of the pond after the rainstorm. Someone had driven a BMW into the pond and then stamped over the muddy tracks to try to disguise them. If Mr. Wattlesbrook, drunk and stupid, had driven his own car into the pond, then who had covered his tracks?

She came back up, breathing rapidly.

Don't think too hard yet or you'll freak out. You are like Jacques Cousteau. You are investigating underwater wildlife, like algae and sunfish and Beamers. That's all. Keep breathing.

Down she went again. She kicked hard till she could grab the door handle and peer in the window. Little light filtered through the dirty water and car windows, but if there'd been a body at the wheel, she could have made it out. As near as she could tell, there weren't even keys in the ignition. The windows were rolled down partway, as if welcoming in the water, and the doors were locked. Something was dangling from the ceiling of the car. Her motion caused it to slowly spin. It was a glove, pockets of air in the fingertips suspending it in the water. In natural light, she guessed, it would be yellow.

Charlotte swam around to the trunk and tried to pry it open with cold, awkward fingers. Locked.

There's a body in there, she thought.

Suddenly her lungs did fine imitations of rabid dogs, snarling and snapping at her. MUST HAVE AIR, they said. Her eyeballs hurt, the cold pressure of the water unbearable. She released her held breath in a flurry of bubbles and beat her way to the surface.

Charlotte came up with a shudder and a gasp. She swam lamely to the side and hoisted herself onto the grassy bank.

"You're trembling," said Eddie, putting his coat around her shoulders.

"Colder than I thought," she said, even though it was exactly as cold as an English pond in midsummer should be. But she was definitely trembling. There was a BMW sitting on the bottom of the pond. And that's a heavy, expensive piece of scenery to dump underwater. And there was no logical reason Colonel Andrews would have put it there as part of his little Gothic mystery. And that meant someone else had for other reasons. And the only reason she could think of was—

"Let me take you inside," said Eddie.

"Body," she said.

"What?"

"I . . . yes, inside. Please."

The only reason to dump a car in a pond was to hide it, since the owner wouldn't be driving it home. Because the owner was dead. And stashed in the trunk. Surely the guards at the gate, under Mrs. Wattlesbrook's orders, wouldn't allow any car through to disrupt the Regency ambience—any car besides the master's, that is. His would have been the only car on the premises that night, the only one to leave those tracks in the mud. Mr. Wattlesbrook was in the trunk of his car at the bottom of the pond, and the murderer was likely someone at Pembrook Park. Someone who'd been on-site to kill him, leave his body in the secret room, dump it out the window after the game of Bloody Murder, get it to the car, and drive the car into the pond to conceal the dirty deed.

She was barely aware that she was wearing Eddie's black jacket. His arm went around her as they walked back. Neville was dusting the dinner gong in the front hall. He looked over Charlotte in her chemise drippiness.

"Mrs. Cordial fell off her horse and into the watering trough," Eddie said. "It can happen, you know."

"Quite, sir," said Neville. He eyeballed Charlotte's dry dress hanging over Eddie's arm, perhaps wondering why Charlotte had undressed before falling into a trough.

Eddie winked at him and walked Charlotte to her room.

"Do you require any further assistance?" Eddie asked.

"Thanks, I'm just going to get out of these clothes and bathe off the pond scum."

"Are you going to ring for your maid?"

"No. I'd rather not have to explain why I'm soaked."

"I could help with the laces," he said.

She laughed and wagged her finger. Sly dog, such a womanizer, even though I'm his sister—ew, is that creepy?

But his expression was serious.

"Well . . ." she said, considering his offer. A corset was hard enough to take off without help, maybe impossible when wet.

He entered the room and shut the door behind him, the click like an alarm bell.

Charlotte backed away, her fingers and toes tingling with adrenaline. Why had he shut the door? He *knew*. About Mr. Wattlesbrook. And the car in the pond. And the only way he would know was if—

"Shy, dear sister? I promise not to look." He kept coming forward.

"Why did I want to swim in that pond today?" she demanded of him.

"Because you are half mad?" he said with a smile, innocent dimples showing.

"You know why, Eddie, don't you?" She backed into the window, and her fingers searched for the latch. If she screamed, would someone hear?

He raised an eyebrow. "I cannot fathom the complexities of your thoughts. I gave up understanding women long ago. Charlotte, you are the only woman I dare comprehend, and right now even you have left me leagues behind."

"I have?"

"Speaking of behind, turn yours toward me so I can undo you. I don't like how you are shivering."

She was shivering, her arms around her chest, her chemise clinging to her skin like a frog's tongue to dinner. But was he here to kill her? She'd shown her hand. Colonel Andrews had said that Eddie hit Mr. Wattlesbrook in the face. That showed an inclination for violence toward the man. Did they have some history? If Eddie had killed him and dumped his car, Eddie now knew that she knew, and that she knew that he knew that she knew too. There was a lot of knowing going on. But then why not just kill her at the pond and bury her there as well?

"No . . . I'll . . . I'll do it. You can go."

Eddie made a noise of exasperation and closed the space between them. Should she call for help? Why was she hesitating? Scream already!

He grabbed her by the shoulders and turned her around. She squeezed her eyes shut and inhaled sharply, but the scream lodged frozen and useless in her chest. His cold fingers lifted her wet hair from her neck and placed it over her shoulder. She clenched her jaw, anticipating his hands circling her neck, tightening, trapping her breath in with the unscreamed scream till everything turned dark as midnight.

Except his hands left her neck. She felt light tugging on her back, and in moments her corset was loose on her chest, held up by her arms alone. His hands dropped away. She opened her eyes.

"That was fast," she said, still not turning around. She spoke softly, her heart beating so hard it shook the breath out of her. "You must have practice."

"One of the many duties of a gentleman. Now I will leave you to your mysterious womanliness."

And he left.

He hadn't killed her. Just a few moments before she'd been sure he was going to kill her. And she'd submitted her corset lacings to him without a plan of escape or attack. Because he was Eddie. And she was nice. Wow, that's an eye-opener.

Since she was still alive and breathing, she took a bath. There wasn't a lock on her bathroom door either.

She submerged her head under the warm water and saw again the car, sunken like a child's toy in a goldfish bowl. If Mr. Wattlesbrook, inebriated on fine sherry, drove the wrong way in the dark till he found water gushing in the car windows, he would either drown in the car or flee. He certainly wouldn't remove the keys and lock the doors.

She dressed for dinner sans corset—since she only had the one and it was sopping—and hoped no one would notice. Would a drowned BMW be enough evidence to merit calling the police? Perhaps, but she still had no idea who'd done it, and that was the whole point of a whodunit, after all. Besides, she felt compelled to figure this out, exactly in the way she hadn't figured out James. She needed a direction to point her finger, but rifling through everyone's personal belongings to look for a bloodstained dagger might not be exactly Regency appropriate.

She came out of her room just as Miss Gardenside emerged from hers.

"Good evening, Charlotte," she said without a trace of worry.

Just how could Miss Gardenside immerse herself so completely in a different character? And what had happened to that dreadful consumption?

Charlotte smiled uneasily and hurried ahead, taking the stairs alone. Coming up was Mrs. Wattlesbrook. She barely acknowledged Charlotte. Her eyes were hooded, as if she hadn't slept well for days. Gnawed by guilt? She recalled the glimmer of a smile on the woman's face when Charlotte had claimed her fictional husband had died a painful and tragic death.

Charlotte leapt down the last three steps and entered the dining room. The maids continued preparing for dinner, their glances taking her in. Suspiciously? Charlotte tried not to make eye contact. Neville approached, his thin arms behind his back.

"May I be of service?"

She was too freaked out to attempt a casual inquiry. "Neville, how many servants are employed here?"

"Let me see . . . kitchen, maids, stables, gardeners—seventeen all told."

Seventeen!

"They all live on the property? Do any of them come and go?"

"They return home to visit family. However, all seventeen remain here for the duration of our guests' stays."

She nodded. She didn't know what else to ask except, Hey, are any of your staff potential murderers?

"Forgive me for the observation, Mrs. Cordial, but you are curious. It reminds me of what happened to the cat."

Charlotte swallowed. Was that a warning from a man so

infatuated with his mistress he'd kill for her? Or from a butler who wished her gone from his tidy dining room?

She scurried out, shutting the doors behind her.

The usual six were in the drawing room, and all their faces turned to her as she entered. Her heart stuck to her ribs, too frightened to beat. Someone in here was probably a murderer. Did they suspect what she knew? Or were they staring because they noticed she wasn't wearing a corset?

"I propose a game," she said. "I've been inspired by the colonel's mystery. Let's say . . ." She cleared her throat, starting to lose her nerve. "Let's say there's been a murder in the house, and one of us is guilty. The victim could be, oh . . . Mr. Wattlesbrook," she said casually, "since he hasn't returned."

Mrs. Wattlesbrook choked on nothing. Mr. Mallery looked up sharply. Eddie shook his head. Miss Gardenside shifted in her chair. Miss Charming gasped, delighted. Charlotte felt her face go red hot, but she didn't blink.

"Splendid!" said the colonel. "A locked-door mystery."

Encouraged, Charlotte ventured forward. "We'll go to everyone's room one by one and search for murder weapons, clues for a motive, that sort of thing."

"Yes, yes!" Miss Charming clapped her hands. "Blood splatter on dress hems and bottoms of shoes, clues in pockets and purses, and I'll write up a list of what everyone has in their room, then, all detective-like, we'll come back here and decide who's the guiltiest."

"I do not find this appropriate," Mrs. Wattlesbrook said.

"Oh come now, madam," said Colonel Andrews. "It is just a game."

"I don't mean to offend you," Charlotte said. "I just thought we could pretend, you know? Anyway, it would be nice to have everyone involved, including you. All of us in this together."

Miss Gardenside stood. "I have always said, Charlotte, that you have a very clever mind. Does she not, Mr. Grey? A very clever mind. Would you not agree, Mr. Mallery?"

"Very clever," Mr. Mallery said.

"Right-o, pip-pip," said Miss Charming. "Just give us all a tit, or a tat or whatever, to go straighten up first."

At once, all were on their feet, moving toward the door.

"No, we have to stay together!" said Charlotte. "If one of us is a murderer, we can't separate, remember?"

"Right, right, Mrs. Cordial," Colonel Andrews said. "But hold that thought for ten, and then we shall begin."

"It has to be spontaneous or people can hide evidence!" Charlotte pleaded.

"I'll leave out my murder weapons, but no one is seeing my toiletries bag," said Miss Charming, the first to the drawing room doors. "Ooh, I hope I'm the murderer!"

"Meet back in the drawing room in ten minutes, all!" Colonel Andrews called.

And like that, Charlotte was left standing alone. No noise but the ticking of a clock. It sounded scoldy—*tsk, tsk, tsk*. She reached into its chest and murderously held the pendulum till it stopped. She knew she'd messed up; she didn't need some obnoxious mantel clock going on about it. If the murderer was one of the drawing room denizens, he or she likely guessed that Charlotte knew. Evidence would be hidden. How to catch the murderer now?

Her plan was foiled, but perhaps she could still glean information. She went upstairs, shut the door to her room as if she were inside, and secreted herself behind the drapes of a large hallway window. The servants pulled them closed in the afternoon to protect the paintings on the walls from bright sunlight. She stood perfectly concealed, one eye peering through the lace edging. She waited.

Seconds later, someone emerged from down the hallway. Through the lace she could only tell that it was a man. He paused at her door as he walked past, then kept going toward the spiral stairs.

Her insides itched with curiosity. The hallway was empty, the doors all closed. She left the safety of the drapes and followed.

The night of Bloody Murder, Charlotte had been confused by the rules of the game. If a murderer was hiding in the house, why would they seek him out? Wouldn't it make more sense for the players to hide from the murderer? Yet here she was in real life doing just that, seeking a murderer instead of hiding. She wanted answers, and she was tired of being afraid.

No one was on the stairs. Up she climbed, the spiral unraveling. She could see only a few steps at a time. Anyone could be lurking. Perhaps she should just wait at the bottom to see who came down. But knowing who left the game to go upstairs wasn't evidence of murder.

The second floor was still. The servants were probably downstairs preparing for dinner. Should she check all the rooms? She approached Mary's room and heard the squeak of a mattress. Someone was in there. Coming toward the door? Charlotte panicked and fled, opening the secret door and hurrying inside.

And she almost collided with Mr. Mallery.

home, years before

WHEN THEY WERE LITTLE, BECKETT and Lu loved to play chase. Charlotte would zoom around the kitchen, and they would flee, laughing and squealing and even screaming.

Upon the shout of "Safe, safe!" any noncarpeted place automatically would become safe—a chair, a stool, a bed, a book, a blanket. They'd need a moment to know they were okay, but they'd never stay still for long. Seconds later, they'd take off again, hoping Mom was on their heels.

What fun was safe?

austenland, day 11, cont.

MR. MALLERY LOOKED UP AT the sound of the door. His hand was on the lid of the black Chinese vase Charlotte had inspected so often. He withdrew it hastily.

"Mrs. Cordial," he said with surprise. "What are you doing here?"

Charlotte felt sick to her stomach. What could she do? Well, when Beckett had a stomachache, she'd tell him to lie down and drink some soda pop and eat crackers. But as practical as that advice was, it didn't apply to this moment. Stomachache aside, what could she do? Run? She didn't want to run. She had to have evidence so she could put this mystery aside and go to the ball with—wait! The night of Bloody Murder, Mr. Mallery acted as if he hadn't known anything of the secret room. Had he lied?

"What are *you* doing here, Mr. Mallery?" she asked.

He did not answer. And he most certainly did not look pleased.

"Oh, I wish it wasn't you," she said with a groan.

Shut up, her Inner Thoughts warned.

Charlotte didn't pay them any mind. She was deep in the story now, feeling it acutely. Reading Austen had felt safe, like sitting on a big sister's bed and hearing stories about the far-off world. But now that she was actually in Austenland, there were no guarantees. Miss Jane the narrator wouldn't swoop in to make sure all turned out well for the heroine. Real life was dangerous. Pembrook Park was dangerous. Mr. Mallery was dangerous. Charlotte knew this without thinking it aloud, and yet in the moment, she found herself responding like a narrator, commenting on the action instead of acting. It was still a story. It wasn't real yet.

"What is it that you wish, Mrs. Cordial? Perhaps it is in my power to grant it."

"I wish you weren't the murderer, I really do."

"You have found me out." He bowed formally. "Now, who did I kill? Your game has a victim—Mr. Wattlesbrook, is it?"

"Yes, because he'd done away with the other estates, and he planned to divorce Mrs. Wattlesbrook and sell off Pembrook Park too, and you couldn't have that, because . . . because . . . why? Why, Mr. Mallery? Do you love it here so much? I can almost believe it. You do seem to *belong* here."

Mr. Mallery squinted and tilted his head to one side. "I'm afraid I'm not following."

"You, Eddie, and Andrews carried Mr. Wattlesbrook off and locked him in a room. Someone let him out. Then I found a body in here and . . . and how did you know about this room?"

"I believed you. If you said there was a room without a door, then you must be right. You are a clever woman. I sought it out for a time before discovering it, though I never found any corpse."

"But . . . but what are you doing here now?"

"Searching for evidence in support of your game, though I am afraid it grows more complicated by the moment."

"Evidence. His car. I saw it."

"Whose car?" Mr. Mallery asked.

"Mr. Wattlesbrook's. I saw it in the pond."

"Did you see that old thing down there?" Mr. Mallery smiled. He had such a dazzling smile. She'd never noticed that before. Or was this the first time he'd fully employed it? "You are enterprising, I must say. How did it look after all these years?"

"Years?"

"Hm? Yes, Wattlesbrook drove his car straight into the pond one night while drunk. That was two . . . three years ago? The vehicle he purchased after that one is probably still in a ditch near York, where he last left it. He does go through BMWs like handkerchiefs, though I suppose I should not talk about it. Don't mention this to Mrs. Wattlesbrook, will you? She knows I think her husband is a complete pillock, but speaking frankly of modern things with the guests crosses her line."

This Mr. Mallery was different. Eddie and Colonel Andrews allowed glimpses of their non-actor beings to peer through, as did Mrs. Wattlesbrook and the ladies. But Mr. Mallery had always been solidly Mr. Mallery. Now he showed cracks. Why did this, his actor self, feel less true than his character?

"Let's not mention the car, all right? It will upset Mrs. Wattlesbrook. But I am game for your game, my dear. Come, let's return and I will play your murderer."

The car. It *could* have been in the pond for years. Why hadn't that occurred to her before? There was a reason why she was so sure the car had been sunk recently, wasn't there? She looked at Mr. Mallery's patented smolder and couldn't remember a thing.

The door was behind her, Mr. Mallery a few paces away. Her heart was pounding in an uncomfortable manner, and her head felt swimmy, but one thought floated to the surface: *I am still an idiot.* This was the universal truth she had always believed in.

Charlotte emitted a squeak. Then a laugh.

"I did it again. I told myself I wouldn't get caught up in the story, but I did, and I really believed there'd been a murder and you were the murderer and . . . and—"

She laughed harder, and with the laugh and spinning reality, she forgot Regency etiquette and leaned into Mr. Mallery, laying her head and hands on his chest, laughing into his cravat. She could feel his heart beating against her head at a galloping pace. Why did his heart race? Was it her nearness, just as his nearness was spazzing out her own heart? And did this mean she was in love with him? Or he with her?

Stop it, Charlotte, said her Inner Thoughts. You can be so dense sometimes.

But wait. An actor can pretend to fall in love, but he can't *make* his heart beat faster, can he? The thought made her stomach feel icy, and she stepped away from him, talking rapidly.

"I can't believe I was such a ninny. Yeah, that's the word I'm going with—'ninny.' A goose, a half-wit, a mooncalf, any of those old words that mean 'naive idiot.' I fit right in with the silly girls Austen poked fun at, though hopefully she might care for me anyway, as she seemed to for Catherine Morland. Did you ever read *Northanger Abbey*? Well, she was a guest in an old house and convinced herself there'd been a murder, just like I did. I mean, I fought the idea because I knew it was ridiculous, but I just kept convincing myself anyway. I don't know what's wrong with me."

His smile took her in, approving. His admiration, combined with her acute embarrassment, made her feel as if she'd downed a jug of beer in one breath. She licked her lips, her head giddy, and began to talk faster.

"Maybe that's why you're so steady-minded, so unaffected. Maybe novels really do fill your head with fluff, like the characters in *Northanger Abbey* who don't read books seem to believe. Reading too much makes a house seem full of ghosts when it's just the creak of wood; it makes thunder seem like a metaphor instead of just the weather; it makes heart-throbbing romance seem possible, when it's not."

He took a step closer to her, his approving smile suggesting something even more, something that made her swallow and look away and talk faster.

"I know I'm making an even bigger idiot of myself," she said with a laugh. "But I can't seem to shut myself up."

"Please don't. You are so charming."

"No, I'm not. I'm really not." She twisted her hands and asked softly, "Am I?"

"You are charming when you speak like a sparrow in the morning. You are charming when you are silent." He took her hand, felt it between his fingers. "You are even charming when you think me a murderer."

She gave a little laugh at that. He smiled with fondness.

"You have charmed me." He nodded, as if surprised he'd spoken the words. "You have indeed. I do not know if I fully realized just how much until this moment. Mrs. Cordial . . . Charlotte . . ."

He paused as if afraid of speaking more, and pressed her

fingers against his lips to stop his words. Charlotte's heart was frantic.

It's a game. It's all a game, she told herself.

The murder mystery wasn't real, and neither was Mr. Mallery's affection. But did it matter? A man was looking at her in that scrumptious way, as if he wanted to kiss her. Not really, of course, but he *was* a real man and he was really looking at her. Good grief, but was she lonely.

"Charlotte . . ." he breathed. He opened her hand and rubbed a thumb across her palm. "I feel as if I have been dead, and your eyes have awakened me."

So this was it. She'd assumed that each guest would be the recipient of a fake but well-spoken proposal of marriage, since all of Austen's heroines were so lucky. But she hadn't imagined it happening in a dark, dusty room where she'd once run into a dead body. Or thought she had.

Her own body didn't mind the macabre environs. Her heart was rattling out a rhumba; her stomach felt all fluttery and wonderful. Even when her mind clamped down, getting stubborn and practical, her body still relished the farce. Her body floated.

"I knew from the first that you were a formidable woman. I thought I could keep my heart safe, but your honest looks and gestures leave me defenseless, your beauty undoes me." He ran his thumb lightly over her freckles. "I knew you were a dangerous woman, but I did not care."

Wait, was the actor speaking or Mr. Mallery the character?

"Let's not play chase any longer—let's not play anything. I am impatient to leave pretense behind. Please, Charlotte, tell me I do not love you in vain. Please assure me of your own attachment, or I know I will die."

He had to be acting, right? And couldn't she just pretend for a time? Couldn't she stop inventing murders and mayhem and problems to fix and simply enjoy the story? Yes, she could! She was about to assure him of her attachment, and to use archaic verb formations in the process just to get into the mood, when he reached out and smoothed a strand of her hair off her forehead, tucking it behind her ear. Exactly as James used to do, back when he loved her.

Charlotte reacted as if she'd been zapped with electricity. Mr. Mallery was like James was like Mr. Mallery was touching her, alone with her, seemingly adoring her. She stumbled away, her mind screaming, This is crazy! How do I process? I can't process! Her hip knocked a little table, and the black Chinese vase and its coy little lid tipped and fell on the ground with a crack. Something tumbled out of its previously empty interior.

A key. The key was attached to a big fat key ring, like the kind that came from the dealer, branded with the car's make. A circle divided into fourths, white and blue. The BMW logo.

That vase had been empty. Mr. Mallery had put the key in there. Why? Because she'd suggested a room search, and the key ring was too big to flush down the toilet. The night after Bloody Murder, Mr. Mallery had returned to this room, dumped the body out the window, gone downstairs and carried it to the trunk of Mr. Wattlesbrook's car, then driven the car into the pond to hide it. But perhaps out of habit, he'd locked the doors and pocketed the key. And now, threatened with exposure, he'd naturally returned to the room where he'd hidden Mr. Wattlesbrook, a room that most people did not know existed. As far as he knew, Charlotte had accidentally stumbled into it the night of Bloody Murder and never gone back. So Mr. Mallery had concealed the clue of the key in his favorite hiding spot until he could dispose of it permanently. And he did all that because he'd murdered Mr. Wattlesbrook.

Charlotte saw the key, processed the murder, and had one

second to react. Time seemed to slow. She could try to play innocent. But Mr. Mallery already knew: Charlotte was clever. She could not undo such a thing as proven cleverness.

How inconvenient clever women must be to men like Mr. Mallery. If only she'd been frivolous, light-minded, vapid even. Generally speaking, when a man is a murderer and a woman uncovers the unmistakable clue pointing to him, it would be so much easier if that woman were dull-witted. A clever woman can get herself killed.

The second passed, and clever Charlotte had no clever plan. She looked from the key to Mr. Mallery. He looked back. His expression was no longer alluring.

"Oops. Do you think Mrs. Wattlesbrook will be angry I broke the vase?" Charlotte said, adding a desperate bat of her eyelashes. "I hope it wasn't valuable."

Mr. Mallery did not blink. He said, "I wish you had not seen that."

She nodded. Her rush of words was gone, the giddiness in her head emptying like a tipped goldfish bowl.

"You've made things much more difficult, Mrs. Cordial."

"Sorry," she said.

Yes, she apologized to a murderer for uncovering his bloody crime. Even in this moment, about to be killed, Charlotte was aware enough to cringe at herself.

"I do not know what to do with you," he said.

"Take me to the ball?" she suggested with a hopeful smile that she managed to scavenge out of the hopeless dread. "You can have the first two dances."

He studied her face then looked down. "I know what I must do, but I do not want to. Killing Mr. Wattlesbrook was one matter, but you are another entirely." He met her eyes again. "Can you offer me a way out?"

"Yes! Of course. A way out. Let's talk about it. What do you need from me? I'm a very reasonable person. I can be your partner in this secret. With pleasure!"

Her cheery speech was spoiled somewhat by the intense shaking of her hands and the sickly tremble in her voice.

Hold still! she commanded her hands. Be cool! she told her voice. They didn't obey. Traitors.

Mr. Mallery's frown deepened. He took a step toward her. She took a step back.

"I wish I knew I could trust you," he said. "But are you as you seem? Or are you someone else entirely? So many secrets in this place. So many falsehoods."

She heard a slick scrape as he pulled a knife from his belt. She barely processed the silver flicker of the blade before she turned and ran for the door.

Her finger slipped on the hidden knob, but on her second press, it opened. She leapt away from the swinging door and heard it collide with Mr. Mallery behind her.

Mary peered out her door and blinked at Charlotte, as if she had been expecting to see someone else.

"Run for help," Charlotte pleaded. "Mallery killed Wattles-brook."

Charlotte barely got out the words when he grabbed her from behind and pulled her back into the room with such force that she tumbled across the floor.

She looked up to see Mary not running for help but holding open the door and staring at Mallery. Even in her thoughts, Charlotte could no longer muster up a "mister" title for him.

"Do you have need of me, sir?" Mary asked, her voice mostly breath.

"Mary, you've always been a very good girl," he said. His

hair had pulled free of its restraint and hung loose around his face. He looked wild.

"Mary, hurry!" Charlotte shouted.

Mallery approached Mary leisurely, and the girl held still, waiting for him, faintly trembling, a mouse caught in a cobra's gaze. He moved Mary's hair behind her shoulder and ran a finger along her long, white neck in a way that seemed practiced. Mary's faint trembling escalated to a full-body shiver. She gazed at Mallery with wet eyes.

Oh no, Charlotte thought. Mary would throw herself into a volcano for him. That does not bode well.

He fingered the neck of Mary's blouse and slipped it off her shoulder. Her collarbone was tense and standing out like a skeleton's.

"Would you give us some privacy to take care of business," he whispered into her neck. "And then I will come find you. To thank you. You have proven to me that you are the only woman I can trust."

Mary seemed scarcely able to move, let alone speak, but she managed to nod jerkily.

"Mary, please, he'll kill me," Charlotte said, pulling herself to her feet with a grunt. The bruises she felt forming on her hip were added to her Things Not Regency Appropriate list.

Mallery held his face close to Mary's and touched her lips with a finger. "You know how much I value your discretion."

He kissed the corner of her mouth, a tease, the promise of more, then stepped back and nodded, as if giving her permission to depart. She took a deep, unstable breath.

"Excuse me," Mary said shakily and shut the door on her way out.

Charlotte was trying to wrench open one of the windows

when she heard a skin-crawling rasp behind her. Mallery had pushed a highboy to block the door. He considered his knife before putting it away. Maybe he wouldn't hurt her after all! Maybe he just wanted to chat about stuff.

Or maybe he just preferred to kill her without a lot of blood.

"Hold still," he said, sounding so reasonable. He came at her, and his hands looked as dangerous as any knife.

Charlotte dodged, putting furniture between her and those hands. He followed. He didn't say anything. He was focused on catching her. And then what?

Charlotte didn't think about what James's reaction would be when he heard she was murdered. She only gave her children a passing thought before her mind fled in white-hot panic from the idea that she could be taken from them. Instead, she thought of Eddie, and how she very much wanted him to save her. Yes, if she could choose any man in the world to save her, it would be Eddie. But he wouldn't, would he? Because no one knew she was here, except Mary, who'd been mesmerized into submission by the predator. Charlotte was starting to suspect that Mary was seriously messed up.

Stupid Charlotte, she screamed at herself. You believed you were clever, and that made you more vulnerable.

When the chase drew her near the window, she plucked a naked lamp from the debris and slammed it against a pane, hoping to break the window but only managing a few cracks.

"Help!" she screamed.

"You do not need to do that," he said.

Mallery and his hands were coming at her. She ran from the window, weaving through clutter and broken furniture, trying to keep that man as far away as possible. But he kept following.

Stupid Charlotte, she screamed at herself again. Two minutes ago you considered falling in love with him!

Those fluttery feelings of new love—those lung-tickling, heart-kicking, squealing sensations of hot and cold and pulses snapping and lips wetting—they were as false as cravats and corsets. They were merely sensations, like the wrenching drop on a roller coaster that warned of impending death. She wasn't really going to die on a roller coaster (probably not, though some were pretty scary). And just because she felt tangled up and swoony with a man didn't mean she was in love or could be happy with him ever after.

Duh, Charlotte. Duh. You're not going to die on a roller coaster, but you are going to die in this room.

"Help!" she yelled again.

Mallery lunged and missed. He would get her sooner or later. It would probably take several minutes to die by strangulation, his hands around her neck, her lungs burning like they had when she'd spent too much time underwater, her eyes wide open with the awareness that she was almost gone.

A sob punched her throat. Imagining how she was going to die wasn't exactly helping her morale.

"Listen, listen," she said, angling to keep a broken sofa and a stack of boxes between her and Mallery. "I don't want to die, so you have a lot of bargaining power."

He came around the side. She fled again, kicking up dust on her way to the stack of chairs. She could see him through the cage of legs.

"You write up something, I sign it. A promise that I never speak a word about my suspicions. I know Mr. Wattlesbrook was an unpleasant man, clumsy with fire and sherry and probably very gassy . . ." What was she saying? Focus, Charlotte, don't be a ninny. "You don't hurt me, and I let you get away with murder. You see? We all win!"

She tried to smile. Still, he didn't speak.

Nice try, said her Inner Thoughts. He already knows you're too moral to do that.

Help me or shut up! she yelled back.

His hands flexed. Charlotte ran again.

The cat-and-mouse might have gone on much longer, but Charlotte stepped on her hem. It occurred to her, the split second before she hit the floor, that men invent fashion. Men who want women in ridiculously long skirts so just in case they murder someone and a woman figures it out, she'll be so hampered by her ridiculously long skirts that she can be killed too.

She scrambled backward and blurted desperately, "I have kids. Two kids. Beckett and Lu."

Mallery didn't slow. He came at her like a man at work, his hands the tool to get the job done. He really was going to do her in. A small part of herself had been hoping she was wrong, but nope. Pessimism wins again.

Killing her would hurt her kids too. She knew this with the pain of a wound. It didn't matter that Lu hadn't wanted to talk to her on the phone or that Beckett had called Justice "Mom." They would suffer if she died. They would cry and ache and need years of therapy, and would James pay for it? Probably not. So they'd have to submit to school counselors who might not be properly trained because of budget cuts, and what if that wasn't enough and the grief sent them into drugs and alcohol and depression and meaningless sex and regrettable tattoo choices and petty crime leading up to serious crime and jail and shock therapy? What if lobotomies came back into vogue? And the surgeon messed up and they died?

And it would all be James's fault. Wait . . . and Mallery's too! It was as if Mallery had cornered not just Charlotte but also Lu and Beckett, as if he was coming at them with dangerous hands and intent to strangle, and they were scooting back and pleading for mercy, but he had none. No mercy for her children? That was *so* not okay.

In the old stories, this was the part when the heroine, overcome with terror, would faint, and the dastardly bastard would throttle her alabaster neck and leave her body for the wolves. Right?

No.

This was the part where Charlotte, heroine, remembered she was a twenty-first-century woman and a mother. This was Charlotte saying, Hell no!

Charlotte screamed.

But this wasn't a scream for help. This wasn't a plea, a panicked, earsplitting supplication for immediate rescue. Charlotte screamed the cry of attack.

Clearly, Mallery did not recognize the subtle difference. Showing no alarm, he was still on offense, and he knelt over her, his hands on her throat. That hurt, but her body, with or without her mind's help, had a plan. She'd sat in on enough of Beckett's martial arts classes to learn a few self-defense moves. When an attacker is strangling from the front, his hands are occupied, leaving every part of him open. Charlotte formed her fingers into spearhead shape and jammed them as hard as she could into his throat. He choked and his grip lessened. She took a deep breath and kicked him in the 'nads, as Beckett would say.

He was on the ground, and she stood up, but she didn't stop kicking. A spare chair leg lay nearby, practically begging to be used as a club. Charlotte complied.

"You're the ninny!" She hit him again. "You hear me? YOU'RE THE NINNY!" She hit him again and again. "No one just *falls* in love, you idiot. You *chose* to not love me anymore. You *chose* to leave me. You *chose* to leave the kids. One weekend a month and one month a year—that's parenthood? You don't go to marriage counseling, you don't give me a chance to fight back. No, you sneak around. You sleep with Justice for weeks and come home to me all smug with yourself. You sick, sick, sick son of a—"

Charlotte gasped. She was solving more than one mystery. "It wasn't just weeks, was it? That's why you had me put your name on my accounts. You were already affairing around and preparing to dump me! You duplicitous, conniving, hardhearted, not-nice nincompoop. And you never even apologized!"

"Sorry," Mallery mumbled desperately, one arm protecting his head, the other over his pummeled manhood.

"Not you, you idiot! Though you're a ninny too."

He made a scramble to get upright, and she cracked the chair leg on the back of his head. He crumpled with a groan. For an inherently dangerous man, he sure didn't seem accustomed to getting beat up. She shoved over the tower of chairs, pinning him to the floor.

It took her a minute to push the highboy far enough from the wall to open the door and squeeze out.

"Help!" she screamed, running for the spiral stairs. "Bloody murder! Bloody, bloody murder! I'm on the second floor, and there's been some seriously bloody murder up here!"

She was halfway down the stairs when Eddie reached her, followed by Colonel Andrews, Miss Charming, Miss Gardenside, and Mrs. Wattlesbrook.

"Are you all right?" Eddie asked.

"Mallery did it," she said quickly. "He killed Mr. Wattlesbrook."

"I say, Mrs. Cordial," said the colonel, "you are spoiling the ending. We were supposed to go on this murderer hunt together, and I had prepared my own things to look remarkably guilty."

Where had all the oxygen gone? Was she underwater? She looked to Eddie like a buoy in mid-ocean.

"He tried to kill me, Eddie. He's in the secret room." The air in her lungs seemed to be tied to a string and yanked out of her. She tried to grab hold of the end of that string, but it was getting so hard to see.

"I've got you," she heard Eddie say before she straight-up passed out. And she wasn't even wearing her corset.

Well, Charlotte, that was done like a true romantic heroine. You are on your way.

home, six months before

CHARLOTTE'S SISTER-IN-LAW WAS responsible for Charlotte's eighth postdivorce blind date, with a dentist called Ernie (a family name). They met at the bar of a restaurant for drinks and appetizers. They conversed easily, their sentences fitting together like one long monologue instead of disjointed back-and-forth. He looked at her more than at his drink.

Charlotte got a little light-headed and tickly-chested, though her drink was just a soda. Maybe she wasn't quite as numb as she thought. Maybe she could thaw just a tad, just enough to know this Ernie, to dip her toes in this possibility. As they left the restaurant, Ernie asked her out to dinner. She said she'd like that, and that's when he leaned in to kiss her.

Charlotte would replay the next few moments over and over again for months to come, usually while she held a pillow over her head:

- His lips touched hers.
- She recoiled.
- She said, "Ew."

Had his breath smelled of calamari? Had his mouth been hot and dry like a shedding lizard's skin? No. Nothing was wrong. Ernie kissed in a very reasonable and appropriate manner. But Charlotte felt repulsed—not by him, but by herself. It was disgusting, she'd thought as he leaned in, disgusting for a married woman to kiss another man. She'd felt like a dirty, horrid cheater.

But Ernie, ignorant of her tortured internal monologue, only heard "ew." He nodded, turned, and walked away.

Did Charlotte call Ernie and explain? No, it'd been too humiliating. Besides, what business does a woman who still feels married months after her divorce have going on a date with anyone?

She reopened her arms to numbness and let that cold void settle deeper into her chest, as deep as night.

austenland, day 11, cont.

CHARLOTTE WAS ONLY OUT FOR a moment. She knew Eddie was carrying her because she recognized his smell. She hadn't realized her brain had stored that information, but she tucked her head against his neck and breathed in.

He placed her on her bed, then he and Colonel Andrews rushed out again. Things got confusing, with ladies and servants coming and going, Charlotte shouting warnings about Mallery and Mary.

"You are certain?" asked Mrs. Wattlesbrook from the doorway.

Charlotte nodded. "I'm sorry. Mallery admitted he . . . he killed your husband. And I saw his BMW submerged in the pond."

Mrs. Wattlesbrook nodded. For a moment Charlotte thought the proprietress might cry, but instead she said, "Let us adjourn to the drawing room. Mrs. Cordial's bedchamber is inappropriate for a gathering."

As if all that matters anymore, Charlotte thought.

But it mattered to Mrs. Wattlesbrook. Eddie was back by then and eager to carry Charlotte again. She protested at first but gave in, curious to see what it felt like in his arms now that she was more awake. Perhaps that dreamy, delicious sensation that had filled her hadn't been his nearness but just the remnants of a fainting dream.

It wasn't.

"I wanted you to save me," she said as he brought her into the drawing room and set her on a chaise longue.

"I wish I had." His face was grim.

"It's okay. I didn't die."

He told her that Mallery was tied and locked in one of the second-floor spare rooms, and that Justin, the most robust of Neville's lads, stood guard. Charlotte could only think of him as "Mallery" now. But why had he done it? She couldn't quite reason it out. Mallery the character would want to protect his family's estates and perhaps even kill to do so. But why had the actor crossed over? Was he simply crazy?

Eddie said Mallery gave him very little fight since she'd already beaten the life out of him.

"I just wanted to be sure," she said. "In movies you think the bad guy is done in, then he rises again."

"Yes, I think you made certain there would be no unexpected rising."

Maids came in to report that Mary was missing, and they

plopped down on the abundant settees, the illusion of the classes cracking under the pressure. Neville gazed over the scene, disapproving but not speaking. Mrs. Wattlesbrook was not present. Surely she was at the inn calling the police.

"Neville, you knew Mary from Windy Nook?" Charlotte asked while the maids chattered away about how Mary liked to personally wash Mallery's breeches.

"Yes. I am alarmed by this outcome."

"But not surprised," said Charlotte.

"No, I suppose not." He stared at his interlaced fingers. "She was raised by her grandmother, who had been in service herself. As a child, Mary would run errands between the village and Windy Nook, and I could tell she hungered for what that house represented. I'm the one who hired her as a maid when she came of age." He sighed. "She started in the kitchen, but since she had spent years taking care of her grandmother, Mrs. Wattlesbrook thought she would excel as a lady's maid. Mary's behavior was eccentric, and Mrs. Wattlesbrook wasn't going to transfer her here when Windy Nook closed. But I . . . I intervened. Mary's grandmother had died and there was nowhere else she felt at home. Perhaps my pity was misplaced."

"Mrs. Wattlesbrook brought you to Pembrook Park as well. Clearly she trusts you more than any other, and she's a smart lady."

His eyes shone.

"And you could see that Mary was enamored of Mallery?" Charlotte asked.

"Well, yes. He stood apart. When the guests weren't around, the actors relaxed, you know. Became themselves. Mr. Mallery never relaxed. I suppose he was himself."

"He was himself," Charlotte repeated softly.

Miss Charming plonked down beside Charlotte.

"You figured it all out." Miss Charming didn't bother with her British accent even though the men were present. "Wow. You're like Jessica Fletcher."

"I am in shock," said Eddie. "Andrews, you and I were most likely the last to see him alive."

"Mallery must have returned to Wattlesbrook right after dinner, and then joined us in the drawing room as cool as anything," Colonel Andrews said. "Perhaps he'd only intended to give him a talking-to?"

"Gave him a talking-to, all right," Eddie said.

"I guess Mary saw him with Mr. Wattlesbrook," said Charlotte.

"She played our garden ghost, you know," said Colonel Andrews. "I told the lads I'd need a helper for my charade, and Mallery suggested Mary. He said she'd do anything for him."

That's proving true, Charlotte thought.

If she were in an Agatha Christie novel, she supposed, this would be when the story would end, with the murderer caught. But she still had three more days in Austenland. Speculation and chatter continued, and Charlotte's head felt too muddled to be indoors. As soon as she could, she slipped outside.

It was dark already, the sky firmly black. The air was pleasantly cool, but she shivered.

I wonder if I'm going to have a nervous breakdown, she thought calmly.

"Charlotte?" Eddie called.

"I just need some fresh air," she said without turning. She wasn't surprised he'd followed. It felt right. "I don't want four walls around me. I thought I was going to die in that secret room."

She held out her hand without thinking, and he took it. They walked to the side of the house, out of sight of the road where the police would shortly be coming. She didn't want to see anyone right then, except Eddie.

They leaned against the house and looked at the stars.

"So you really did find a body in that room," he said.

"I guess I did."

"Here you've been, a spider in the corner, observing, weaving Charlotte's web of mystery."

"Or stumbling around, confused and pathetic."

"I'm sorry I didn't believe—" he started to say, then snorted with a laugh. "It is kind of ridiculous."

"Yeah." She snorted too.

He laughed again.

Then the dam broke. Charlotte leaned over and laughed so hard her stomach strained, laughed till she wept, then the weeping took over, and she cry-laughed and laugh-cried. Eddie held on to her, and she put her head on his shoulder and ached with crying and laughing.

"He was trying to kill me for real," she said. "He really was."

"That must be surreal."

"It is. That's just the word for it. Maybe I'm going crazy?"

"Going?"

"Oh man, he lied to me, lied a lot."

"Mallery lied to all of us."

"Not Mallery—I mean, James, my ex. Mallery just wanted to kill me, which should top the list of relationship enders, but what James did feels even worse. Still, the whole attempted murder is not going to help me much long-term, is it? I mean, my ability to trust in men has got to be permanently damaged, right? Eddie, tell me truthfully, are all men—" She stopped.

"Are all men despicable scoundrels?"

"I don't really believe it. Because you're not. Though there was a moment I thought you were the murderer and were going to kill me."

"Really?" His eyes seemed happy. "That's kind of you. I like the idea of seeming dangerous. But . . ." He lifted his hands as if to say, I am who I am.

"No, you're not dangerous. You feel safe. And that's nicer." She smiled at him. "I like you, Eddie. I like you lots."

Charlotte had to stop talking, because Eddie was looking at her. And he was quite a bit nearer than was normal for an acquaintance or a brother or anything. His face was in her personal space, but it didn't feel invasive. He was gazing at her curiously. He lifted his hand to touch her jaw with his thumb, as if he just wanted to feel her. Her head lightened with that touch. She felt as sharp as a star. She held still and hoped he was touching her because he, Eddie, the real Eddie, wanted to. Because that was what she wanted.

"What are you doing?" she asked.

"Attempting to woo you." He kept glancing at her lips. "Is it working at all? It's been a long time since I sincerely wooed anyone, and I can't remember how. All I know is I want to look at you."

She was afraid to move, afraid even the slight nod of her head would move his hand and he would give up and go away. She couldn't seem to form words, so she hoped he could see the yes in her eyes.

Say yes, she screamed at her eyes. Sparkle or something! Come on, babies, twinkle for Mama!

And he kissed her. His arms went around her and he was kissing her really well. And her only clear thought was that Eddie was wonderfully tall. James had been just her height, and for the sake of his vanity, she could never wear heels.

Eddie withdrew enough to look at her face. "That seemed to work?"

Charlotte didn't answer. She hadn't caught her breath, or her equilibrium. The kiss had shifted the whole world forty-five degrees, and she was still falling. Except that his arms were around her, so maybe they were falling together.

"Um . . ." she said, and touched his lips with her fingertips. It was all the language she could muster at the moment, like Caveman for "Kiss me again, please."

And he did. He kissed her and she kissed him, and he held her so tight she felt safe from the whole world. It was wonderful to feel really safe again, and glorious to be kissed. The world kept tipping, and maybe she was upside down now, blood rushing to her head, feet in the stars.

With warm cheeks and starry feet, she realized that she'd been yearning to be this close to Eddie all along but had resisted for some reason. Why had she? Oh yeah, because he was—

"Wait!" she said.

He stopped, alarm in his eyes.

"It needs to be said that we're not really brother and sister."

He nodded sagely. "Yes, it does. It needs to be said."

"Because I want to kiss *you*, not that character. I don't have any incest fantasies, thank you, and I don't want to be involved in anyone else's. So . . . you're not really my brother; I'm not really your sister. We're not related in any way."

He was holding her hands, rubbing her fingers against his chin. "Not a whit."

"And my name's not 'Charlotte Cordial' when I'm kissing you. I'm still 'Charlotte,' just not the 'Cordial' part."

"Understood. And the name's not 'Grey,' nor 'Edmund' either. It's 'Reginald.'"

"What!" Charlotte recoiled. "Don't be serious. 'Reginald'? Really?"

Reginald shrugged. "Family name."

"Family curse."

"But 'Eddie' will do. I rather fancy being 'Eddie,' when you say it." Eddie smiled. He kissed her fingers. "Tell me something else. Something true."

"I'm a mom of two kids, and my ex-husband found me less interesting than a woman named 'Justice' who keeps reading one book over and over again called *A Fragment of My Heart*, and it's about a man who is in love with his neighbor for sixty years and does nothing about it and she doesn't find out until he dies and she discovers his journal, and Justice sent me a copy and harassed me via e-mail until I read it, and you're supposed to weep at the end but I laughed, and I judge her for that."

"Tell me something true about you."

"Okay . . ." She mentally rifled through birthplace (Portland, Oregon), college major (sociology), astrological sign (Virgo), favorite movie (*The Apple Dumpling Gang*—don't judge), until she hit a fact that wasn't completely mundane. "One of my favorite things in the world are those charity events where everyone buys a rubber ducky with a number and the first person's duck to get down the river wins."

"Why?"

"I like seeing the river teeming with all those outrageously yellow and orange ducks. It's so friendly. And I love the hope of it. Even though it doesn't matter if you win, because all that wonderful, candy-colored money is going to something really important like a free clinic downtown or cleft palate operations for children in India, you still have that playful hope that you *will* win. You run alongside the stream, not knowing which is your duck but imagining the lead one is yours."

"And this is the essence of your soul—the ducky race?"

"Well, you didn't ask for the essence of my soul. You asked for something true about me, and so I went for something slightly embarrassing and secret but true nonetheless. Next time you want the essence of my soul, I'll oblige you with sunsets and baby's laughter and greeting cards with watercolor flowers."

He squinted at her thoughtfully. "No, so far as I'm concerned, the yellow duckies are the essence of your soul."

"Okay." She smiled. "And you—Julia is real, isn't she?"

"I'm an alcoholic. Her mother isn't actually deceased. We weren't married," he said without hesitation. "I've been sober for thirteen years, but I botched things badly in the beginning, and Julia's mother doesn't care to have me around. I only see Julia a few times a year. But that will change."

"Yes, it should."

"It will. I promised her so in the letter. She may not be as excited about that prospect as I am—yet—but I'm terrifically fond of the girl. Let's see, what else . . . I have a 1955 Jaguar XK140 that I inherited from my father, as well as the compulsion to keep it mint. When I'm not here, I read the paper from cover to cover every day. I've also read every Terry Pratchett novel at least three times over."

"I'm not familiar with Terry Pratchett."

"You will be."

"Okay."

Eddie moaned sadly.

"You sound unhappy," said Charlotte, surprised.

"I'm in a quandary. I'm riveted by your every word, and yet when you speak, your lips move, you see."

"They do? How shocking!"

"Isn't it? More than shocking—it's obscene. I look at them, and looking makes me want to taste them again, and yet I wouldn't interrupt the conversation . . ."

He leaned closer, but stopped a breath from her mouth and pulled back and moaned sadly.

"What shall we do, Eddie my love," said Charlotte. "Kiss or speak?"

"I'm finding both options delightful. You decide."

Before decisions could be made, a shrill voice shouted for Mr. Grey, and they both jumped away from each other and hurried into the open, trying to look as casual as possible and therefore seeming extremely suspicious.

Mrs. Wattlesbrook glared at them. "It is high past time for dinner."

"But where are the police?" asked Charlotte.

"They will be here soon enough. And in the meantime, we go forward. All this . . . this *nonsense* is not reason to behave uncivilized. We will dine at once." Mrs. Wattlesbrook looked daggers, but her hands, gripped together at her waist, shook. And Charlotte considered that what the proprietress of Pembrook Park, who had just discovered that her husband had been murdered, needed right then was a formal dinner in a grand dining room with people in Regency attire, as if everything were crazily normal.

"Here we come," Eddie said.

She turned and went into the house. Eddie made to follow then turned back suddenly, put an arm around Charlotte's waist, and pulled her to him. He gave her one long, slow kiss.

"I couldn't leave the matter hanging like that," he said quietly, their faces still touching.

"Of course not," she said. "You're a gentleman."

He nodded, offered his arm, and escorted her inside.

The night was darker in than out, the hallway candles dimmer than stars. Charlotte felt the weight of the old house like a coffin lid. She knew, in the way a rheumatic can feel oncoming rain, that she was going to struggle to sleep tonight.

* * *

DINNER WAS A QUIET AFFAIR. It was impossible to talk about the murder in front of the victim's widow, especially as no one was certain if said widow was heart-stricken or relieved. Little was consumed and conversation was a round of this sort:

"Is that . . . are those potatoes there?"

"I am not certain. Would you like them?"

"I guess so."

"Is there bread down at your end?"

"Yes, here it is."

"I wonder if it will rain tonight."

"Most likely."

"Do you think it will be sunny tomorrow?"

"Hm."

Charlotte kept looking out the window. Where on earth were the police?

When everyone returned to the drawing room, Charlotte followed the proprietress into the nearly dark morning room.

"I'm surprised the police haven't come yet," Charlotte said.

Mrs. Wattlesbrook sat at the desk with a groan. She placed her candle carefully in the center of the desk and folded her hands together.

"I would have thought—considering the gravity of the crime and the fact that the suspect is hog-tied upstairs—I would have thought they'd have put the pedal to the metal . . ." Charlotte squinted at Mrs. Wattlesbrook. "You didn't call them, did you?"

The woman kept looking down.

"Mrs. Wattlesbrook, you have to call the police."

"If I do, they will be here for a long time, running all over the place, marching in and out of rooms. Just the idea makes the house feel dirty."

"Dirtier than murder? He killed your husband."

Mrs. Wattlesbrook pursed her lips. "You make it sound more dramatic than it actually is."

Charlotte gaped.

"Not the murder part," Mrs. Wattlesbrook said, shuffling papers around on the desk. "The husband part. He was not . . . dear to me. I suppose you think I should have divorced him. To my mind, divorce is vulgar, common, modern in the worst way. Besides, Pembrook Park was his family home. I used to be proprietress of three estates. Now, because of him, this is all I have."

"If your husband had forced you into a divorce, he would have kept Pembrook Park and then sold it."

"The bank took Bertram Hall and would have claimed Windy Nook as well, if we had not found a renter. Though this estate was my husband's before our marriage, Miss Charlotte, my inheritance fixed it up, my savvy created a business with enough income to maintain it. He would have let wild animals roost in the sofas and damp rot the wood. He never cared for this place, but he insisted on playing a part in the cast, most likely so he could ogle the women. Well, some time ago he went too far, was aggressive with one of my guests, and I finally put my foot down. So he wanted to divorce, sell the Park, and split the profit. And I would lose the only thing I love."

"And Mallery knew this."

She nodded. "He has been a part of our repertory cast for years. True, he sometimes exhibited irritation with the clients, but only when they did not adopt proper respect for the house and their own characters. Nevertheless, he was visually pleasing to the ladies. Three years ago he suffered some personal loss—a dead mother or a sister or such. After that, he wanted to stay on as a permanent cast member, without breaks. During winter holidays he lives here as caretaker. He loves this house."

She spoke with pride.

"You felt a kinship with Mallery," said Charlotte.

"He was the one person who wanted to live in this bygone time as much as I."

"And he was so determined to stay that he killed your husband."

Finally the woman showed some emotion, her forehead agitating. But she reasserted her calm.

"Perhaps. Now, if you will excuse me." She turned back to her papers.

"He was your husband for a long time," Charlotte said. "It's okay to grieve a little."

"I don't need to."

"Even the jerks earn some of our affection. We can be glad they're gone and yet still mourn the good parts. Were there good parts?"

Mrs. Wattlesbrook started to cry. She cried like someone who didn't know how it was done. Her face contorted at the unfamiliar sensations, and she smeared the tears aggressively with the heel of her hand.

"Is that what you do?" Mrs. Wattlesbrook asked in a wet, strained voice. "You admit you are glad your husband is gone and yet still hold in your heart the few memories that are precious? Is that how you maintain your queenly poise?"

This caught Charlotte off guard, and her chin started quivering.

"No. I'm a wreck," she said in the squeaky high voice of one who is determined not to cry.

"You do not seem like it," Mrs. Wattlesbrook squeaked back.

"Thanks," Charlotte chirped. "I do yoga. Ninety percent of confidence is posture."

"I didn't know that," Mrs. Wattlesbrook cheeped. "How fascinating."

And with gazes averted and voices strained and high as mice, they talked about yoga some more, as well as the pros and cons of corsets, the most comfortable sorts of chairs, and the weather, just for good measure.

CHARLOTTE MADE CERTAIN THAT EDDIE accompanied Mrs. Wattlesbrook directly to the inn to phone the police, and the drawing room gabbers broke up for the night. There were only so many times anyone could exclaim, "I can't believe Mr. Mallery killed Mr. Wattlesbrook, what-what!"

Charlotte was dead tired. Was this really the same day she dove into the pond and spied Mr. Wattlesbrook's German-engineered coffin? That seemed weeks ago, but her corset still hung over the radiator, its dampness proof.

She considered knocking at Miss Charming's door to ask for a sleepover, but she was too beat. Besides, Mallery was well tied and guarded by Justin, and the police would be there any moment.

She took off her dress, laid it on a chair, and went to the bathroom, flicking on the electric light.

"Mary!" she said.

Mary startled, dropping Charlotte's toiletries bag onto the floor. Eye shadow and lipsticks rolled, and loose powder escaped in a puff. The runaway maid was still in her serving garb, though it looked dirty, as if she'd been crawling through unswept places.

"I didn't hear you come in," Mary said guiltily.

"What are you doing here?"

"I . . ." Mary looked around, as if unsure. "I had something. I was going to do something."

This girl was missing a few cards. Or a few dozen. Charlotte backed out of the bathroom.

"No one could find you earlier."

"Yes, I was hiding." Mary looked at the ground, fidgeting with her skirt. "I never should have left him alone with you. I should have protected him."

"Mallery is not what he seems, Mary."

Mary tilted her head, contemplating Charlotte as if she were an alien, and said matter-of-factly, "He's the most perfect man who ever lived."

"He killed Mr. Wattlesbrook."

"Perhaps," she said, her eyes unfocused. "I saw him take the old man into that room and come out alone, only I didn't snoop because *I'm* a good girl. I fetched him some gloves from the kitchen when he asked. He trusted me to wash the pond mud out of his clothes. And I trust *him*. If he had to kill someone, then I'm sure he had a good reason."

"He also tried to kill me."

"Obviously because he couldn't trust you. It's your own fault."

"That's for the police to decide," Charlotte said.

Mary's crazy eyes burned a little crazier.

"I can't stand it. I can't stand to think of him locked up. He'll be so unhappy. He's like a dog that needs to get out and run."

Charlotte was close to the bedroom door. She moved slowly so she wouldn't alarm Mary, but she also felt no hurry. Mary was slight. If it came to a fight, Charlotte thought she could handle this girl.

"Locked up forever, no sunshine, no country air, no chance he will ever touch me again . . ." Mary touched her own neck, and a shudder ran visibly through her body.

"Mary, trust me, that's a good thing."

"I'll die for him!" Mary stood in the threshold of the bathroom, the light behind her lining her pale hair in bright yellow.

"No one wants to kill you, Mary. There's really no call for—"

"I'll die for Mr. Darcy."

"Um . . . did you just say 'Mr. Darcy'?"

"No."

Mary's face seemed to cool, the red splotches of emotion fading. She reached around the far side of the bathroom door, picked up a rifle that she had placed just out of sight, put it against her shoulder, and pointed it at Charlotte.

"Holy crap!" Charlotte said, as Beckett might. "I thought England was all famous for not having guns!"

"The gentlemen go hunting."

"Is that a prop gun?"

Mary cocked the rifle. The *click* sounded ominously real.

The door to the hall was just a step away. Charlotte glanced at it. Did she dare run? Would Mary get spooked and shoot?

"*You* did it," Mary said, her hands shaking dramatically, the tip of the rifle aimed at Charlotte's head, at her neck, at her feet, now at the wall. "You're responsible for Thomas's capture. No one would have cared if the old man had just disappeared. But you spoilt everything. And Thomas loves me! He practically said so!"

"Then I'm very happy for you two," Charlotte said shakily.

Mary's eyes narrowed. "I didn't like how he'd look at you. Perhaps he was pretending to love you. I don't know, I don't know . . ."

That swaying rifle was pointing in the region of Charlotte's head way too often. She decided fleeing was worth the risk.

Mary adjusted her stance, the bathroom light falling over her face, and Charlotte could see that the girl had put on makeup, apparently from Charlotte's own stash. Her cheeks were well blushed, her lips pink, and one eye sported brown shadow all the way up to her eyebrow.

"Mary, you look pretty," she said.

Mary hesitated; the rifle lowered. And that's when Charlotte ran.

A gunshot rang in her ears as she threw open the door and fled into the hall.

"Mary's got a gun!" she yelled, racing for the stairs. Miss Charming and Colonel Andrews poked their heads out of their bedrooms then quickly ducked back in again. Charlotte couldn't blame them. She took the stairs two at a time.

Oh, come on already, police, she thought. Come on with your vicious billy clubs and beat the love crazies out of this psychopath!

Charlotte had no plan except to get out of the house. Maybe the house wasn't a sentient, ancient beast that swallowed corpses whole, but it sure lodged a lot of nutjobs.

Another shot splattered plaster in the wall above her head. She screamed, nearly tumbled down the rest of the stairs, and knocked into the front door. Someone opened it from the outside.

"Charlotte," said Eddie, "what's—"

She pushed him out and ran for the gravel drive. "Mary. She's back. With a gun."

The front door opened and Mary came out, rifle on her shoulder.

"You should have left him alone!" she yelled.

A shot fired into the night. Eddie pulled Charlotte down flat then sprang back up, tackling Mary to the front stairs. He ripped the rifle from her hands, flung it away, and grabbed her fast. Mary struggled weakly for a few moments then started to weep. Her cry was high-pitched and rhythmic, reminding Charlotte of a wounded bird. Eddie didn't let go, but after a moment, he did began to mutter, "There, there."

Charlotte almost said, Hey, she just tried to shoot me in the head! Don't *there, there* her!

But she couldn't really blame him. Her cry *was* pathetic.

Mrs. Wattlesbrook stood over them, arms folded. "Really,

Mary, you cannot expect to work here while engaging in such behavior. And your hair is a sight."

Charlotte was lying on the gravel, her ears still ringing with the sound of rifle fire, and she wondered how many people had twice been the object of attempted murder on the very same day. She was special, that was sure, part of an elite club of other unknown almost-victims. Maybe she'd get a special citation from the queen. Maybe Lu would think she was cool.

"Are you going to faint again?" Eddie asked, kneeling beside her as the police cars rolled in.

"No . . . I think I'm getting used to it all," she said, her voice sounding hollow and far away. "Attempted murder is becoming so mundane."

He pulled her up into his arms. She closed her eyes.

"Oh no, Eddie," she said, alert with a new thought. "You know what Mary would do first, before coming to kill me?"

Eddie groaned. "Let Mallery go."

When the police went upstairs to the locked room, it was empty. Cut rope lay on the floor. Justin the guard was sound asleep in the hall beside a cup of tea, likely drugged and brought to him by Mary.

"At least it wasn't yew tea," said Eddie.

Charlotte had to push through half an hour of questions with the detective sergeant and wait outside with everyone else while the police conducted a thorough house search. There was no sign of Mallery. By the time the detective agreed that the rest of the questions could wait till morning, Charlotte felt more than half dead—at least two-thirds dead. The police were pretty well occupied with questioning their rifle-shooting prisoner, setting up a perimeter to catch an escaped murderer, and dredging a car out of a pond.

"I'm so sleepy," Charlotte said, leaning into Eddie as they

walked upstairs. Her speech was getting slurred and slushy. "I guess too much adrenaline in the system has some side effects, huh?"

Her eyes were closed when he picked her up and carried her into her room. She was going to accuse him of carrying her just so he could show off his manly strength, but speaking required so much effort. She'd removed her dress before the Mary incident, and handily she'd gone sans corset ever since her swim, so he slid her dressed as she was beneath the sheets. He lay down beside her.

"What are you doing?" she said, though it was barely intelligible.

"Staying beside you, making sure you aren't attacked again tonight. If I don't have that privilege, then no one should."

"Okay," she said. She turned on her side and looked at him once more before closing her eyes for good.

"You're safe," she mumbled. "I love that. I love that so much."

home, before

ANOTHER UNIVERSAL TRUTH IS THAT endings trump beginnings. Charlotte's memories of James began to warp and darken, like photographs held too close to heat, till all his past kindnesses were tainted by how he'd ultimately hurt her. James had been sweet at first only to make her ache all the more when he wasn't.

Now that she thought about it, his name should have been a red flag: "James." What kind of a person is so fussy he can't dress down to a decent "Jim"? She didn't need a "Jimmy" necessarily—though she wasn't opposed to it. And there was always the "Jamie" option. But no, it was *James* all the time. His name, his betrayal: all cold, calculating, and self-important.

At least one memory remained vivid: once or twice each night, James would turn over in his sleep, his back to her, and play a long note on the buttocks bassoon. Hey, Justice, enjoy that adorable quirk.

austenland, day 12

CHARLOTTE WOKE BEFORE EDDIE. The light from the windows tasted of late morning, and Charlotte guessed he'd stayed on guard for much of the night. She adjusted her pillow and looked over his face. Watching someone sleeping was an intimate act, something reserved for longtime lovers and parents of small children. She thought she should feel guilty, but she didn't.

She found herself smiling as she noticed his abdomen lift with each breath, his fingers twitch as if caught in the net of a dream. He wasn't hers to keep. She knew that. This was a two-week vacation, nothing more, and it didn't matter if waking next to Eddie made her feel more content than anything she could remember.

He woke slowly and said, "What are you looking at?"

"You."

"It's morning? I'm glad you're still alive."

"Me too."

He reached out to take her hand. "Have you been awake long? You must be famished."

"No, I'm fine," she said. Then her stomach interrupted her with a loud, hungry squelch.

He left her to get dressed. She opened her wardrobe, stared at it for a few beats, then shut it again. Reality was leaning over Pembrook Park, breathing into its windows, and she could not take herself seriously in a corset and gown. She put on a robe over her chemise and went into the bathroom.

A black bag lay in the corner. In their searching, the police must not have realized that it wasn't hers. Charlotte unzipped it: canned food and bottled water.

Mary, she thought. She must have come back for food. Maybe killing me was an afterthought.

Eddie met her on the stairs, dressed in breeches and an untucked white shirt, collar open, no cravat. They held hands as they went down the stairs, letting go before entering the dining room.

Detective Sergeant Merriman's questions lasted well past breakfast. When Charlotte was released, she went outside to watch the police tow the BMW, the body from its trunk already bagged and hauled away. Off in the distance, where the garden wall met up with the trees, Charlotte saw something twinkle. Something smallish, handheld.

A camera.

Charlotte looked around. Eddie, Miss Charming, and Colonel Andrews were strolling among the police cars, but not—

Miss Gardenside started to emerge through the front door.

"Alisha, stop!" Charlotte hissed in a stage whisper.

Miss Gardenside froze, hearing the warning in the use of her real name. Charlotte placed herself between the girl and the camera and pushed her back inside, hurrying her to the dining room.

Eddie rushed in. "What is it?"

"I think someone sneaked onto the grounds to take photos," Charlotte said. "We don't want Alisha exposed."

Eddie nodded and rushed out again.

Alisha sat down. "So you guessed why I'm here."

Charlotte hadn't. "Whatever reason, I'm sure you don't need your name associated with this vacation-turned-murder for the rest of your career."

Alisha's expression was forlorn. "It's nice of you to think the best of me. Not everyone does."

"You've always been so in character, Lydia—or . . ." Charlotte hesitated. Lydia Gardenside had never worn such a lost expression. "Alisha. I figured you wanted not to be yourself for a while, and paparazzi taking pictures of you here—it's like catching you sunbathing nude."

"Been there," said Alisha.

"Wow." If someone photographed Lu in the buff, Charlotte just might justify murder. She thought of leaving, but Alisha seemed to want to talk. How much Charlotte would have given to sit in a room like that with Lu, to have Lu leaning toward her, her expression willing.

"I'm glad you're feeling better," Charlotte said gently. In her experience, young girls spook easier than wild horses.

"'Consumption' was Mrs. Wattlesbrook's code for 'addict,'" Alisha said without emotion. "I needed some time to get off the painkillers, and sitting in an asylum somewhere talking about my feelings is not my style, is it? I've gone that route twice already, thanks. Give me a microphone and a stage, or a camera and a character, and I'm cozy. Put me myself in a room of inquiring minds and I want to commit bloody murder."

"Then coming here was a great idea—well, except for the bloody murder part."

"I had to go somewhere. Mrs. Wattlesbrook was willing to play along. I think she even searched the staff and guests to make sure no one brought painkillers. Besides, my mom's always been an Austen fan, and I thought she might . . . approve." Alisha shrugged again.

Charlotte leaned in and hugged her like a mother would. Alisha hugged back and sighed a little, as if she were glad.

"So . . . not consumption. I'd wondered, but the illness, the coughing . . ."

"Withdrawal. Isn't that a boatful of fun?"

"How in the world did you find the energy to keep up the act?"

"Easier to suffer as Lydia with consumption than as Alisha with withdrawal. Lydia doesn't get depressed, so that made it easier. I like that you didn't assume the truth, Charlotte. I hate that I'm such a cliché. Poor, troubled young star turns to prescription meds. You'd think the shame alone would keep me clean."

"You are an incredible woman, Alisha," Charlotte said as Eddie came back in.

"Do you mean to do that?" Alisha asked. "Make people feel amazing? That night I sang at the piano, I'd been pretty low. I was so caught up in the character of Miss Gardenside that I didn't want to go back to being Alisha. Ever. But I sang as her, as myself, and what you said to me after—I felt like I could be me again and be okay."

Eddie beamed at Charlotte. "I rather suspect our Charlotte has been a hero to one and all."

"Stop it, or I'll get a big head and I'll have to be refitted for my bonnet," she said lightly, but really she felt ashamed by their words. Charlotte wasn't a hero—she'd failed in her marriage, disappointed her children and her own self. At least, that used to be true, but even as she thought those words, they didn't feel quite as solid as they had before.

"The police chased off the photographer," said Eddie. "And I spoke with Detective Sergeant Merriman. She's confident she can keep Alisha's name out of this since she wasn't directly involved."

While Alisha met privately with the detective, Charlotte tried to call her kids at the inn, though, once again, there was no answer.

Eddie walked her back to the house, his silence accompanying her own. Ever since she'd almost died, Charlotte's longing for her kids had magnified. It was just fine that Beckett called Justice "Mom" and that Lu seemed more content there than at home. Of course it was. She wanted her children to love their father and stepmother, right? She would not selfishly insist on being the sole recipient of their affection. Don't be ridiculous.

And maybe this came at a good time. Before, she never would have considered extending her vacation. But if her kids were okay, then she could . . . could . . . could what? Hang out interminably, like Miss Charming, so she could spend more time with Eddie? What was she thinking?

She wasn't. It was time to just feel a little bit and do something about it. So there.

"Reginald . . . Eddie," she said, "what are you like when you're not here? Are you an actor?"

Earlier he'd retrieved a practice foil from the secret room, and now he wore it hanging from his belt so he could be armed. Charlotte thought he looked like a Regency secret service agent.

"I'm more of a dancer than an actor, but that's a game for twenty-year-olds. I've done my share of West End productions with Pembrook chaps over the years and recently signed on here myself. Mrs. Wattlesbrook advised me to adopt a character most in keeping with my natural self. Easier to maintain. The women who come here, you can tell they are lonely. It's a pleasure to dote upon them, to see them smile in earnest."

"It's not real love," Charlotte said softly.

"It mirrors it, doesn't it? My take is, we're here to treat the women kindly and send them home reminded of what affection feels like."

"And so I became one of your projects."

His smile was slightly exasperated. "You weren't supposed to be. I'm scripted for Gardenside. But you caught my eye, curse you." He lifted her hand to his mouth and kissed it. "I have a confession."

She'd been waiting for this. "You're married. You're dating someone. You're gay."

"You are horrid at guessing. No, no, and no. I never thought Mallery deserved you. You're different, Charlotte. You're genuine. You deserve better than you've had. I don't know what you've had—besides the Mallery incident, that is—but I know you deserve better."

"You're just dazzled by my exceedingly fine deductive skills," she said.

"I didn't believe for a moment that there was a real murder. I used it as an excuse to stay close to you. I know, I'm uncommonly clever."

The tow truck and most of the police cars were gone. She had two more nights. If the kids had answered the phone, she'd planned to tell them that she'd be staying longer. Though Eddie hadn't asked.

As they entered the front doors, Eddie let go of her hand. Charlotte expected that, but it still felt a little jarring.

"There they are," said Mrs. Wattlesbrook, holding court in the dining room. Colonel Andrews and Miss Charming were eating hamburgers, clearly purchased from town. Alisha was snacking on ice cream.

"Have a seat, Mrs. Cordial, Mr. Grey," said the proprietress. "We are discussing our remaining time."

"I don't want to go home yet," Alisha said.

"Given the circumstances, I expect the ladies may require a refund." Mrs. Wattlesbrook lifted one eyebrow and looked around, her tight lips betraying her anxiety.

Charlotte shook her head. "It's not your fault one of your cast members turned out to be a crazed killer."

The other ladies concurred, and Mrs. Wattlesbrook's shoulders relaxed.

"But what about you?" said Charlotte. "If you want to close up shop early, I'm sure we'd all understand."

"No," she said, terror widening her eyes. "I do not wish to sit somewhere and *think*. This is my home. I . . . like having you here."

This produced silence. From Mrs. Wattlesbrook, the declaration was almost sentimental.

She cleared her throat. "As for the ball . . . it was meant to be tomorrow night."

"Ooh, let's still have it!" said Alisha.

"Of course we'll still have the ball," said Miss Charming, confused. "What kind of Austen joint would this be if we didn't have a ball?"

Charlotte felt strange at the thought of putting all the clothes back on, pretending to be Mrs. Cordial again. She let her hand dangle at her side. Eddie did the same, and underneath the table their fingers touched.

"I'd like to stay for the last two days," she said.

And more, she thought.

How much more? asked her Inner Thoughts.

Charlotte didn't have an answer to that.

"Naturally, for you, Mrs. Cordial," Mrs. Wattlesbrook said, "I will secure a new partner."

"Oh." Charlotte hadn't thought that part through. Her fingers were still touching Eddie's.

"And we shall do our utmost," said Colonel Andrews, arising to bow formally, "to ensure that this one doesn't try to murder you in cold blood."

"Thanks," she said, "but don't put yourselves out on my account."

"Never fear," said the colonel. "It is now Pembrook Park policy to take each new actor aside and ask, most sternly, Are you or do you plan to be a murderer? And if he answers yes—"

"Or if his eyes shift suspiciously," Eddie added.

". . . then he shall be turned out on his heels!"

"Quite," Mrs. Wattlesbrook said with a sniff.

Neville echoed her sniff.

"I don't know if I remember the dances," said Alisha.

There was a slight pause, and Eddie, pulling his hand away from Charlotte's, arose.

"In that case," he said, "shall we hold our own ball rehearsal tonight?"

"And pajama party," said the colonel. "There will be time for corsets and cravats tomorrow. I am rather fancying the ladies in their robes."

He waggled his eyebrows at Miss Charming. She made a kissy face back, as if at a favorite dog, and took another bite of her hamburger.

BY DINNER HOUR THE HOUSE was scrubbed of strangers. The police had cordoned off Mr. Mallery's room, Mary's room, and the hidden chamber on the second floor, the blue-and-white tape a visual reminder that all was not normal in Austenland.

They ate a casual meal in the drawing room. Miss Gardenside played jaunty dance tunes on the piano until Eddie wound up the music box so she could dance as well. Charlotte entreated Mrs. Wattlesbrook to stand up with Neville, and they both complied more readily than Charlotte would have guessed. Neville danced like he ran, skinny limbs akimbo. His grin was uncontrollably huge.

Charlotte nodded in satisfaction and turned to watch Eddie and Miss Gardenside dance. They were all grace and perfection. She stopped watching.

"We should get some rest," Mrs. Wattlesbrook pronounced after a few dances. "The ball is tomorrow, and despite our recent setbacks, I promise it will be up to Pembrook's usual standards."

Eddie followed Charlotte upstairs. It had been lovely, so lovely, to talk with him, to kiss him behind the house, to wake up and see him sleeping. Being with Eddie made sense, here and now, around midnight in Austenland, but she had a nagging fear that when she departed for home, the fantasy would dissolve into mist like Brigadoon. Sure she could stay a few extra days, but then what? She tried her best to ignore her pessimistic thoughts, especially her Inner ones, as they kept observing how often Eddie had danced with Miss Gardenside.

"I don't want to leave you alone," said Eddie.

"I'll be fine. Mary is in jail, and Mallery is probably in outer Liechtenstein by now."

Perhaps she would have invited him in her room anyway, but Mrs. Wattlesbrook was in the corridor too, so Charlotte just said goodnight.

She slid into bed, reminded herself that she had no reason to be afraid, and blew out the candle. The darkness in her room came alive with movement. How normal it had all seemed in the light, but now the dark swirled and swelled, shifting like the water of the pond. She imagined seeing the car before her, the rubber glove floating behind the window. The darkness formed faces that vaporized when she tried to focus on them. One face-shape didn't disappear, an oval lightness at about the right height as a standing man. Charlotte shuddered. What was it really—her pink bonnet hanging on a hook, perhaps?

She thought, Perhaps it's Mallery come back to haunt me.

The thought stuck. She sat upright, as if suddenly fitted in a full iron corset, and whispered to the dark, "Mallery isn't in outer Liechtenstein. He's still here."

home, before

THE FIRST FEW NIGHTS AFTER James left, Charlotte was okay. Stunned, sure. But as soon as the kids went to bed, she would close her bedroom door, watch TV, and not think. She didn't miss James next to her—not that much. He'd been gone a lot lately anyway. (Doing what? Don't think about it, Charlotte. Don't think!)

About a month later, James was set up in a larger apartment, and he invited Lu and Beckett to sleep over. And Charlotte was alone in her house overnight for the first time.

It was different than being alone in a hotel room on a business trip. Here she was solo with vastness. So many windows. Why didn't she get all of them covered? James had thought that putting blinds on the windows facing the fenced-in backyard was pointless, but really, people can climb a fence. Peeping Toms, burglars, serial killers—all excellent fence climbers. She went to the kitchen to rustle up some dinner and worried about how best to peel the carrot and drain the tuna fish. Would a watcher judge her for not rinsing the carrot, for the ragged way she cut open the can? Would a serial killer think badly of her if she used too much mayo?

Alone at home for the first time, she felt anything but *at home.*

austenland, day 12, night

CHARLOTTE GRABBED HER ROBE AND slippers and ran out of her room. No candles burned in the hallway. The night filled it with dark blue, as if it were a submerged hold in a sunken ship, and she found herself holding her breath, just in case she were in fact underwater. She prayed as she ran that she was alone. That no one watched her. That no one chased. Eddie's room, just four doors down, seemed freakishly far away.

His room was dimly lit by a single lamp, but she could see he was wearing pajama pants (Regency appropriate?) and had just removed his shirt. As she barged in, he looked up and grabbed the practice foil leaning against his bed.

"Do you really expect to do something with that?" she couldn't help asking.

"Perhaps. Is something chasing you?"

"I don't think so. I just realized, Mallery is still here."

"Where?" Eddie pulled her behind him, brandishing the foil like Errol Flynn.

"I'm not sure. I've been trying to figure Mallery out, and if he killed Wattlesbrook to preserve Pembrook Park, if this place meant that much to him . . . well, he'll stay as long as he possibly can."

"The police searched—"

"Mrs. Wattlesbrook said he was the caretaker during holidays. We know there's one hidden room. What if he discovered others? He could be anywhere. He could be here."

They looked at the walls, the wardrobe. Eddie shook his foil at the fireplace.

"Come out, come out, big bad wolf."

"He will. He'll have to. Mary dropped a bag of food in my room. I think they were hiding together and she came out to get supplies. But she made a pit stop to put on my makeup. Isn't that tragic? She just wanted to be pretty for him."

"Also, as I recall, she wanted to kill you."

"Yeah, but that was probably an afterthought."

They stood back-to-back, as if expecting Mallery to come out of the walls at any moment.

"He's probably not in my actual room," Eddie whispered.

"Probably not," Charlotte whispered back. "He might have realized by now that Mary's been captured. If he's still hiding, he won't stay put for long. I'm going to seriously flip out if he gets away again. We should hunt him out. Immediately."

He looked at her over his shoulder. "Are you afraid?" he asked.

"Not too bad actually. Not right now, anyway."

"Oh. Could you pretend you are for a moment? It's just that you look bewitching in that white chemise, and I'd like an excuse to comfort you. My ghost, my Charlotte, my own private haunting . . ."

She whispered even more quietly than before, barely breathing the words, "Eddie, I'm terrified."

He put his arms around her. Her hands felt the muscles of his bare back, her cheek rested against his neck. It was like diving into warm water, the touch of his skin.

"There, there," he said as if comforting her, and they both laughed a little, but neither let go. "Feeling better?"

"I could use a little more comforting," she said against his chest.

He kissed her neck, his hands tight on her back, and she closed her eyes and felt extremely angry at Mallery for needing to be hunted out. This was really inconvenient timing.

Forget Mallery, said her Inner Thoughts.

Eddie started to kiss her shoulder.

Forget who? Charlotte asked.

She was kissing Eddie now because, though he was brave,

surely he needed some comfort as well. It was the nice thing to do. All thoughts, Inner and Otherwise, turned off for a few moments. When Practical Charlotte tried to reclaim her brain, she found herself pressed against the bedpost, her arms around Eddie's neck, her hands clutching his hair. She disengaged her lips.

"Mallery?" she said breathlessly. "Danger? Police?"

"Right," said Eddie. "Call. Now."

He looked over her face then slowly let her go, seeming bewildered as to why he would willingly do such a thing.

"I hate him," Eddie said with real sadness.

Charlotte nodded.

She and Eddie held hands as they ran down the gravel drive. The air was warm and cool at the same time, and for just a moment, her running strides slipped into a straight-up skip.

The inn was unlocked, and they phoned Detective Sergeant Merriman, who sounded sleepy but willing to come out.

"It will take her half an hour at least," said Eddie after he hung up. He raised one eyebrow. "What shall we do?"

"Go wake Mrs. Wattlesbrook," said Charlotte. "See what she knows of this house's other secrets."

He sighed. "Why are you so practical?"

Mrs. Wattlesbrook was not happy to be awakened and told that the police were coming yet again. She gruffly asserted that there were no other hidden spaces in the house besides the room on the second floor.

"Must we uproot the entire household at midnight for yet another fruitless search? Perhaps you could have left well enough alone."

"I guess it was well enough for her," Charlotte said as she and Eddie made their way back outside. "She wasn't the one imagining the pink bonnet on the hook was Mallery coming back for a second chance at her throat."

They sat on the front steps of the house, waiting for the police.

"Sorry, Eddie. I just felt so sure."

"There may be secrets about this house that even Mrs. Wattlesbrook doesn't know."

"But how do we ferret him out?"

"I'd wager Mary knows where he is."

"And she'll never tell." Charlotte started to make a wish on a star peeping through a hole in the clouds, till she realized it was a satellite. "You know, when Mary came into my room last night, her clothes were dirty, as if she'd climbed through a dusty space. But the dirt was black. Maybe not just dirt, but soot. Ashes."

"A passageway through a fireplace?"

"Or maybe . . ."

Charlotte stood up, looking off into the distance. Eddie stood beside her.

"Pembrook Cottage?" he said.

"Yeah."

They ducked into the morning room, grabbed a couple of candles, scrawled a note to the detective to meet them at the cottage, and left it on the front steps under a rock.

They'd intended to wait for the police outside the cottage, but once there, neither could resist creeping through the burned-out front door to look for signs of Mallery. Footsteps had scuffed the layer of ash, but for all Charlotte knew, they were the mark of firefighters. Without speaking, they made their way through charred rubble to the back of the house, where walls and roof were stained with smoke but intact.

Eddie was scanning the floor for clues. Charlotte meant to search, but she was distracted by the way the walls seemed to undulate in the candlelight. How could there be so many shadows when the only light came from a thumb-size flame?

"What a creepy little house," Charlotte whispered.

Eddie made no response, and she thought he must not have heard her. Or perhaps the house swallowed up sound. She walked down the hall, her feet probing for creaking boards to convince herself sound was possible in this place. Would Mallery really prefer to skulk in an ashy, dark half-of-a-house than to run to freedom? It didn't seem likely anymore.

At the end of the hallway, just before the stairs going up, she found a small sitting room. The smoke had barely touched the walls and ceiling, leaving intact a small table with chairs and a bookcase. Charlotte held up her candle, curious what books lined the shelves. She read titles under her breath.

Charlotte frowned. The bookcase seemed to be coming slowly forward. She shook her head, sure it was just her candlelight creating false motion on the bookcase's uneven surface. She was about to remark on it to Eddie when a hand grabbed her wrist and pulled her into the wall behind the bookcase. All in the same second, the bookcase/door shut, a breath blew out her candle, and a hand covered her mouth.

"Don't scream."

Charlotte, you're so stupid! screamed her Inner Thoughts.

Yeah, thanks, I've figured that out, she thought back.

Being in a hidden room with Mallery again—her heart doing that manic tickety-tack, tickety-tack—felt so familiar.

Mallery whispered, "Do you promise to stay quiet?" she nodded under his hand.

"I won't hurt you," he said, letting go.

"I don't believe you." She hadn't meant to keep her promise. She'd planned on screaming bloody murder to alert Eddie, but it was hard to talk at all. She felt as if she were underwater, her lungs tight, the pressure of the pond pushing her head down.

Mallery guided her to a small sofa in the dark and invited her to take a seat. Her head brushed a ceiling that slanted down, and she realized they were in the space under the stairs. This scarcely qualified as a secret room—more of a secret hole, or nook, or niche even, perhaps a cavity or alcove . . .

Come up with synonyms all you want, said her Inner Thoughts. It's not distracting me from the fact that you're stupid.

"I am happy you came to me, Charlotte," Mallery said, sitting beside her.

Uh-huh. "Eddie is out there. And he's . . . he's *armed*. And the police are on their way."

Mallery ignored this, but the calm in his voice was forced, fraying at the edges. "I would not have done what I did if there had been another way. Wattlesbrook did not deserve to live. He had no respect for women or ancient edifices."

She had a sudden image of Mallery the night Pembrook Cottage was burning, running to the pond for water and racing back to the fire, tossing bucket after useless bucket on the growing flames. He must have been mad with frustration. The fire had burned fast, the firefighters had come too late, and the pond water had done nothing. Not that night. But he'd returned to the pond two days later, and then its waters had been very effective at swallowing a car with a body in the trunk. That is, until Charlotte had taken an afternoon plunge.

"You know it's not really 1816, right?" she said. "You're not delusional. Pembrook Park was never your grandfather's, and killing Mr. Wattlesbrook to protect your workplace seems extreme. So, why?"

He didn't answer.

"Wattlesbrook burned down the cottage, lost Windy Nook and Bertram Hall because of his incompetence, and planned to divorce his wife and sell off Pembrook Park. Why do you, the real you, care so much? Is it because you belong here, as Neville said?

I can believe that. You know it's fantasy, but it's as real as you can get to being where you feel you belong. Maybe killing him seemed like a necessity. You were protecting yourself, as you saw it anyway. It was practically self-defense."

His voice was a raw whisper. "Self-defense of the most sublime nature."

"But you tried to kill me, and that wasn't self-defense."

No response.

"One thing I admire about this era that you love so much is the civility. Etiquette is observed, respect maintained. Whatever your reasons, strangling me in the storage room was pretty darn uncivil, and I'd like a real apology."

"I am sorry I tried to kill you. I am, Charlotte. I am seared with regret. At the time . . . I . . . I saw no other way."

His voice did sound sincere, and that, for some reason, made her spitting mad.

"What you're doing to Mary is cruel, you know. You don't really love her."

"She has desires that don't fit in her world. I help her realize them."

"She covered up your deeds. She attacked me. She'll probably go to jail for a long time."

"I am sorry she was captured, but all she did was her choice."

Charlotte felt his finger touch her cheek.

"Charlotte?" she heard Eddie call. He sounded far away.

"You killed a man." She couldn't help trying to make him feel some regret for the murder. "He was alive and you killed him. Whether or not he was pond scum, that wasn't your choice to make."

"But it was," he said, his whisper so low now there was no tone in it. "He was worth less than the damage he did. It was within my power to stop him, and so it became my responsibility."

"You could be hundreds of miles away by now," she whispered. "Why did you stay? What are you really afraid of, Mallery?"

He put a hand on the back of her neck and pressed his forehead against her temple. She could feel the breath from his whisper on her cheek.

"I do not know where else in this world I can exist."

He sure sounds delusional, her Inner Thoughts said.

Charlotte wondered if she would have recognized the crazy much earlier if he looked more like Steve Buscemi than Mr. Medieval Hotness. She was about to, in appropriately ladylike terms, ask him to get his hands off her, when his lips were on hers. It was so surprising she didn't move.

He withdrew his lips but left his fingertips on her face. "I know why you made me nervous, Mrs. Cordial. To yearn for you, and yet be forbidden to touch you."

"Your character was scripted to love me," she whispered, almost feeling sorry for him. He sounded heartfelt. "None of that is real."

"It is all real, Mrs. Cordial. All."

"Charlotte?" Eddie called, his voice still faint but perhaps closer.

Charlotte saw a flicker of light. There must be a small hole in the bookcase for spying out, she thought. Eddie was probably in the sitting room, for the moment anyway.

"Eddie—" Charlotte breathed.

Mallery kissed her again, longer, his arms wrapping around her. It is such an awkward thing to be the recipient of an unsolicited kiss. She didn't want to kiss him back, and yet she was afraid he'd feel bad.

Had she really just thought that?

She put a hand on his cheek and pushed him away. "You need to turn yourself in now."

He pulled her to her feet and stood behind her with one arm tight across her diaphragm.

"You know how much it grieves me that I hurt you," he whispered in her ear. "You will not put me through that again, and I will not hurt you so long as you don't hurt me, Mrs. Cordial. I cannot stay here any longer." His voice cracked at that. "You will accompany me off Pembrook property, and then I will set you free. Unless you wish to stay with me."

He listened by the hole in the bookcase. All was silent.

"Now behave yourself," he whispered and pushed the wall, opening the bookcase like a swinging door into the sitting room. The bookcase clicked closed behind them.

Behave herself, huh? Absolutely. Charlotte elbowed Mallery in the gut, right where she was pretty sure she'd previously bruised his ribs. He let go.

"Bloody murder!" she screamed.

"Halt!" Eddie shouted, rushing into the room and pointing the tip of the foil at Mallery's chest. Charlotte leapt to the side.

Mallery eyeballed the blunt tip and knocked the blade away impatiently. Eddie whipped him with it on the top of his head.

"Ow," said Mallery.

He took a menacing step forward, but Eddie whipped him again on the shoulder.

"Stop that!" said Mallery.

The two men stared each other down.

"I have a knife," said Mallery, pulling one from his belt.

"Mine is longer," said Eddie.

Boys, Charlotte thought, with an internal roll of her eyes.

He whipped Mallery's hand, and Mallery dropped his knife. They stared again. Charlotte found it all very dramatic. Mallery faked as if to pick up the knife but ran instead, dodging Eddie to get down the hall and out the charred front door. He didn't look quite so menacing when he ran.

Eddie and Charlotte chased after him, leaping over debris and coughing on the ash his flight kicked up. Car headlights met them outside, coming from the direction of the house. The police! Mallery swerved and made toward the wood.

"That's him! That's him!" Charlotte yelled.

The detective's car left the drive and crossed the lawn, the tires churning up the grass.

"Mrs. Wattlesbrook is not going to like that," Charlotte said.

Police scrambled forward, shouting, a couple of them pulling out guns. More guns! Weren't they supposed to just use billy clubs in England? Where had she been getting her information? The detective's car cut off Mallery's route to the woods, and he stopped, hands in the air.

Eddie was beside her.

"Are you happy you got to use your foil?" she asked.

He smiled, his dimples like full moons.

"I think I owe you some kind of an apology," she said, "about how I misjudged your prowess with a weapon and how you really are dangerous."

His arm went around her waist.

"I am officially the happiest man alive."

After questions and explanations, the police sent Charlotte and Eddie back up to the big house. It was silent, most of its inhabitants asleep and clueless about the happenings at the cottage down the lane.

Soon Charlotte found herself once again in bed, in a room without a lock, awake long after midnight. But something was different tonight. Something was missing. She looked around her room, patted herself as if searching for lost keys, ran her fingers through her hair. Something large, something usually present, was just gone.

I'm not afraid, she realized. I don't feel the least bit afraid.

She thought of the dead body in the secret room. Nothing. She imagined her brother in a mask chasing her through a dark house. Nada. She thought of Mallery trying to kill her, and Mary in her room with a gun, and murdered nuns and ghosts and a house that might eat corpses alive . . .

She sighed, rolled onto her side, and fell asleep.

home, thirty-one years before

"LET'S PLAY CASTLE," SAID CHARLOTTE'S loud and bespectacled friend Olga. "I'll be the princess, and you be the lady-in-waiting."

"Okay," said Charlotte.

She watched Olga traipse about with Charlotte's plastic tiara on her head and felt a mild ache that her lot was to sit on the basement carpet and pretend to weave a tapestry. But Olga looked really happy, and being the lady-in-waiting wasn't so bad. She still got to be a part of the story. Even if she wasn't the heroine.

austenland, day 13

CHARLOTTE POURED MILK IN HER TEA, dabbed the corner of her mouth with a napkin, and said, "Last night Eddie and I found Mallery hiding in Pembrook Cottage."

The sounds of chewing, tinkling utensils on plates, and subdued breakfast conversations hushed at once. Even Neville, just entering the dining room from the kitchen with a plate of sausages, gaped openly.

"The police arrived," said Eddie, "but not before Charlotte was nearly taken hostage."

"What happened?" Miss Gardenside asked.

"Oh, you know," she said, waving her hand as if it were all so typical. "He was hiding behind a trick bookcase in a secret alcove. Or was it a nook? Anyway, he pulled me in. He apparently had been dying to apologize for almost killing me. Then he kissed me."

Eddie stood up, rattling the table and knocking over a glass of orange juice. "He what?!"

"He kissed me?" she said, more apprehensively this time. She hadn't expected a table-rattling, juice-spilling reaction to that news.

"Did you let him?"

"Yeah. NO! It wasn't . . . it was . . . well, he needed closure, I guess. He's like those old heroes—or villains, maybe—those tragic princes and tortured Heathcliffs and Rochesters. At least, *he* sees himself that way. He wouldn't have lasted long in that little cubbyhole, and I think he was waiting for a finale of sorts before he left this old world behind. He was still calling me 'Mrs. Cordial.' After everything that's happened—*Mrs. Cordial.* He's that far gone. But he wanted that final moment, right? He wanted to end it with a kiss. And now that he's in jail, his last free action wasn't trying to kill the lady, it was kissing the lady, and he can live with that. You know?"

Miss Charming rested her cheek on her hand. "What was the kiss like?" she asked.

"Well, it was very dark, I couldn't see him, and suddenly—"

Miss Charming put her hands over her mouth and squealed

with delight. Eddie slammed down the empty juice glass he'd just picked up. Colonel Andrews and Miss Gardenside were looking back and forth from Charlotte's fumbling to Eddie's fuming.

"Never mind," said Charlotte. "It was just a kiss. It doesn't matter. I just wanted to tell you all, so you knew that Mallery is no longer a threat."

Charlotte gave Eddie a stern look, warning him to calm down. He sat and reached for a piece of bread, then tore it apart over a plate.

"I just don't like that he took such a liberty. I should have been there to prevent it."

"It's really okay, Eddie. I'm okay. Mallery tried to kill me, but I still feel sorry for him. It's not easy to be him in this world. He doesn't deserve much, but maybe he did deserve his final moment."

Eddie laughed, and Charlotte shrugged.

"I know," she said. "But I'm nice. It's what I do."

It was the heroine's prerogative to give the villain a final kiss, and she had decided to be the heroine after all. Jane Austen had created six heroines, each quite different, and that gave Charlotte courage. There wasn't just one kind of woman to be. She wasn't afraid anymore. She was feeling at home at last in Austenland, and she meant to enshroud herself with that boldness and take it home with her.

And she meant, quite specifically, to damn the torpedoes and fall very much in love with Eddie, even if it was temporary, even if she didn't quite know what she meant to him.

They weren't alone for the rest of the day. Miss Gardenside, Colonel Andrews, and Miss Charming were always hovering nearby. Eddie didn't say anything significant to her, such as "I love you," or "Please stay forever," or even "I'm going to go brush my teeth—meet me in your room in ten." He stood near her, his attention on Miss Gardenside.

Evening drew close. Mrs. Wattlesbrook chased the last of the police away and the guests to their rooms. The ball would be starting soon, and Charlotte could hear musicians tuning and smell pastries baking. She had no expectations. That made her feel a little bit lonely, but a little bit lonely was nicer than a whole lot numb.

Eddie would be back in character and dancing with Miss Gardenside tonight. Charlotte didn't feel much motivation to spruce up, but her ball gown lay neatly on her bed. She'd been measured for the gown on her first day, and it must have just arrived from the seamstress. Its newness seemed to make it glow, as if a magic wand had only just zapped it together from rags. She held it up. The length from high waist to low hem was longer than her everyday dresses, accentuating her height. The cream-colored organza was delicately embroidered in a pattern of flowers and curlicues and embellished with beads that winked in the window light. Seventeen years of fashion changes had rendered her wedding dress laughable, but two hundred years hadn't hurt this style. The gown was beautiful.

Mary was no more, but Charlotte was certain that if she pulled her bell cord, some downstairs maid would come help her dress. No matter. Charlotte had been doing her best to dress herself for the past week. She could ask Miss Charming to do up the unreachable buttons and help her with her hair. Or maybe Colonel Andrews. Something told her he'd be a whiz at an updo.

There was a knock at the door. No one had ever knocked at her door besides Mary, and the last time Mary had come around, she'd been exercising the right to bear arms.

Eddie's voice asked, "May I come in?"

"Sure," she said.

He entered, still exercising his own right to tote a practice foil.

"Here's my bodyguard."

"You've proved to need one."

"Do you think you'll have another chance to use that?"

"A chap can dream."

"It's got a blunt tip."

"In my dream it's sharp as a tack. Also, I get to keep whipping Mallery's face with it till he cries like a baby."

"Quite a detailed dream."

"And I haven't even gotten to the part where I'm a racing driver."

He stood by the door as she touched up her makeup in the bathroom and turned his back when she pulled off her robe and slid into the ball gown.

"Um . . . I could use some help with the doing-up," she said.

He sighed. "Truly?"

His reluctance made her blink. "I can ask Miss Charming if you're busy."

He trudged over, showing unwillingness in every movement. Like a big brother annoyed with his pesky sister? She bit her lip as he fumbled with the gown's many buttons, determined not to speak and annoy him further.

"You drive me mad."

"Sorry, brother of mine," she said flatly.

His hands paused. "Please don't call me that." She felt his fingers continue up her back. "Since our outing to the abbey, when you were concerned you were letting me down by not being clever enough, you have kept me laughing and longing too. Your kindness is genuine. Do you know how rare that is? Your presence absorbs me, and yet I'm not supposed to notice. It was hard enough to pretend indifference when you were bathing in the pond. Loosening your corset about undid me. And yet here I am again, so near you yet unable to carry you off to be my own. I must be a masochist."

She remembered to empty her lungs, but after she could only inhale in quick, shallow breaths.

"So you'd prefer I didn't call you 'brother'?"

"Not in private, please." She felt him rest his forehead against her neck, and his exhale raised goose bumps on her back. "Please. I don't know how to have you here, when I am not me. I don't know . . ."

She nodded. He put his arms around her waist, holding her from behind. She put her arms over his and they stood there in a silent embrace. Her heart was beating so hard she could see her bodice shake, yet she felt oddly calm.

This would have killed me when I was fourteen, she thought with sudden insight. I remember *that* much of my younger self.

The romance and awkwardness and sublime uncertainty would have broken her heart and driven her crazy. *What next, what then, what should I say, what if I turned around, what will we do?* But age gave her the peace, at least, to live inside that moment like a poet—to not sacrifice the beauty to the anxiety of What Next, but to just observe. The warmth of his hands under hers. His heartbeat against her back. The moment he adjusted his head to the side, as if he wanted to feel her skin against his cheek. The way his arms subtly tightened—conscious of her waist, feeling her there, enjoying her. How she felt from inside her throat down her middle toward her legs—all zingy and cold and light too. This was why she'd come here. Nothing else ever need happen again. She'd had her moment in Austenland, and even unfulfilled and uncertain, it was perfect. She leaned her head back till it touched his own, and she heard him sigh.

"I will be dancing with Miss Gardenside tonight," he said.

"It's okay."

"It's not okay."

"It's why you're here. Why she's here. It's supposed to happen this way."

"I wish it weren't."

Charlotte was about to say what she wished when her door opened. She moved out of Eddie's embrace, and he whipped out his foil.

Miss Charming screamed, raising her hands in the air. "Don't shoot, don't shoot!"

Eddie lowered the weapon, his face flushed. "Sorry. I—sorry."

"He's standing guard in case there's yet another person in this house who wants to kill me," Charlotte said.

"Good thing I want you alive, then, so you can do up my back," said Miss Charming. "Don't want to ring for a maid. Don't trust any of them anymore, crazy-eyed, trigger-happy lot."

She turned her back to Charlotte and submitted to the buttoning, then fixed up the mismatched mess Eddie had made of Charlotte's buttons, chatting all the while of past balls and favorite dances and the squelchy excitement she always got in her tummy whenever the music started. Her faux-British accent had taken a holiday ever since Mallery had tried to murder Charlotte.

Miss Charming volunteered to do Charlotte's hair and dragged her to her own room. Through the open door, Charlotte could see Eddie in the hallway, holding his foil uncertainly.

"Go get dressed, Eddie," she called out. "If any hopeful murderers attack us, Lizzy has promised to beat them with her curling iron."

Charlotte thought it a reasonable threat, and Eddie must have agreed, for while he hesitated for a moment, he soon nodded and left.

"You really are more beautiful than you seem at first," Miss

Charming was saying, sticking a plastic Bumpit under Charlotte's hair to add volume.

"Thanks?" said Charlotte.

"You've got a look that a person's got to get used to, then after a while, *voilà*, you're beautiful. My Bobby totally would have tested out a mattress sample with you."

"Okay."

"'Course, not that you woulda. You're not one of those dangerous women, Charlotte. You're nice."

CHARLOTTE HEARD THE BALL BEFORE she saw it. Music floated upstairs and lured her out to the landing. It was remarkable how different she felt in a ball gown—like someone special, someone princessy.

Miss Charming and Miss Gardenside met her on the landing. Strangers in formalwear swirled through the front door, handing cloaks and hats to servants, laughing as they made their way to the great hall. Charlotte had to wonder where Mrs. Wattlesbrook found them all. A casting agency? The local YMCA? There must have been three dozen fresh bodies in Regency clothing. From this vantage, Charlotte couldn't see the police tape on Mallery's door or the bullet hole in the wall. Austenland was primped and pretty.

"Each time it's like the first time," Miss Charming whispered. "Each time, I think, This is the ball when everything changes."

"Does it change?" Miss Gardenside asked.

"Sort of. But maybe . . . not quite enough."

Colonel Andrews strode to the bottom of the stairs. Like all the men that night, he wore a black jacket and breeches, white shirt and cravat, the Regency version of the tuxedo. He put one hand behind his back and lifted the other up, an invitation.

"Do not require me to grovel, Miss Elizabeth, for you know I will. Come to me and make me the happiest man in the world, or I will grieve to the heavens of the injustice. I will tantrum until the gods take pity and strike me dead to save me the agony of a broken heart. I beg you, be my lady!"

Miss Charming pressed her gloved hands to her chest and gasped with delight, then jogged down the stairs with much roiling and shaking in her upper regions. Colonel Andrews flew up the stairs to meet her halfway, as if he could not wait another moment to touch her.

He took her hand, kissed it, then sighed to the ceiling. "She is a goddess, I say. A goddess!"

Miss Charming's eyes sparkled, and she seemed about to cry but giggled instead as he led her away.

Before Charlotte and Miss Gardenside could descend the staircase, Eddie appeared, waiting at the bottom. He did not look at Charlotte.

"Miss Gardenside, I must speak out. I, for one, find your behavior this evening abominable."

"I beg your pardon?" Miss Gardenside asked with mock offense.

"As you should. Think on the other ladies, Miss Gardenside. Think on their delicate natures, their wounded vanities. It is not enough for you to be merely attractive, but must you outshine your entire sex so egregiously? I say, for shame."

"Perhaps I might powder my nose with mud or pour grease on my hair?"

"Provocative suggestions, but I think my presence at your side might dim the splendor effectively."

Miss Gardenside took his arm and, with an affected American Southern accent, said, "Honey, you could catch a fish without a hook."

"If my lady desires fish, my lady shall have fish." He gestured to the ballroom and they proceeded in.

Still not meeting her eyes, Eddie said over his shoulder, "Good evening, Charlotte."

"Hello, Eddie."

Mrs. Wattlesbrook waved a hand to get Charlotte's attention. She wore an extremely lacy dress and feathers wiggled in her hair. Without her marriage cap, she seemed quite festive. "Mrs. Cordial, may I present Lord Bentley, a very old friend of our family. He has expressed a desire to meet you especially. Sir Charles, Mrs. Charlotte Cordial."

Lord Bentley was a tall man, taller than must be comfortable for everyday living. Sure, Charlotte was a tall woman, but partnering her with the Chrysler Building seemed like overkill.

"Mrs. Cordial, I daresay this is a pleasure. Am I presumptuous, are you otherwise engaged, or may I request your hand in the first two dances?"

So here she was on yet another blind date. Another man forced into it by a friend—or in this case, because he was paid. Did that make him a gigolo? Weren't they all, then, essentially gigolos? Ugh.

Charlotte took his arm and entered the ballroom. Hundreds of candles dazzled in the chandeliers, the music dazzling right back. Couples were already dancing, and the swirl of dresses was as beautiful as a coral reef. Tables along the walls were heavy with punch bowls and pastries that emanated sweet, crunchy aromas. Charlotte gasped. Never had Austenland felt so real.

"It's beautiful," she said.

"So are you," said Lord Bentley.

Oh gag, said her Inner Thoughts.

Charlotte danced with Lord Bentley, sometimes watching Mr. Grey dancing with Miss Gardenside. And sometimes Mr. Grey watched Mrs. Cordial dancing with Lord Bentley.

"I have heard much of you from Mrs. Wattlesbrook," Lord Bentley said as they waited their turn to sashay down the middle.

"Have you?" Charlotte asked. Eddie and Miss Gardenside were sashaying. Charlotte wanted to laugh. It was hardly a romantic dance. Then again, he *was* holding her hands.

"You intrigue me," said his lordship. "I rode in from London just to meet you."

"That's a long way," she said.

"It was worth it," he said. Then they sashayed. It was a bouncy passage down the middle, sidestepping at a skip. She hoped no one held a hidden camera. She didn't want this to end up on YouTube to embarrass her children.

The second dance was a little less Virginia reel and had more style. Partners stood opposite, coming together then away. Lord Bentley seemed to have given up conversation in favor of smoldering looks. After having been professionally smoldered by Mallery, she found Lord Bentley's attempt to be just sad.

At one point in the dance, ladies crossed to the gentlemen on their right. Charlotte lifted her hand. Eddie took it. All the magic and smells and dazzles surrounded her with that touch. She was no longer observing; she was inside Austenland. She was real.

"I'm sorry," Eddie said softly.

"Don't be."

They crossed behind other dancers and met again.

"It's not right," he said.

"That's not for me to decide," she said. But she wished it was.

They returned to their partners. Lord Bentley was all eyebrows and brooding looks. She discovered a new appreciation for Mallery, who had probably smoldered from birth. Even his sweat had been broodish.

The dance was over. Miss Gardenside took Mr. Grey's arm, and they walked off together.

"Excuse me, I've got some . . . lady business," Charlotte said as awkwardly as possible, in hopes of avoiding any inquiries from her date. Lord Bentley bowed and she hurried away. Was she being dishonest? Perhaps she was just being clever. But that wasn't likely, given that she had stalking in mind, and her stalking track record wasn't impressive.

Charlotte followed Eddie and Miss Gardenside at a discreet distance. The couple wandered into the conservatory. Charlotte stopped at the doorway, hidden behind a fern. The air in the glassed-in room was tropically warm and felt as sweet as a sweater on her bare arms.

Mr. Grey took Miss Gardenside's hand and spoke. This was the moment. This was the proposal, the one Charlotte would have had from murderer Mallery. It was an all-inclusive vacation, including meals, wardrobe, outings, and a marriage proposal. Right now, elsewhere in the house, Colonel Andrews was probably proposing to Miss Charming for the umpteenth time.

The couple strolled between plants, their voices low, their heads leaning toward each other. Miss Gardenside's hand rested on his arm. His hand lay atop hers. Charlotte's throat constricted. She was torturing herself, that was all. Would she have wanted to peer into a motel room at James and Justice? Certainly not. She started down the hall.

A moment later she was back. Eddie was holding Miss Gardenside's hands, speaking earnestly. She seemed elated. Were they going to kiss? Yes, any moment, they would certainly kiss. The moonlight was angled in the window just so, as if propped up for this scene, and the air was heady with love and plant sap. No kissing please. Charlotte couldn't bear that, even if it was supposed to be pretend. If Eddie kissed Miss Gardenside, it meant he wanted to, didn't it? Alisha was so beautiful and young. Maybe Eddie was more like James than she'd thought. Charlotte's heart bounced inside her chest, encouraging her to flee.

She put a hand over her eyes and sought after her Inner Thoughts.

What do I do?

Her Inner Thoughts skipped forward, happy to be asked. Leave 'em alone and go get some punch. But stay away from Lord Bentley, 'cause he gives me the creepos.

But what about Eddie?

Nothing's real here, including him. Nice people don't mess up someone else's expensive romantic moment, especially since you're clearly not ready to love Eddie for real. Get out before you make an idiot of yourself or get that heart broken again. We're still aching from the last time, thanks very much.

No, said Charlotte, surprising herself. I am ready. I'm ready to love again, and I choose him. I don't know how, with two kids in one country and this man in another. But I can't imagine anyone else I would want to be with besides Eddie. Is that selfish? Does that mean I'm not nice?

Yeah, said her Inner Thoughts.

Well, forget you. I'm going to be the heroine in this story.

She started into the room just as the couple, apparently concluding their conservatory business, was starting out.

"Charlotte?" he said.

"Eddie," she said, not knowing what else to say. But she was spared the formation of words by the mercifully loquacious Miss Gardenside.

"Oh, Charlotte, is it not wonderful?" she effused, hurrying to Charlotte's side.

"Is it?"

"Now do not tease. Though I know you will mock me for being so blind, I am not as arch as you, my dearest, sweetest friend. You can find out a murderer, but I could not see true love when it formed before my face!"

"Don't beat yourself up," said Charlotte. "True love can be so easily mistaken for other things—friendship, humane concern, indigestion . . ."

"Stop it, you delightful thing. Now that I look back over the past two weeks, I see the mark of it running through everything that happened. Mr. Grey's gallantry, his constant attention, his reluctance to dance even. Why, I simply thought him uneasy, given it is our last night. But in truth he was harboring a secret all along! Do not think I mind for my own sake, my dear Charlotte. You are sly, but I understand, though I should scold you amazingly. Sometimes one does not mean to fall in love. Sometimes it just happens."

Charlotte was about to argue this point. She had a year's worth of thoughts and impressive opinions on the subject of choice in love, but she stopped herself, because suddenly she was confused. "Wait . . . what?"

Miss Gardenside studied her face, her expression kind. "You really don't understand, do you? Then do I get to tell you the news?" She glanced at Eddie but didn't wait for permission. "He's in love with you, Charlotte! He is desperately in love with you! And not really your brother, of course. All this time, he took my arm out of obligation, but I free him from that freely now! You are free to love!"

"What?" She couldn't seem to soak in what Miss Gardenside was saying, perhaps distracted by her liberal use of "free."

Alisha whispered, "He fancies you for real."

She smiled and squeezed Charlotte's hand.

Charlotte dared look at him now. He smiled broadly, showing

teeth, his cheeks fully dimpled, his eyes wide, as if slightly fearful of her reaction.

"But . . . he's scripted for you."

Alisha—it was definitely "Alisha" now, in accent and manner—screwed up her mouth and shrugged one shoulder. "I'm not here for the romance. To tell the truth, I find it all fairly weird."

She kissed Charlotte's cheek with a smile and left without another word, and Charlotte was left in the warm breath of the conservatory alone with Mr. Edmund Grey. Or with Reginald, perhaps. But certainly with Eddie.

"Not quite the way I imagined this moment," Eddie said.

He'd imagined it! Charlotte pressed her icy fingers to her cheeks to cool them down.

"What did you have in mind?"

"'Shall I compare thee to a summer's day,' that sort of thing. It always works, doesn't it?"

She was near him now, though she didn't remember walking into the room. Perhaps she was floating like Colonel Andrews's ghost-on-wheels. "Why not give it a try?"

His smile softened. His hand was warm in hers.

"You are more like an autumn day. Your presence makes me sure that change is coming, and it is a change I want and welcome."

"I'm sorry I spoiled your evening with Lydia. I hope you won't get docked pay or anything. But I . . . missed you. Is that silly?"

"Wisest thing I've ever heard."

They were sitting on a bench, though Charlotte didn't remember walking there either. She seemed to be floating all over the place. Someone could tie a string to her and sell her at carnivals.

"I have a confession to make," said Eddie. "I have a friend, a former cast member here, who fell in love with one of the clients.

I thought he'd confused fantasy and reality and imagined he was in love when he was just acting a part. I hadn't thought it truly possible. But you made it possible."

She laughed. "This is crazy!"

"I have yet another confession: I love crazy."

He kissed her.

You were wrong, Charlotte told her Inner Thoughts.

The Inner Thoughts nudged her kindly then took off, giving them some privacy.

And he kissed her.

And Charlotte thought: *He seems to like me. He really does. Maybe* (oh my, if he keeps doing that, I won't be able to breathe), *maybe there's nothing really wrong with me.* (Holy everything, he has the most delicious lips.) *Maybe James would have snookered me for Justice no matter what I did. Maybe* (good gracious, I could kiss this man forever), *maybe it wasn't about me after all. Maybe I'm not broken and unwantable. Maybe I'm . . .* (Is a man holding your face while he kisses you the sweetest thing ever? Because it feels like the sweetest thing ever.)

And still he kissed her.

Now that they'd stopped talking, Charlotte could hear the music through the walls, through the windows, an echoey, spectral sound. It was sad and eerie and beautiful too, and Eddie pulled her to her feet and they danced. He held her hand, held her back, and spun her around the room. She supposed it was the waltz, or nearly. She didn't really know what her feet were doing.

It must be near midnight by now, Charlotte thought and idly wondered if her dress would turn to rags, and horses, née mice, would come to fetch her home.

But I'm not ready to go home yet, she would tell those pesky, homebound mice. And she wouldn't care if her dress turned to rags and she was barefoot before Eddie, the dazzle magicked away. She wouldn't care as long as she could stay. And for the first time, she felt confident that he would want her to.

They danced to the ghostly music until it stopped. Then they kissed well past midnight and talked till dawn.

home, last year

"I'M NOT LEAVING YOU," JAMES told the children as he emptied the closet of his clothes.

"I'll always be your father. I'll never leave you," he said as he packed up some boxes and left.

austenland, day 14

IT WAS DAWN. EDDIE AND Charlotte walked slowly up the stairs, the pale light from the windows pushing down on them like gravity. Her body felt like a sack of straw, but her mind buzzed, and her hand tingled where Eddie held it. They passed Colonel Andrews and Miss Charming heading for bed, and Eddie still held on.

At Charlotte's door, they stopped, too tired to do anything else and too sorry to let go.

"I have two weeks off before the next session," he said, his voice hoarse with morning.

"I'd like to stay," she said. Could she stay two more weeks? Would her kids be okay? She hoped so. But what then? It didn't matter. She was in love, and her heart felt brand-new.

She went into her room before her practical mind could wake up worrying.

She didn't bother wrestling out of her ball gown. It turned out it was possible to sleep in a corset, though perhaps not advisable. She shut her eyes against the growing light and dreamed instantly of a truck carrying crates of cabbages.

Her Inner Thoughts grumbled. Come on! There's nothing the *least* bit romantic about cabbages. After a night like that, at least you could shoot me something hot and steamy.

Charlotte, asleep, shrugged. Couldn't be helped. Dreams chose themselves, and that morning, it was cabbages. In a truck.

She woke feeling shy. And sore. Really, it's worth the time to remove the corset. The sun was high—she'd slept past breakfast. She was hungry but embarrassed too. Today was The End, and she wasn't sure how she was going to wrangle a permanent happily-ever-after into it. She definitely wasn't sure two more weeks could form something strong enough to withstand the Atlantic Ocean when it rushed between them. And after they put Austenland behind, would it become weird between her and Eddie? Would he realize that she was normal, would he make excuses and send her home?

He's worth the risk, she told herself. Don't go back to being numb.

After bathing, Charlotte put on the corset one last time—feeling sentimental about the constricting, torturelike undergarment—dressed, and went out.

"Good morning, Charlotte," Miss Gardenside said. "You missed breakfast."

"I was up late," said Charlotte.

Miss Gardenside/Alisha gave a low, throaty chuckle.

"Thanks for giving me Mr. Grey," said Charlotte. "He was meant for you."

"Gross! He's old enough to be my dad."

He probably wasn't, but Charlotte smiled anyway.

"Could I ask a favor?" she asked. "This is probably going too far, but . . . do you think you could write a note to my daughter and tell her you think I'm cool? Or something? She worships you, and she thinks I'm . . . well, I'm Mom."

"For my dearest, sweetest bosom friend? Absolutely."

"That's . . . that's amazing. Thanks. And if you don't mind, I'm going to write a note to your mother, telling her how wonderful I think you are."

Alisha's smile was sad. "Actually, I don't mind at all."

Charlotte planned to write it longhand on fine paper. Perhaps she'd even use a quill pen.

Alisha gave Charlotte a hug and two cheek kisses and left to pack. Charlotte wandered by Miss Charming's open door.

"Are you staying on?" she asked.

Miss Charming was sitting on the floor, painting her toenails a bright coral. "Yeah, why not? This session didn't feel really real, with the murders and guns and everything. I don't want to end with *CSI: Pembrook Park*. Besides, Colonel Andrews will still be here for another two months, and I should keep him company."

Charlotte sat on her bed. "Are you two really an item?"

"Naw, the colonel doesn't swing for me. We love each other in our own ways. That's probably all I need."

"Is it?"

Miss Charming's lower lip began to tremble. She screwed the brush back into the polish, leaving several toes unpainted. "I don't know what to do. I don't know where to go. I can't imagine leaving, but I can't just stay forever. Can I?"

She looked up at Charlotte with wide, wet eyes and a little quivering chin.

Charlotte took Miss Charming by the arm and marched her down to the morning room, where Mrs. Wattlesbrook was tidying up her desk.

"Mrs. Wattlesbrook, may I present to you Miss Elizabeth Charming. You have known her as a guest these many months, but she has much more potential. Miss Charming has a keen interest in seeing Pembrook Park remain afloat. She might also consider restoring Pembrook Cottage and renewing the activity of Windy Nook. She is a savvy businesswoman and was half the partnership that built a single mattress outlet into a successful chain of eighteen stores across three states. She has loads to invest and a superpower for eyeballing real from fraud. Miss Charming, in short, is your new bosom friend. I think it's time you two talked business, ironed out a partnership, and got this place back on its feet."

Miss Charming gasped three times during her narrative. Mrs. Wattlesbrook was not unaffected. Charlotte could tell by the way her hands flitted about, patting her hair, resting on her chest, finding her lap. But she kept a stern expression.

"And I suppose with the offer of money and partnership will come meddling? Just what do you have in mind, Miss Elizabeth?"

"Well, this is sudden," said Miss Charming, fanning herself with a hand. She sat down primly. "Here are a few thoughts off the top of my head: You don't have to shut down all winter, you know. The winter coats and mufflers and what-not are *soo* cute. Imagine Christmas at Pembrook Park! With more marketing power, you'd have no trouble drumming up new clients, especially if you make some menu changes."

"Strict observances of the culture of the era—"

"I know, and that's all well and good, honey lamb, but the

food, missus. The food! Does it have to be *so* authentic? What about having a few dishes each meal that are more human-friendly and still keep one or two that are straight from your Regency cookbooks? I'm not saying Pop-Tarts and corn dogs, just a dish or two people will actually recognize. Are sheep's eyeballs *ever* necessary?"

Mrs. Wattlesbrook shrugged, a little hurt.

"Listen, you still be proprietressy, write up the characters for all the actors and guests and their love affair plots and make sure we're still old-fashioned-like. Let Colonel Andrews plan the entertainment to keep things lively. He loves when we put on the theatricals you wrote, planting mysteries, and he has scads of other ideas. Meanwhile, let me do the business work. You don't have to be *soo* secretive and exclusive. Increase security and let's advertise, bring in fresh clients, do some weekend stints instead of only two- or three-weekers. And we need more men! Two men to each woman, I say, so everyone has a choice, and let them go visit the other estates, make calls on the guests at Windy Nook, and make eyes at their men too, and it'll be so exciting!"

"Perhaps . . ." Mrs. Wattlesbrook sat down, her hands in her lap. "Perhaps we could talk numbers?"

"Land's sake, yes, I love talking numbers! Math was my best subject. Math and anatomy."

"I'll leave you to it," said Charlotte.

As she shut the door, she saw Mrs. Wattlesbrook lean back with a sigh of relief.

Charlotte walked to the inn for the last time.

The kids will be fine, she told herself as she dialed James's number. They'll love staying with their dad a couple more weeks. And after that? Could she move to England? Well . . . no. Lu and Beckett had gone through enough upheaval the past year. She could visit Eddie from time to time. Would that be enough?

Her newly spry heart seemed to slouch a bit in her chest, but she ignored it the best she could. Beckett had just answered James's phone, and the sound of his "hello" pricked her eyes with tears and made her heart swell. Oh, she loved that boy.

"Hi baby!"

"Mom?"

"Yeah, it's me. I'm sorry I haven't been able to get a hold—"

"Hang on."

Sounds of walking, a door shutting.

"What's going on?" she asked, imagining scenarios where James and Justice had been killed and Beckett was being held hostage by violent kidnappers.

"I just came into Dad's office to talk. I don't know why I couldn't sleep in here. I hate that stupid couch."

"I'm sorry. We should work out different sleeping arrangements for you next time."

"Yeah. At least this visit's almost over."

"Weren't you loving it?"

"No," he said, which sounded like a synonym for "stupid."

"But . . . but your dad said you were having the time of your life, and Justice said you called her 'Mom.'"

"By accident, duh. She's weird. She gets in your face all lovey and cutesy for a few seconds, then every night she locks herself in her room so we can't bug her. And Dad turns on the TV like he doesn't know what to say to us, and lately they go out for dinner and leave us with a pizza. It's weird not having dinner all together, you know?"

"Yeah."

"I really miss you, Mom."

He missed her. He hadn't said anything like that since he was little.

"I miss you tons, Al," she said, using his nickname. As an

infant, he'd resembled Al Gore to a disturbing degree—the VP era, not the bearded era.

"You're coming back tomorrow, right?" he asked, his voice worried.

Charlotte hesitated for three seconds—three seconds to imagine her two weeks with Eddie, three seconds to weigh her hoped-for happiness against Beckett's. She did her best to keep any regret out of her voice when she said, "You bet."

"Good," he exhaled.

Charlotte cleared her throat and forced herself to smile so he could hear the smile in her voice. "How's Lu been?"

Beckett snickered. "A huge pain in the—"

"Beckett."

"Yeah, okay. But really, I wouldn't hate it here so much if she weren't so mopey."

"She having a hard time with Justice?"

"Maybe. I don't know. She's always on the phone or with her friends complaining about Maggot Boy—don't get mad at me, that's what she calls him."

"Who?"

"Maggot Boy. That guy, what's-his-name."

"Pete?"

"Yeah, she loved him *sooooo* much, and then he was a jerk apparently and now she hates him forever and ever. That kind of thing."

"What did he do?" Charlotte asked casually.

"Two-timing, I guess."

She knew it! Charlotte just knew it! And now her daughter was boyfriend-less! Yes! Wait—no! Oh no, poor Lu. Oh, ouch, poor thing. Why were boys so stupid? She'd kill that Pete! Well, maybe there'd been enough murder, lucky for him. Lu would find someone better. Charlotte believed that, and even hoped for it.

"Is Lu there?"

"Yeah, hang on."

She could hear Beckett open the door and call to his sister, who yelled something back.

"She says she's on her way out."

"Let me just talk to her for two seconds."

"Two seconds!" Beckett yelled.

A pause. Lu said, "Hi."

"Hi baby. I just wanted you to know that I miss you."

"Yeah. I got your letter."

"You did?"

"Yeah. I've gotta go."

"Okay, I'll see you tomorrow."

Then Beckett's voice again. "She read that letter like a hundred times."

"Shut up, Beckett!" Lu yelled from the distance.

Beckett laughed. Charlotte did a little dance.

Next, the phone made it to James's hands. She could hear him walking while making idle chitchat, and another door closing. He was probably in his bedroom.

"We're not going to be able to take the kids that weekend next month," he said, a slight *hem* in his voice the only sign of shame.

Charlotte pursed her lips. Normally she would say "okay" and be done. But someone had tried to kill her, by golly, and she'd just given up hope of being with Eddie. After that, a person is entitled to a few questions.

"Why not?"

"Well, with my conference coming up—"

"Your conference is in November."

"Right, so it's only three months away and I need to prepare—"

"All weekend, every weekend next month, you'll be preparing for your November conference."

His voice slipped into a half whisper. "Justice never had children, you know. And these past weeks have been hard on her. I'm not sure a full month each summer is the best idea."

Charlotte took a very deep breath, a breath that pulled right up from her toes and smoothed over the shout that had been building up in her chest.

"James Nathan Kinder, we are going to have this conversation one time, right now, and then never again. You are Lu and Beckett's father. A father puts his children first. Before your new wife, before your work, before yourself. That's what parenthood means. They love you, poor kids. They *need* you. And you will do everything in your power to make sure they know you love them too and are constantly, without hesitation, their father, on call day and night, their biggest supporter, their biggest fan, and the one man who will always open his home to them."

"Of course, sure, in an ideal world, but—"

"No *buts*. Not a single *but*. This is a simple issue, Mr. Kinder. And in this single conversation that will never be repeated again, I'm going to give you a little incentive, since your heart appears to have shrunken to Grinch size and can't be depended on to help your head make good choices. You think you're safe because I signed divorce papers? Don't sit back on your bank account. You were having an affair for months before our divorce, weren't you? You were already breaking your marriage vows when you asked me to add your name to my accounts. You know Lenny wanted to go for the jugular during the negotiations, but I held him back. What do you think he'll do if I give him a second chance?" She could almost hear James quivering on the other end. Lenny was an excellent lawyer, and James was fully aware Charlotte had muzzled him. Whether or not a renegotiation of the settlement was possible now that the divorce was final Charlotte didn't know—but then, neither did James.

"We have your credit card statements for the past several years. You are a creature of habit, Mr. Kinder, and I suspect you left a trail of evidence—restaurants, hotel rooms, gifts. You also burned through a number of old friends who might have interesting testimonies to add. I have no doubt Lenny can prove that you were acting in ill faith long before you had rights to my money. And when he does, say good-bye to your nest egg."

Silence.

"Excellent point," she said. "Well put. Without my money padding your lifestyle, Justice might have to get a job. What do you think will be more inconvenient for her—being an adequate stepmom or losing a fortune? So I'm telling you, go curl up in a corner somewhere and lick your little wounds and get over it. The moment—and I mean, the *moment*—I detect you are being a less-than-enthusiastic father, I will go mama bear on your ass. Have no doubt that I can and will do it. Can you hear it in my voice? A tone perhaps unfamiliar to you? More than confidence. It's absolute surety, Jimmy boy. If you do not behave like the decent father you once were, I will do everything in my power to strip you of that ill-gotten gain and protect my children. Are we clear?"

More silence.

"I have Lenny's number on speed dial—"

"Clear," he said quickly. "We're clear, yes."

"Good. Enjoy the rest of your visit with the two most wonderful children in the world."

Charlotte clicked End and sat down, breathing out as if she'd been holding it in for some time. And perhaps she had.

She started the walk back toward the manor, slow as a funeral march. Tendrils from home seemed to touch her now, slowing her walk, tugging her gently away. She imagined sleeping in sweats, waking to the beeps and explosions of Beckett playing video games on a Saturday morning, the clanking of Lu's spoon in her cereal bowl. Those were things to look forward to. She didn't feel sorry to be leaving. Not really.

She was thawed, her heart raw. She was feeling again. Keenly. Even though a twinge of heartbreak was burrowing into her chest, she couldn't regret anything. What a magical thing to meet Eddie, to know that there are good men in the world, and to have had a few days loving him. She hoped the awe and warmth could sustain her for however long it would take her to get over this new heartache.

I'm in love, she told herself, and knew it was true. But it didn't change the two children waiting for her in Ohio, or the fact that Eddie was an actor who lived in England. She'd told Beckett she was coming home, and after talking to James, she knew she had to be the parent who was always there. Always.

You're not going to find someone like Eddie on those blind dates, her Inner Thoughts said.

No, Charlotte agreed. I'd be comparing everyone to him, and no one will measure up.

So you're probably going to be alone for a long time, and that's lame.

Yeah, probably. But that's just the way it goes.

Whatever, said her Inner Thoughts, annoyed beyond arguing.

The manor was close, and panic filled Charlotte's chest. She didn't want to face Eddie just to say good-bye. And why should she? This was not, after all, a date. She'd been freed of worry about saying the right things, making the best impression. This was a place without anxiety (non-murder-related, anyhow). The expectations had been clear: come for two weeks and go home again. And perhaps Eddie had enjoyed the final scene last night in the conservatory in the same way Mallery had sought his own final moment in the cottage. It was all fantasy. Home was real.

Charlotte would go. Now.

She did a pivot turn and hurried back toward the inn. The

only things that were hers in the house anyway were her toiletries. She would write Mrs. Wattlesbrook and ask her to send her makeup to Mary in jail. Charlotte's luggage awaited at the inn. She could change and call a hired car to take her to the airport.

She didn't look back. Now that she'd decided to go, the thought of seeing Eddie again filled her with terror. His face would weaken her resolve, his words would make it so much harder. She was just one of those love-starved ladies he'd talked about, someone he could take pleasure doting upon for a couple of weeks. Whether or not he really wanted her to stay, he'd be kind, and that would hurt.

The sky was soupy, the clouds having no particular shape or shade. Mist crawled the grounds, making her glad of her bonnet and longer sleeves. The gravel was loud beneath her footsteps. Wet fog and crunching gravel seemed to make up the whole world. She could feel the manor house behind her but she didn't look back. She could live without the grandeur, the corset and feet-tangling skirts, the lack of solitude, the feeling of always being watched, even in her own room. She could live without Austenland.

But you're going to miss Eddie, said her Inner Thoughts.

I know, she said. But as you'll learn someday, this is the kind of necessary choice you have to make as a grown-up, even when it hurts.

It sucks, said her Inner Thoughts. I'm sorry.

Thanks.

Charlotte couldn't allow herself to dwell on how it felt to hold Eddie's hand—as if all that mattered in the world were expressed in that touch; as if she would be safe and happy forever because this wonderful man wanted to be beside her; as if doves had come to nestle and coo beseechingly in her bosom. No, she really couldn't allow herself to dwell on that, especially if doves were involved. Doves crossed the line. As they often do.

She was at the gates of Pembrook Park when she heard someone call out, "Mrs. Kinder!"

Charlotte started at her real name. She was both disappointed and relieved that the voice was not Eddie's.

Detective Sergeant Merriman was standing outside her car on the other side of the gate.

"Look at you! All made out like a lady." Detective Merriman smiled. "Oh, I had such Austen fancies like you wouldn't believe when I was a girl. Good thing I grew out of them."

She smiled good-naturedly, but when her glance flicked back to the manor, a moment of wistful longing passed over her eyes.

"Good morning, Detective Sergeant," said Charlotte, just stopping herself from curtsying. She did remove her bonnet. It was one thing too much.

The guard opened the gate and Charlotte stepped through.

"I need to talk to you about Thomas Mallery," said the detective.

"Is that his real name?"

"It is, in fact, and one reason this case continues to complicate. He claims that he didn't kill John Wattlesbrook and that his attack on you was simply part of the charade."

Charlotte rolled her eyes.

"Yes, yes, I know, but it is a rather smart move. There was that ongoing mystery of the nuns, and the game of Bloody Murder, and so his 'pretending' to be a murderer could be passed off as a continuation of the game. He did not actually kill you, you see. His fingerprints were not on Mr. Wattlesbrook's car, nor on the keys you found. He must have wiped them off before hiding them."

"And wore kitchen gloves," said Charlotte. "There was one in the secret room and another in the car. Do the gloves have his prints?"

"I'm afraid not. He must have worn his personal gloves under the kitchen gloves. Protects the latter from his prints, and the former prevents any DNA evidence. Smart man."

"Mary is a witness," Charlotte said. "I think she saw Mallery go into the secret room with Wattlesbrook and come out alone. And after he pushed the car into the pond, she helped him wash the mud out of his costume."

"That's an avenue we will pursue, but in your opinion, how readily will Mary testify against him?"

Charlotte sighed. "Not very."

"I wouldn't be surprised if she tries to confess to the whole lot. So I'm afraid the only strong piece of evidence we have against our man is his confession to you."

"He was pretty direct about it in the cottage, and that was after a couple of days of hiding. I don't see how he'll claim that was still part of the game."

"He'll try. I'm very sorry, ma'am, but I have some bad news for you. I can't have you leave the country right now."

"What?" This possibility had never crossed her mind. "But I can't stay. I'm leaving today. Right now, actually."

"I know it must be a terrible inconvenience. You have a job to return to?"

"Yes. Well, no, I can work from anywhere. But my kids . . ."

"Of course. Could you find a place for them to stay? Or even bring them here?"

Charlotte felt as if she were filled with helium and floating just above the ground.

"Bring them here . . ."

"Yes, I'm afraid that if you don't stay, you'll be coming and going an awful lot, and as you make up the entire case against a murderer—"

Charlotte began to pace. "No, no, I understand. I *have* to stay. You're *ordering* me to stay."

"Well, I might put it differently—"

"I'm essential to the case. My testimony is paramount. I would be neglecting my humane duty if I went home now. Everyone will have to understand. You need me."

"I suppose, in so many words . . ."

"If I went home now, I'd practically be as guilty as the murderer himself!"

"Well, I don't know . . ."

"Charlotte!" Eddie stirred the mist as he ran, and it swirled around him like dancing ghosts. "Charlotte, you're going, aren't you?"

"I was . . ."

"For shame!"

She'd been right to try to slip away. Just the sight of his face made her legs feel soft, and it's hard to run away with soft legs.

"You want me to stay," she said, believing it already.

"Of course I do!" he shouted.

"That's good," she called back, "because Detective Sergeant Merriman has absolutely forbidden me from leaving the country! It's Mallery's fault. He made me a key witness."

Eddie was running faster. "You mean, you must stay here, in this very county, for the foreseeable future?"

"Indefinitely!"

"I know it must be a terrible inconvenience?" the detective mumbled.

But she didn't say any more when Eddie reached Charlotte. He put his arms around her and lifted her, spinning around.

Charlotte used to wonder why people did the spinning thing in books and movies. Now she knew. She felt it. Eddie's arms were around her and they were together, they were one, solid in the center of everything. Outside, the world was fast and blurry and dizzying and strange. Inside, everything made sense. Inside, the only clear things were Eddie and Charlotte. Both Charlotte and her Inner Thoughts were thinking the same thing: *hooray, hooray, hooray.*

"Indefinitely," Charlotte said again as if it were the most important word in the world. The great expanse of the Atlantic became irrelevant. It would not flood between them. She would stay in England.

He put her down, his arms still around her waist.

"I woke up with a cold fear that you would talk to your children and feel guilty and decide that I probably don't really feel anything for you so it would be better just to leave quickly."

Charlotte gasped. "How did you—"

"A woman without hobbies is dangerously self-negligent. Looks like I owe Mallery for keeping you around. Happily, these trials can drag on forever."

"Months and months," she said.

"Years, even," he said.

"I'll fly my kids over."

"And perhaps rent a flat in London."

"Do you know a good neighborhood?"

"I rent near Chelsea."

"I've always wanted to live in Chelsea. At least, I would have always wanted to live in Chelsea if it had occurred to me before. As it has now. It has definitely occurred to me."

"You'll love London. I love London. I'd love to see you in London."

"I've seen London. In fact, I've seen France."

"Do go on," he said, his eyes turning all bedroomy.

She kissed him. It was all she wanted to do. Kiss Eddie. She dropped her bonnet and let the wind blow it away to part the mists and put her arms around him and kissed him. Her eyes were closed and she felt as if the world were still spinning.

Remembering their audience, Charlotte peeked. The detective was sitting in her car and watching Eddie and Charlotte without shame, as if they were silhouettes on a screen at a drive-in movie. She rested her hand and cheek against the window and sighed.

"Come on," said Charlotte, taking his hand. "Let's go for a swim."

He squinted. "Truly?"

"I'll protect you from the dangerous fishies."

He picked her up and carried her across the lawn. His arms were becoming a common means of her transportation.

"As you wish, my darling. After all, I have become an expert at your buttons and lacings."

home, present

HERE'S THE THING ABOUT HOME: you can create it most anywhere, as long as you gather your people around you. Charlotte was surprised by how readily Beckett took to the move, plied with promises of stateside trips to visit his friends. Lu seemed at home at once, especially after meeting Eddie's daughter, Julia, her mentor in all things British. The chance to meet Alisha also sweetened the deal. James would fly over periodically to have some quality time with his kids without stepmother Justice, who didn't have a passport and refused to get one for mysterious ideological reasons. Charlotte's other people—her friends, mother, and brother's family—loved the excuse to visit England, especially on her dime.

And then there was Eddie. He already felt like home.

Charlotte was filled with plans that made her fingers tingle with anticipation. After exploring the country's flora, she could expand her business to a new continent. And she was determined to collect some hobbies along the way. Hiking was second on her list, though no one but her Inner Thoughts guessed her ultimate goal of Kilimanjaro. But first, she was going to learn to dance.

acknowledgments

I AM INDEBTED TO THE many people who nurtured this story from concept to printed book. Lovely cheek kisses for all the folks at Bloomsbury: Victoria Wells Arms, Mike O'Connor, Maureen Klier, Liz Peters, Sabrina Farber, and Rachel Mannheimer. Special slobbery kisses for Barry Goldblatt, Janae Stephenson, Shelby Ivory, Jen Jones, Meghan Hibbett, Stephenie Meyer, and Jerusha Hess. A movie kiss on the mouth for Dean Hale. And a grateful curtsy to Jane Austen.

While writing this book, I enjoyed delving into many Gothic tales, particularly *Rebecca* by Daphne du Maurier, *The Haunting of Hill House* by Shirley Jackson, *Jane Eyre* by Charlotte Brontë, many Agatha Christies, and, of course, *Northanger Abbey* by Jane Austen.

Finally, apologies to nuns everywhere for the sad fate of Grey Cloaks Abbey, and most especially to the Poor Clares of Perpetual Adoration of Our Lady of Solitude in Arizona, who wrote to tell me how much they appreciated the dedication in *Austenland*.

Reading Group Guide

THESE DISCUSSION QUESTIONS ARE DESIGNED to enhance your group's conversation about *Midnight in Austenland*, another charming adventure set in Pembrook Park, a Jane Austen–themed country manor house for women in search of nineteenth-century romance.

About this book

Charlotte Kinder's husband has just left her for another woman. Another woman named "Justice." And Charlotte's two children might be calling their new stepmother "Mom." Clearly, Charlotte needs a vacation.

Charlotte hasn't been a Jane Austen fan for long; she's used to reading spooky Agatha Christie mysteries. But *Pride and Prejudice* and *Northanger Abbey* have inspired her to take a trip to England, and her travel agent has just the thing for her: two weeks at Pembrook Park, where it is always 1816, and ladies are wooed by actors dressed as proper gentlemen. Charlotte's assigned love interest is Mr. Mallery, a dark and brooding gentleman who would stop at nothing to protect and preserve Pembrook Park. But when the manor's owner goes missing, Charlotte seems to be the only one who suspects foul play. Meanwhile, she finds herself falling out of character and falling in love with Edmund Grey, another guest's love interest. As Charlotte tries to solve the mystery of the murder at Pembrook Park, she realizes that her feelings for Eddie matter more than her desire for an Austen-inspired fantasy life.

For discussion

1. Charlotte reads two authors before her trip to Pembrook Park: Jane Austen and Agatha Christie. Compare how each author influences Charlotte's expectations of her vacation. When does she seek romance and propriety, and how does she find mystery and murder instead?

2. Before most chapters of the novel, there are flashbacks to Charlotte's life prior to Austenland. How does this backstory add to Charlotte's character? What do we learn about her personality and her history through these sections?

3. Charlotte is most often described as "nice." When does she act the nicest, and when does she break out of her usual easygoing personality? Does her niceness make her an unusual heroine?

4. Discuss Charlotte's business savvy. How does she wind up running her own company? How does she handle her unexpected success? How has her business affected her marriage?

5. Consider Charlotte's first impressions of Mr. Mallery. Why is she attracted to him at first? Why does Mr. Mallery appear "too untamed and, well, *dangerous*, to enter the prim world of the drawing room" (32)? How is Mr. Mallery, in fact, even more dangerous than he appears?

6. Discuss Charlotte's belated romance with Eddie, the "safe" character of Pembrook Park. When does Charlotte first realize that she is falling for Eddie instead of Mr. Mallery? How does Charlotte come to trust her feelings for Eddie?

7. Charlotte's "Inner Thoughts" are often heard on the page. What does Charlotte's internal commentary add to the story? When are her Inner Thoughts correct, and when do they mislead her?

8. Charlotte often finds herself worrying about her children back in America. Why is she anxious about Beckett and Lu during her vacation? How does Charlotte manage to escape her worries about her family?

9. Considering the artificial world of Pembrook Park, Charlotte wonders, "What kind of person would desire this full-time?" (123) Compare the two characters who are stuck in Austenland: Miss Charming and Mr. Mallery. Why do these two characters prefer to stay in Pembrook Park rather than face real life in the twenty-first century?

10. While Charlotte fights off Mr. Mallery, she finds herself "solving more than one mystery" (194). What does Charlotte realize about her marriage and divorce? How does she take out her anger at James on Mr. Mallery?

11. Miss Lydia Gardenside confesses that she always reads the last page of a book first: "happiness, marriage, prosperity . . . That is how all stories should end" (120). Do you agree with Miss Gardenside that all endings should be happy? Why or why not? Does *Midnight in Austenland* have the kind of happy ending that would satisfy a reader like Miss Gardenside? Explain your answer.

12. "Here's the thing about home: you can create it most anywhere, as long as you gather your people around you" (272). How does Charlotte's definition of "home" change over the course of the novel? What kind of home is Charlotte likely to create with Eddie in England?

13. At the end of the novel, Charlotte realizes, "Jane Austen had created six heroines, each quite different, and that gave Charlotte courage. There wasn't just one kind of woman to be" (240). In the end, what kind of heroine is Charlotte?

14. Imagine a movie version of *Midnight in Austenland*. Which actors would best fit the parts of Charlotte, Eddie, and Mr. Mallery?

15. If you've read *Austenland*, discuss how that previous novel compares to *Midnight in Austenland*. Which of the first novel's characters were you happy to encounter again? How does Charlotte Kinder compare to Jane Hayes, the heroine of *Austenland*?

Suggested reading

Shannon Hale, *Austenland*; Jane Austen, *Northanger Abbey*; Karen Joy Fowler, *The Jane Austen Book Club*; Jane Austen and Seth Grahame-Smith, *Pride and Prejudice and Zombies*; Beth Pattillo, *Jane Austen Ruined My Life*; Laurie Viera Rigler, *Confessions of a Jane Austen Addict*; Jon Spence, *Becoming Jane Austen*; Emma Campbell Webster, *Lost in Austen*; Amanda Grange, *Mr. Darcy's Diary*